RULES TO THE GAME

SHERRYL D. HANCOCK

VULPINE
PRESS

Published by Vulpine Press in the United Kingdom in 2019

ISBN 978-1-83919-300-2

Cover by Claire Wood

www.vulpine-press.com

Also in the *MidKnight Blue* series:

Building Empires

Empires Fall

Where Loyalties Lie

Treachery Rising

Betrayals Stand

For all Intents and Purposes

Blood in the Water

Means to an End

Past in the Present

Just for Now

Here and Now

CHAPTER 1

Donovan Curtis stared down at his answering machine, listening to Jeanie's voice telling him she hadn't heard from him in a while and she just wanted to make sure he was okay. To say that he'd become apathetic in his love life was a safe bet. He depressed the erase button. He didn't pick up the phone to call Jeanie back, instead finding the TV remote and clicking on the television. Going to his dresser, he took off his holstered gun and badge. He removed the ammunition magazine from the gun and pulled back the slide to unload the chambered round. Then he stood and emptied the ammunition clip into a box he kept in his dresser.

When he opened the top drawer to put the box away, the diamond ring he'd given Jeanie years before slid to the front. Donovan stared at it emotionlessly. The ring didn't even faze him anymore. There was a time when he'd see it and feel sick at what he and Jeanie had lost. Now, it just seemed like another piece of jewelry, albeit an expensive one.

Closing the drawer, he sat down on the bed and took off his boots. He finished undressing and put on sweatpants, lying down to watch TV. He flipped through the channels, not staying on anything for too long. So proceeded his evening, just like the nights before. If he wasn't working, he wasn't alive anymore. At 8:15 Erin called. He let the machine pick up and listened to her message as she left it.

"Donovan, it's me, Erin. How are you? It's been a long time since

1

I've seen you... I didn't know if you were just working a lot or what... Anyway, call me, okay? I miss you. Bye." Erin's voice was soft and undemanding, as always.

Donovan stared at the machine, his lips curling in derision. Again he reached over and erased the message. He fell asleep an hour later, still lying on his bed with the TV on.

The next day he went to the office, needing to check in with Spider and file some paperwork on the case he was ready to wrap up. He spoke briefly with Spider, explaining when he wanted to do the arrest; Spider agreed and told him to contact Joe for a back-up team. Donovan walked back out to his desk and sat down to go through his mail and phone messages. There were four from Jeanie and three from Erin. He scanned the names and then crumpled up the messages one by one, tossing them into the trash. There was also one from his sister, Randy, asking him to come to dinner on the Sunday that had just passed. He crumpled that message up and tossed it too.

He finished up the report he'd emailed to himself from his laptop at home. His email came up with three messages. Two were from Jeanie, one was from Erin, all saying the same things they had said everywhere else. *Haven't seen you, wanted to make sure you were okay, blah, blah, blah*. He deleted them without replying.

He pulled up the report and worked on it until 12:30. He printed it out to read over it again before handing it in to Spider. Spider was at lunch, so he dropped it in his in-basket.

Walking over to the status board, he marked himself as "out," then went to his desk and picked up his jacket. He pulled out his keys and locked his desk and computer, then headed for the elevators. He

2

got downstairs and was just outside the front doors of the building when he heard his name called.

He turned and saw Jeanie walking over to him. He stood and waited for her, pulling out his sunglasses and putting them on.

"You don't call, you don't write…" she said, grinning.

Donovan looked down at her, his face stoic. He shrugged. "I've been working a lot," he said tonelessly.

Jeanie looked up at him, searching his face. Then she nodded, dropping her eyes. "Okay, no problem. I, uh, I gotta go," she said hesitantly. "Take care, Donovan," she added over her shoulder as she walked away.

"You too," he said, then turned and walked down the steps.

Jeanie made her way to the bathroom, closing herself in a stall and leaning back against the door. She forcibly held back tears, gritting her teeth. Things with Donovan were becoming more and more strained. When she sat down and thought about it, actually counting the months, it had been six since she'd been with him. Every time she'd called him and actually gotten him since then, he would put her off. There was always some reason he didn't want to go out. "I gotta work." "I'm tired, just got in off UC." "I already have plans." There was always something. The six months before that they'd seen each other, but even that had tapered off little by little.

She assumed he was seeing someone else now, but she certainly hadn't heard any rumors like that. *So it was someone outside of the department,* she figured. He'd previously been seeing her and Erin Shandley. She hadn't heard anything about him and Erin in a long time either, so she didn't know for sure what was going on there.

Erin was the woman Donovan had turned to when Jeanie had made the huge mistake of choosing her career over him. She'd been

3

offered an investigator's position with Alcoholic Beverage Control in San Francisco. It had meant leaving Donovan, and she had foolishly done it. Donovan had told her that she was making a mistake, that she needed more street time before she'd make a good investigator. She'd been nasty to him and told him that he was jealous because it had taken him seven years to get a sergeant's position doing investigative work. In the end, Donovan had been very right. Jeanie had been badly beaten by a suspect who had overpowered her far too easily. It was Donovan who'd come for her in the hospital, flying to San Francisco to make sure she was okay. She'd begged him to take her home to San Diego. He had.

Jeanie had realized then what a big mistake she'd made letting Donovan go. She had spent the next six months trying to win back his trust. Things had been fine for a while. Donovan had told her he couldn't commit to a relationship at that point, because he didn't want to get into anything that serious again. She had accepted that, realizing that she'd been the reason for his new reluctance. But now he didn't seem to want to see her at all. He didn't return her calls, or her emails. When she did see him, he seemed to look right through her. She didn't know what had happened. She'd done everything she could to let him control the relationship, hoping to win back his love. She hadn't pushed, she hadn't displayed any of the jealousy she'd felt at seeing him with other women.

She had no idea what she'd done to put her on the other side of the world from Donovan, but she knew he was purposely avoiding her. Part of her mind was telling her to forget him and move on, and she'd really tried to do just that. No man she had dated in the last year and a half even came close to making her feel like Donovan had. Donovan had a way of making her feel like the most beautiful, sexy, smart, witty, wonderful woman alive. He had a way of touching her

4

to make her feel like he'd never seen flesh so beautiful. He made love to her almost with reverence, and that was impossible to find.

Every other guy she'd dated had made it quite obvious that they couldn't wait to get her into bed, whereas Donovan had always treated her like an intelligent, interesting person first and foremost. The last guy she had gone out with spent an hour telling her about how hot the other women he'd dated had been. She guessed he was trying to tell her that she should feel privileged to be considered hot by him too. She hadn't felt privileged; she'd felt used. He'd dragged her to the club that he liked to frequent, wanting his friends to see her. She'd spent half the evening in the bathroom, just trying to avoid the lecherous looks of his friends. Donovan wasn't like that at all. While he'd always seemed proud to be with her, he never tried to show her off like she was some sort of prize he'd won. He'd always treated her like a treasured and loved friend. Now he was treating her like she didn't exist. It was driving her crazy. All she knew was that she was going to have to do something soon. She needed to know what was going on with them, if there even was a "them" anymore.

Donovan was called into Spider's office two days later. The day before he had completed his last case, with the arrest of five suspects and the seizure of a number of illegal weapons, drugs, and $45,000 in cash.

"Hey, Donovan," Spider said, nodding to the younger man. "Good bust yesterday."

"Thanks," Donovan said.

"Got a new one for you." Spider slid a folder across his desk.

Donovan picked it up and flipped it open.

"This one's a little different," Spider was saying.

5

Donovan noted two arrest reports, as well as a pamphlet for a prestigious private college. There was also a class schedule.

"Okay," he said, his brow furrowing. "I'm game."

Spider grinned. "Well, I need to use your youth."

"Uh-huh…" Donovan prompted.

Spider leaned his elbows on his desk, narrowing his eyes at Donovan. "What do you know about Rohypnol?"

"The date rape drug?" Donovan queried. Spider nodded. "Well, I know it's basically a very strong muscle relaxant that's known to induce memory loss in its victims. It's being used primarily in… colleges…" His voice trailed off as he glanced down at the pamphlet. "And you want me to bust someone selling this stuff?"

"Well, it's not that straightforward," Spider said. "The thing is, we've had two young guys busted with a number of these tabs packaged for distribution."

Spider pulled an envelope out of his desk and pushed it across the desk. Donovan looked inside and saw individual packets of white pills.

"Okay, but this stuff is pretty low end," he said.

"Yeah, but it's becoming a big problem in the colleges. And the thing is, both these guys are from La Jolla Village University. And we're talking large quantities here. I want to know where they're getting it from."

"I assume we asked them, right?"

Spider looked back at Donovan, a wry grin on his face. "Obviously," he said. "They aren't willing to tell us anything. Since they're not looking at a lot of jail time here, considering Rohypnol is pretty low level, they don't feel like giving up their source."

6

"So you want me to go in undercover?" Donovan asked disbelievingly.

"Yes," Spider said, realizing from Donovan's tone that the younger man wasn't into the idea.

Donovan sat back, crossing his arms over his chest. It was rare that he thought Spider made a bad decision. He respected the man more than most, but this time he was fairly sure Spider was wasting his time.

"Kinda like *21 Jump Street* time, isn't it?" he said.

Spider grinned at the reference. The show had portrayed police officers who looked so young they were able to go into high schools to make undercover cases.

"Yeah, it is," Spider agreed. "But it's a college, so you won't be expected to have peach fuzz." He grinned, then grew serious. "And this is a serious problem. Young women are being raped by guys using this stuff. We can't make a case against the men they believed raped them because the women can't remember enough about the incident to provide evidence. It's getting way out of hand, and we need to rein it in." Spider gave him a pointed look. "I need you on this, Donovan. You're one of my best narcs, and you look the part."

"Well, I guess I should be happy I don't just look the part, huh?" Donovan said drily.

Spider heard the cynicism in Donovan's voice and wondered at it. He'd noticed that the usually outgoing, affable young man was becoming more and more somber. Spider didn't like the change. He knew that Donovan had been through the wringer in his personal life, and he admired the fact that he never brought his problems to the job; Donovan wasn't one to become a falling-down drunk, or throw angry fits in the office just because things in his personal life

7

weren't going well.

Spider remembered well the literal knock-down, drag-out fights between Donovan's brother-in-law, Joe Sinclair, and his best friend, Rick Debenshire, years before. He remembered all the times Midnight Chevalier's voice would bellow either Joe's or Rick's name when one or the other got out of hand in their anger. There had been a number of fights in the office during the early days of FORS as well, so men like Donovan who were fairly even tempered were a nice change.

"I want to bring in a second person on this," Spider said. "I think a female student is necessary too."

Donovan nodded, saying nothing.

"I'm thinking of using Jeanie," Spider said, watching Donovan for reaction.

Donovan stared back at his boss for a full minute, saying nothing. Eventually, a leading "Okay…" was his only response.

"She got number one on the sergeant's test," Spider explained. "And Midnight intends to offer her any assignment she wants."

Donovan nodded. "And she wants narcotics."

"I thought she might," Spider said. He was silent for a few moments, then sat back in his chair, narrowing his eyes at Donovan. "Is that going to be a problem for you?"

Donovan fixed his teal eyes on Spider. "Why would it be a problem?" he asked evenly.

Spider searched his face, but then shook his head. "I just thought I'd check with you before I offer her the assignment."

Donovan nodded, but again said nothing.

"You're obviously going to be the lead on this. So I'll have you

8

brief Jeanie once you've read up on the whole thing, okay?"

"No problem," Donovan replied smoothly.

Spider nodded, still a bit disconcerted by Donovan's non-reaction. There was definitely no joy there at the prospect of working with his ex-fiancée turned dating partner. There also didn't seem to be any anger or hostility. There just wasn't anything, and it bothered Spider immensely.

***

Joe Sinclair was feeling the effects of non-reaction too, from another member of the Curtis family: his wife. Randy had been working non-stop at her center. She'd named it Sinclair House, after the man who had bought her the building it resided in, her husband. It had been a Christmas present the year before from Joe. The center took in displaced children, kids whose parents had been arrested. Many of them were understandably upset, some violent, some comatose in their shock. Randy's staff dealt with it all. And Randy dealt with a lot on her own. She'd completed her bachelor's degree in child psychology and had started working on her master's degree, planning to go for her PhD next.

Joe had always been supportive of her and her program. He'd understood the long hours it had taken to set it up, and he'd understood her need to be there to make sure things ran the way she'd envisioned. Even in the early months, though, she'd made a point of coming home to be with him and the children. They hadn't made love as often, but that was to be expected.

However, they'd made love at least one time that counted, since Randy had found that she was pregnant eight months after the start of the center. She'd been stunned. Joe had been too; at thirty-nine, he wasn't really ready to have any more children. Their two kids, Kat and JT, had just turned seven and eight years old the month before.

It had almost been a relief when Randy had lost the baby a month later, although neither of them were willing to say as much at that point. The doctor attributed it to the stress Randy was under with the center as well as the fact that she'd been on birth-control pills at the time of conception. At thirty-four, Randy was still as healthy as ever. Randy and Joe had finally talked a couple of weeks after the miscarriage and agreed that it had obviously not been meant to be that they'd have that baby. They'd also decided that they needed better birth control, since Randy was fairly sure it had been missing her pills too many times that had caused the pregnancy. She had talked to her doctor and switched.

Sexually, things had never gotten back on track for them. They had abstained for the appropriate six weeks after the miscarriage. But Joe had found that when it was okay for them to go back to making love, Randy wasn't really interested. They'd made love twice in the following months, both times nothing like what they'd had before. Now, they hadn't made love in two months. Randy was rarely home at night until after Joe had gone to sleep. Even on the weekends, she'd be gone most of the day.

Joe knew something was wrong in his marriage, and he wanted to know what it was.

One night he waited up for her. When Randy got home at 11:30, Joe was sitting on their bed with a glass of Jack Daniels in his hand. She was surprised to see him awake, and sighed inwardly, knowing by the look on his face that he wanted to talk.

Randy had no idea what to say to him. She knew that things were bad between them, that they were so far apart at that point that there was a huge chasm building more and more every day. The thing was, she didn't know why either. She had thought about it a number of times, but when an answer didn't come she'd push it aside and hug yet another child to her. Randy felt like the center had become her whole life. When she made a point to leave early to try and be home with her family, she found herself worrying about little Johnny, who had been brought in the night before, with his sniffles and his asthma. Or little Samantha, whose parents had abused her to the point that she was terrified of anyone that came near her. She worried constantly about them all.

She'd told herself over and over again that eventually things would settle down. But they never seemed to. She knew things were strained with Joe, but she told herself she'd always understood his long hours when he was working so hard in the past. It wasn't her fault that now that he was a captain and things were more stable in the department he didn't work such long hours. She knew she was avoiding things again, but she didn't know what she could do. Joe's answer was always to hire more staff, but that didn't help, because she'd still want to be there to make sure they did what she thought should be done.

"You're up," she said, noting the serious look in his eyes.

"Yeah, I'm up."

He leaned back against the headboard, his knees up to his chest, his arms draped casually over them. He was bare-chested, and had Randy been paying attention she would have noted that he actually looked better now than he had a year before. Since the scare with lung cancer almost two years before, Joe had been determined to quit smoking. In doing so, and being determined not to gain weight, like

11

many who quit smoking were, he'd been working out three to four days a week at the department gym. His chest was more defined than ever, his waist slimmer, his arms as well as his legs more chiseled.

Randy didn't notice. What she noticed was that he was drinking. Which usually meant he was fortifying himself to have a serious talk with her that he really didn't want to have.

Good, she thought. *Maybe if I avoid it a little longer he'll give up on the idea.*

To him, she said, "I'm going to take a shower."

Joe's expression reflected surprised, but he just nodded.

He received a page a few minutes later. He glanced at the number and, figuring Randy would be in the shower for a bit, decided to call it, lest they page again while he and Randy talked.

When Randy got out, Joe was on the phone. She dried off, unpinned her long hair, and brushed it out. Then, without preamble, she got into bed next to him and promptly turned over, putting her back to him. Joe watched her, his eyes widening in surprise even as he continued to talk to the officer on the phone. A few minutes later, he hung up. He moved to lean over her, kissing her cheek, and felt her tense.

He sighed. "What is it, Randy?" he asked, his English accent still clear after years in the States.

"I'm tired, Joe," she replied wearily.

Joe nodded. "Yeah, you're always tired, Randy," he said, his voice taking on an edge.

She turned her head slightly. "I'm sorry, I know this is a strain on you," she said, her voice taking on the monotone it did when she was placating him without really meaning it.

12

"It's a strain on *us*, Randy."

Randy turned onto her back, looking up at him, her blue eyes narrowing slightly.

"Who 'us'?" she asked, trying to discern if he was talking about the two of them or their family, the kids included.

Joe looked back at her, as if trying to figure out why she didn't get it. Which was, in fact, true.

"Us, Randy. You and me."

Randy sighed, shaking her head. "Is this about sex, Joe?"

Joe stared back at her, stunned by her attitude. She wasn't even making an effort to be reasonable.

"It's about a lot more than sex, but yeah, that's part of it too."

"Well, contrary to popular male belief, there is more to life than sex."

Joe's mouth dropped open. He couldn't believe she'd just lumped him with the rest of the male population and the well-known male preoccupation with sex.

"And I just said it was a lot more than that, Randy," he replied disbelievingly.

"Okay, then what?"

Again he stared at her, unable to fathom her attitude. He shook his head slowly, his light blue eyes taking on a cynical look.

"Fuck, never mind, I'm sorry I'm bothering you," he said, moving to get off the bed.

"Joe…" Randy said, her tone still impatient, but she sat up, watching him.

He turned, wearing only faded jeans, and stared back at her for a long moment. He walked over to her then, leaning down to kiss her lips, reaching up to caress her cheek. Her response was lukewarm, and he could tell she was forcing even that. Straightening, he looked down into her eyes.

"Nothing," he said, stunned.

"What are you talking about?"

Joe shook his head. "I get nothing from you anymore, no reaction."

Randy shook her head, looking agitated again. "Joe, I'm tired—I told you that."

"Yeah, you told me," he said coldly. "What you haven't told me is the truth."

"And what truth is that?" she asked wearily.

"That you don't want me anymore," he said softly, as if trying to lessen the impact of that possibility on himself. His light blue eyes again searched hers.

Randy stared back at him, unable to think of a reply. He was right—she didn't—but she didn't understand why. His kisses left her cold now, and she had no idea at all why. But his saying plainly what she'd been thinking in her deepest, darkest thoughts left her speechless.

Joe let out his pent-up breath in a sardonic laugh, shaking his head and looking up at the ceiling, refusing to allow her to see the hurt in his eyes. "I don't know why I thought you'd deny that." There were tears in his voice, and complete surrender.

Without another word, he walked out to their closet and pulled on a shirt and his boots, then went over to his dresser to pick up his gun and his keys before walking out of the bedroom. Randy sat on the bed, too mired in her own thoughts to even think to react. Joe left the house that evening, and Randy didn't sleep for many hours, finally drifting off around five in the morning.

Joe walked into their bedroom an hour later. She woke to the sound of him moving about the room. When she opened her eyes she saw that he was putting clothes into a suitcase. She sat up, her hair falling about her in a long blond silk curtain.

"What are you doing?" she asked.

Joe looked up at her, his eyes points of cold ice. "Leaving."

Randy stared at him openmouthed. After a few moments she closed her mouth, then nodded. She lay back down, turning over so her back was to him, so he couldn't see the tears she was crying. She knew she was allowing this to happen, but she just didn't have the words to make him stay. She knew she wasn't giving him anything, that she wasn't making him happy. And she felt that she just didn't have it in her right now to give. She didn't understand it, no matter how hard she'd tried, so how could she make him? She couldn't, and that was why she was letting him leave without a fight.

Joe Sinclair had been the best thing that had ever happened to her, and she was letting him leave. Was he coming back? Was he divorcing her? She didn't know, and she was afraid to ask, because she had no reasons to give him not to. Closing her eyes, she forced herself to lie there, not turning around, not looking at him. She didn't see him staring at her, wanting to shake her for letting him do this. Wanting to scream at her for making this so damned easy. They'd been together for thirteen years—didn't that count for anything? Shaking his head, he closed the suitcase, picked up his holstered gun, keys, and badge, and left the room. Randy lay in her bed and cried all morning, knowing she was dying but not how to fix it.

15

Joe called in to the office the next day, asking for Assistant Chief Kyle Masterson and telling him he was taking a few days off. Kyle thought it was strange that Joe would call him instead of Midnight, his best friend. Midnight thought the same thing later that morning when Kyle told her about Joe's request. It took all of another two hours for Midnight to get mad enough to call Joe's house to see what was going on. No one answered the phone. She tried his cell phone, and he didn't answer that either. She stewed about it the rest of the day, finally going over to his house that night. Randy answered the door, looking tired and unhappy.

"Randy, what's wrong?" Midnight asked, stepping inside the doorway.

"Aunt Midnight!" Kat and JT screamed in unison, charging up to her and grabbing her legs.

"Hi, you two!" Midnight said, laughing as she knelt down to hug them both.

"You have to see my new car!" JT said, pulling at her.

"No, she needs to see my new drawing," Kat said, trying to pull her the other way.

Midnight glanced up to see Randy watching the scene but still not smiling.

"Hey," Midnight said to the children. "I need to talk to your mommy for a bit. Can I come see you in a few minutes?"

JT looked rebellious, much like his father often did, then finally nodded. Kat agreed readily, and they both ran off back down the hall to their rooms.

Midnight stood up, her eyes surveying Randy. "Come on," she said, nodding toward the living room.

Midnight sat down on the couch, and Randy sat next to her.

"What's going on, Randy?" Midnight asked, knowing without a doubt that something had happened.

"He left," Randy said simply.

"Left?" Midnight asked, stunned, and sure she hadn't heard right.

Randy nodded miserably.

"Why?"

"It's my fault," Randy said, leaning back against the couch with a sigh. "I've been so busy at the center, and I haven't had enough time for him, and when I'm home I'm so tired..." She trailed off, shaking her head.

"Joe's worked long hours for years," Midnight pointed out. "You've stayed with him all that time."

"I know, but..."

"But what, Randy? But it's not okay for you to do that now, when you're finally doing something you're passionate about?" Midnight asked, angry at Joe for what appeared to be selfishness on his part.

"It's not that," Randy said. "You know Joe's always supported me with this center. I mean, Jesus, the man bought me an entire building to help me get started. It's not that," she said again, suddenly feeling desperate to defend him.

"Then what is it?" Midnight asked, searching Randy's eyes.

Randy hesitated for a long time, not sure she wanted to say what the problem was, because she still didn't understand it herself.

"He thinks I don't want him anymore," she said finally.

"And why would he think that?" Midnight asked, sounding wary suddenly.

17

Randy bit her lip, knowing how what she was about to say would sound, but it was the truth. "Because I don't."

Midnight's mouth dropped open in her shock, and she looked much like Joe had that morning when Randy hadn't denied what he'd said. Then she shook her head slowly, as if denying just that.

"You don't want him anymore?"

Randy sighed miserably. "I don't know why I don't, Midnight, but no, I haven't wanted to make love with him for months now."

"Jesus..." Midnight breathed, unable to comprehend it.

She had no idea what she'd do if Rick ever stopped wanting her sexually. She looked at Randy. "Did you tell him you don't want him anymore?"

Randy looked ashamed, her eyes dropping from Midnight's.

"Oh God, you did," Midnight said, suddenly understanding why Joe had called Kyle instead of her; he was depressed, and Midnight would have picked up on it instantly.

"He said he thought I didn't want him anymore, and I didn't say anything," Randy clarified, knowing that not denying it had been just as bad as not saying anything. Midnight's wince confirmed that.

"Randy..." Midnight said, shaking her head dejectedly. "He's been getting more and more sensitive about getting old lately, and now this..." She spread her hands wide to express the helplessness of the situation.

Randy didn't answer. She hadn't been aware that Joe had become sensitive about his age. She realized she'd missed a lot in the last few months. Or maybe Joe hadn't shared his insecurities with her, knowing she didn't have the time or obviously the capacity to help him. It compounded his leaving.

18

Joe answered the door to the suite, knowing before he did who it was. He looked down at his best friend of over seventeen years. Midnight reached up and hugged him without a word, seeing the devastation in his eyes. He accepted her hug, closing his eyes, still extremely hurt. He'd worked on numbing himself against the feeling of inadequacy all day, drinking heavily, but that seemed to only intensify his desolation. Midnight moved him into the room, closing the door behind her. She had no idea what to say. She wished she could tell him he was wrong about Randy not wanting him anymore, but she couldn't, not when Randy herself had admitted it.

"Joe..." she began, searching for something to say.

Joe held up his hand. "Don't, Night. It's okay," he said, his tone dead.

"It's not okay," Midnight said, looking up at him. "You're hurting. I want to help."

"You can't help," he said, shaking his head. "Not with this."

Joe assumed she'd talked to Randy, to at least ascertain that he'd left. Midnight would have made the natural assumption he'd check into a hotel. He was at the Intercontinental, which wouldn't have been too hard to track down. He had no idea, however, what had been said between Midnight and Randy, and that Midnight did indeed know what was making him hurt so much right then.

Midnight bit her lip, uncertain for the first time in a long time, where Joe was concerned. Obviously she couldn't restore his faith in his virility. She grinned.

"Well, I could help, but..." she said, her grin deepening. "Rick would shoot you, and then I'd have to get a new captain in vice, and..." She trailed off as she sighed, shaking her head.

19

Joe's eyes narrowed. "She told you?"

"She told me why you left."

Joe nodded, not looking happy about the prospect that his best friend now knew the nature of the problem. It was a bloody bitch, getting old. He walked over to the couch, sitting down heavily, looking more despondent. Midnight moved to kneel in front of him, looking up into his eyes.

"Tell me what to do, Joe."

Joe just shook his head, not meeting her eyes. "Just go home, Midnight."

"I can't," she said. "I can't leave you feeling like this."

"Night, I just want to be alone right now."

"No," Midnight said, shaking her head.

"Damnit," Joe growled. "I'm asking you to leave me alone."

"Why? So you can mull all this over in your head, over and over again? Make yourself feel worse?" she asked, her anger at her own inability to help him making her tone sharp. Joe looked back at her, his eyes serious, not giving an inch. "Joe, please..." she said, reaching out to touch his hands, noting they were cold. "Let me help you."

"You can't."

"Let me at least be here with you," she said, desperate to take the sadness out of his eyes.

"No," he said, unyielding. "I want to be alone."

"Damn it, Sinclair!"

"Night!" he said, raising his voice to match hers. "You can't fucking help me. You can't give me back my youth, my strength, my fucking manhood." He paused, pinning her with a look filled with impotent fury. "You can't, okay? You just can't."

Midnight stared back at him, sickened by the idea that he thought he'd lost all of that.

"You're not old," she said, her voice a quiet contrast to his anger moments before.

Joe looked at her for a long moment, a sad smile curving his lips slightly. "You're only two years younger than me. If you admit I'm getting old, you'd have to admit the same about yourself."

She was taken aback by his statement. She knew he was trying to justify in his mind why she didn't see what he was so sure he did, but he'd never launched a direct assault at her to justify his own point of view. It proved to her that he was very definitely convinced about what he believed, and it also scared her to death.

"You're scaring me, Joe," she admitted, searching his eyes.

"I'm sorry," he said, his voice indicating that he was but that he had no intention of changing his attitude.

"Will you let me stay with you?" she asked. "Please?"

Joe shook his head, once again refusing to meet her eyes.

"Joe," she said, trying a different tact. "You'd never let me be alone at a time like this."

"You wouldn't give me a choice," he replied, knowing her well.

"Well, I'm not giving you one now, either," she said, standing up and looking down at him.

Joe stood too, his eyes narrowing dangerously. "Don't start with me, Midnight. I said I want to be alone."

"And I said you're not going to be," she replied, not intimidated by his tone of voice or the look that would scare most full-grown men.

21

Joe's jaw twitched as he clenched it, his fingers working at his sides in anger. Midnight's look changed to one of challenge.

"You thinking about hitting me, Sinclair?" she asked dangerously.

"Maybe."

"Try it," she replied, her eyes not leaving his.

There was a tense moment, and Midnight really believed that he wanted to hit her. She could feel his fury just under the surface. She also knew his anger wasn't directed at her, but at his inability to turn the tide of frustration and inferiority he was feeling.

Joe let out a yell of pure fury as he kicked the heavy wooden coffee table behind Midnight, launching it a foot in the air and upending it. Midnight closed her eyes, realizing that could have been her but not willing to flinch from his anger. When she opened them, she was staring into his light blue eyes. She could see the suffused anger on his face, and it actually scared her. It had been a long time since Joe was actually mad at her, and she didn't remember ever being afraid of him before. She took a step back, her expression wary, but she refused to look away from him. Something in Joe's head clicked then— she could see it. He closed his eyes, lowering his head as he grimaced.

"Midnight…" he said, his voice low and so devastated. "I'm sorry. God, I'm sorry." He had seen fear in her eyes, and it hurt him to see her look at him that way. He stared at her then, his eyes pleading with her. "Do you see why I need to be alone right now? I'm not fit for human interaction. I need to work through this one on my own." He reached out, touching her cheek. "Please, Night. I'm begging you."

Midnight stepped forward, wrapping her arms around his waist. "Just promise me you won't hurt yourself."

22

Joe put his arms around her, closing his eyes, knowing that he could make the promise but not sure that he could keep it.

"Joe?" Midnight said, raising her head to look up at him. "Promise me," she said again, aware that he would never promise her something he couldn't deliver. When he didn't reply, she said, "Promise me, or I swear to God, I'll be here with you twenty-four-seven."

He took a slow, deep breath, expelling it in a deep sigh, finally nodding miserably. "I promise."

Midnight smiled, reaching up to touch his cheek and praying inwardly that this wasn't going to be the first and last time he ever broke a promise to her.

"If you need me or Rick, or any of us, all you have to do is call, okay?" she said softly.

Joe nodded, swallowing convulsively.

Midnight left a little while later. Joe went to bed, feeling worse. Now he'd made a promise to Midnight and it felt like he was even more stuck with this feeling of dread, knowing there was no way out now.

***

Stevie was asleep when she felt lips on her bare shoulder. She stirred as they moved to her neck, then her cheek. She was half awake by the time his lips met hers. Her hands moved through black hair as she pulled him closer, kissing him with growing fervor.

"Missed me, did you?" Christian asked.

"No," Stevie replied, grinning as he nipped at her lip for that blatant lie.

23

Stevie opened her eyes and saw that he was kneeling next to the bed, still dressed. She glanced at the clock. It was 12:30 a.m.

"Red eye, Collins?" she asked, sitting up, not bothering to pull the sheet up with her.

"Yup," he replied, sitting on the bed next to her.

His eyes moved appreciatively over her body, unclothed and on show for him. Reaching out, he touched her waist, pulling her to him to kiss her again. That's when Stevie caught a whiff of perfume. She pulled back immediately, her head coming up, staring straight into his eyes.

"I wasn't aware you'd switched to perfume, Collins," she said, her voice icy, her emerald green eyes narrowed.

Christian looked mystified for a moment, then made a disgusted sound in the back of his throat. He shook his head, giving her a "You should know better" look.

"It's Jackie's—she hugged me when we got to the airport. I've told you, she practically bathes in her perfume." His tone was weary, telling her he was tired of having to explain that to her.

"And what was she doing at the airport, Collins?" Stevie asked. "Isn't that a little above and beyond her call of duty?"

"She took me to the airport," Christian supplied, leaning back and looking down at Stevie, his face set in stone.

Stevie nodded, her expression cynical. "Yeah, she had nothing else to do at, like, ten o'clock at night, right?"

"Steve..." he said, his tone cautionary. "Nothing happened, okay? She hugged me and now I smell like her perfume—that's it.

You're gonna have to believe me, because I'm not gonna fucking argue about it for the next two hours." His voice had taken on an angry tone, and Stevie feel his tension.

She lay back on the bed, looking up at him. "Well, take a shower before you come to my bed. I don't want to smell the bitch on you."

Christian sighed, getting up and shaking his head. He couldn't believe he'd honestly wanted fire like hers. There was no halfway with Stevie O'Neil. If she felt something, whether it be passion or anger, you knew it. He loved her, but she drove him crazy sometimes. They'd been living together for over a year now, and there were so many times when he was thankful she was his, and others when he was sure he was crazy for living with a woman like her.

Stevie O'Neil did everything with intensity. She didn't take insults lightly, she kept what she considered hers and would fight for it if necessary. There had been a time when she had doubted Christian's feeling for her, and had shown him her displeasure by totally turning her back on him. It had made him want her more. Then she'd been gunned down in front of him, by a drug dealer she was testifying against. As she'd lain bleeding in his arms, he'd discovered that he loved her. Since that time they'd been together. It had been over a year and a half, but there were still days when he knew he didn't possess her completely. He didn't realize she felt exactly the same way.

An hour later he climbed into bed. Her back was to him. He moved to lie behind her, his body molding against hers. He slid his arm under her neck, winding it around so his hand splayed over her upper torso, his other arm going to her waist, pulling her back against him. Christian could feel her tension, but he knew how her mind worked. It was his turn to make it up to her. He leaned down, kissing her shoulder, caressing her bare skin gently.

25

He moved his lips to her neck, then her ear. "I love you," he whispered, noting the twitch of her jaw as she gritted her teeth, which indicated that she was fighting to resist him.

He brushed his thumb upward over her breasts and across already sensitive nipples, and felt her moan quietly. He smiled to himself, knowing he had her then. Taking his hand from her waist, he reached down to touch under her chin, turning her face to his.

"Collins…" she gritted out, even as his lips covered hers.

She made a disgruntled sound just before she started kissing him back, turning over to press against him. He knew it pissed her off no end that he could make her react to him, and he found it endlessly amusing that she fought it every time.

He spent the next two hours reminding her why she loved him, why she craved him, and why she let him get away with things she would have dumped other guys for. He had a few marks on his back and neck to show for it; unknowingly, she did as well. Their lovemaking was always heated and passionate, and always resulted in both of them being exhausted but completely sated.

Even as she drifted off to sleep in his arms, still lying half over him, Stevie leaned down and bit his shoulder. He flinched, tightening his arm around her.

"Don't ever come to my bed smelling like someone else again, Collins," she said seriously.

"I won't."

She leaned down and kissed the spot she had bitten, then laid her head back down on his chest. They fell asleep that way.

CHAPTER 2

Stevie drove her Trans Am up to the front of the building. She looked good, wearing her black jersey dress and black three-inch heels. Her hunter green jacket was draped over her seat. Her long fiery-red hair was pulled back from her face with a clip, spilling down to her waist in silky waves. Her makeup accentuated her emerald green eyes, but for once it was more conservative. She was going to court today, to keep the man that had killed her brother-in-law—and almost her— behind bars.

Marco Tiempo was appealing his conviction for attempted murder of a peace officer. He claimed that he had never sent anyone to kill Stevie O'Neil. Stevie had been shot three times with an AK47 rifle. She'd come very close to dying, and many were convinced that part of what had saved her life was the fact that Christian Collins had taken the fourth shot, which would have more than likely killed her. They knew for a fact, however, that Marco Tiempo had been trying to have Stevie killed so she couldn't testify against him. She had infiltrated his business, becoming his bodyguard. It had taken a year and a half and the help of Dave Dibbins, but she'd taken down the man that was responsible for the death of her brother-in-law, Jason Templeton. Jason had been killed in a car accident during the pursuit of a fleeing Marco Tiempo, leaving his wife, Rhiannon, Stevie's sister, devastated.

Stevie leaned forward, looking for the familiar figure of Joe Sinclair. He was accompanying her to the courthouse that day, testifying as a ballistics expert for the prosecution as well as ensuring that Stevie was safe. Stevie didn't know the second half of that task; Chief Midnight Chevalier had requested it of Joe, and he'd agreed. Stevie was now a very accepted member of the "Gang". The Gang was, to them, their version of a family, and consisted of members of Midnight's original task force as well as their spouses, children, siblings, and/or significant others. Stevie's significant other was Christian Collins, Joe Sinclair's cousin. It made one crazy to even contemplate the intricate workings of who was with whom and related to whom. It was easier just to know you were part of something that entailed total loyalty.

She spotted Joe coming down the stairs at the front of the building and pulled the car up to the curb. Joe walked over and opened the passenger door, tossing his jacket in the back before getting in. He looked handsome in his dark suit pants and light blue shirt. Stevie also noticed he looked tired and unhappy.

"Everything okay?" she asked, sensing his depression easily.

Joe stared back at her for a long moment, not sure whether she'd heard anything about him leaving Randy. Finally, he just shook his head and blew his breath out in a sigh.

Stevie looked at him for a long moment, not sure if she should pry, and figured that if he wanted to talk about it, he would. "Well, I'll listen if you want to talk," she said, putting the car into gear and pulling away from the curb.

"Thanks, O'Neil," he said, smiling slightly. "What I could use right now is a cup of coffee. Do we have time?"

Stevie glanced at her watch. "Yeah, we've got plenty of time," she said, giving him a sidelong glance. "Coffee pot at home broke?"

28

He caught her look and couldn't help but grin. She was a lot like Midnight; she'd get it out of him no matter what he did to evade her.

"Ah, I guess you heard, huh?" he replied.

She nodded solemnly. "I heard, yes," she said softly.

Joe nodded, looking out the window. He still felt very raw about the whole thing, even though it had been a week. He knew that the Gang had heard, not because of Midnight but because Susan had found out, since she worked in their home. Rick obviously found out from Midnight, while Kyle figured it out on his own, and Spider had too, since he'd had to call Joe back at the hotel rather than at home. Donovan had found out from his sister. Eventually the whole Gang knew.

They were silent on the short drive to the coffee shop. They went in to buy their coffee then came back out to the car. When Stevie pulled out of the parking space, she flipped her hair over her left shoulder as she looked behind her. Joe couldn't help but notice the red mark on her neck, and grinned.

"What?" Stevie asked, catching it.

Joe reached over and touched the mark, just below and behind her ear. Stevie had stopped, waiting for traffic to clear so she could get onto the road, so she glanced in her rearview mirror. She proceeded to groan at the sight of the hickey.

"Oh, great, O'Neil, real professional," she grumbled as she pulled her hair down over the spot. "I'm gonna kill him."

Joe laughed at her rancor, shaking his head and feeling better suddenly. Then he shrugged. "Hey, it's good to know someone is getting some," he said, grinning.

Stevie looked over at him, her mouth dropping open. Joe was sure he'd just stunned her with the impropriety of his statement; this

29

was a work setting, after all. He was thinking he should apologize when she dissuaded him of his original thought.

"She's not giving you any?" she asked, her amazement apparent.

Joe shook his head. "Not recently, no," he said, suddenly feeling stupid for having brought it up.

Again Stevie gave him a more serious look, as she stopped at the next light. "Have you had her head examined?"

"For what? Not wanting an old man?" he said, feeling really vulnerable at that point and not liking it one bit.

"Uh, Sinclair," Stevie said. "You are not old."

"Beg to differ, honey."

She glanced over at him again as the light turned green. "How old could you be? What, thirty-three, thirty-four?"

Joe looked at her for a long moment, a sardonic grin starting on his lips. "Stevie, I'm thirty-nine."

"No fucking way!" Stevie said, shaking her head.

Joe grinned. "I hate to break it to ya, babe—I'm pushing forty."

"Like hell you are," Stevie shot back, still not sure she believed him.

"You wanna see my license?"

"I might," she replied, narrowing her green eyes at him. "I still say she needs her head examined," she added after a long moment.

"Why?"

Stevie looked over at him, her eyes moving from his face, down his body, then back up. "Because if I had what she has, I wouldn't neglect it."

Joe looked back at her for a long moment, stunned. He felt good for a few moments before his mind started telling him she was just trying to help.

Stevie could see the moment his ego quit and his head took over, and she started shaking her head. "And don't go telling yourself I'm just saying that to be nice, Sinclair. I have nothing to gain by admitting that."

"Admitting?"

Stevie bit her lip, even as she accelerated to get on the freeway. They were headed to the next county over, where the appeal was being heard. This was probably now about to become the longest ride of her life.

"O'Neil?" he queried when she didn't reply.

She sighed heavily, getting into the fast lane. "Okay, okay," she said, shaking her head at herself in disgust. "I swore I'd never tell anyone in the Gang any of this…"

"Tell me," he said, his voice softer.

She stared straight ahead as she drove, looking for all intents and purposes like she was testifying in court.

"The first time I met you and Midnight Chevalier was when I was eleven years old. But I knew about you both before that. I'd heard about Midnight from my dad for years. He'd always thought she was really great, and that she would go far in the department. I'd seen her at a couple of the functions that she attended. I decided when I was about ten that I wanted to be Midnight Chevalier when I grew up. And then there was you." She hesitated as she looked over at him. He nodded, his face composed as he listened her. "My dad had said that you were a good cop, that you were working with Midnight to run

31

FORS. I'd never seen you until the day of my dad's funeral. Obviously, I was pretty screwed up that day, but I remember you and Midnight walking up." She glanced at him again, and he nodded. "You were both dressed in black, and I remember thinking that you were both so striking, that you both just seemed so… I don't know, *right*, next to each other. She was so tiny compared to you, and you stood just behind her, like her back-up would…" Her voice trailed off as she shook her head. Then she glanced at him. "Do you remember what you said to me that day?"

Joe thought for a moment, then shook his head slowly. "I remember the funeral, and I remember talking to you, but I don't remember what I said."

"I do," she said. "You knelt down in front of me, you took my hands in yours, and you looked me right in the eye and said, 'I know exactly how you feel right now, Stevie, but you have to believe me when I tell you that eventually it won't hurt so much and someday you'll be able to breathe again.' Those words meant more to me than you could possibly know," she said, her voice tinged with tears.

"I was right, wasn't I?" Joe said softly.

She nodded. "You were right, and from that moment on, I just thought you were a god. I followed everything FORS did—I read every news clip, and kept the articles. I watched the news avidly. When I was about sixteen, when all that stuff happened with Randy being on trial, I followed everything. I even managed to get into the courtroom for your testimony, although I didn't know you were testifying that day—I just wanted to be around the whole thing. But when the lawyer was asking you about your family home, and how much it meant to you, when you looked at her and said that it meant almost as much as she did to you, I was one of the women in the room that sighed so loud everyone heard it. You were this larger-than-life man, this star to me. And when your picture appeared in the paper with Midnight's, I cut it out and kept it. I still have it, Sinclair." She looked straight at him then. "I always wanted to be Midnight, and since I was about fifteen, I always wanted to be *with* you."

Joe was stunned, and he couldn't even think of a reply for a long moment. He finally shook his head and said, "Ah, the dreams of youth."

Stevie grinned. "Yeah, well…" she said, pressing her lips together to keep from saying more.

"What?" Joe asked, his voice taking on a mockingly suspicious tone.

"Nothing," she said, holding back an embarrassed grin.

"O'Neil…"

"What?" she asked, giving him an exasperated look.

"What?"

Finally she shrugged, giving him a roguish grin. "Okay, so some dreams die hard."

Joe's mouth dropped open for a moment, and then he started to laugh, shaking his head. He couldn't believe what he was hearing. He knew he should find a reason to justify why she was saying this to him; it was just too fortuitous timing-wise. What were the odds that he'd find out about this now, when his ego needed it the most?

"What's so funny?" she asked, trying to appear offended even as she grinned.

"Oh, Stevie," he said, still laughing a bit. "You have no idea how much good you're doing this old man's ego."

"Okay, one, you're not old—I don't care how old you *claim* to

33

be on paper," she said vehemently. "And two, why would what I have to say mean anything to you?"

Joe sobered then, trying to keep the grin off his face. "Because, O'Neil, in case you haven't noticed, you're a young, vibrant, beautiful woman, and to have you telling me this is the boost my ego needs right now."

"Well, I'm not doing it to boost your ego," she said, giving him a sour look. "In fact, I could just kick myself for opening my mouth in the first place."

"Why?" he asked; again, his tone was soft.

"Because in case *you* haven't noticed, Sinclair, you're married, in love with your wife, the cousin of the man I'm living with."

"Ah," he said seriously, nodding, but started to grin again immediately. "Speaking of which, how's that going?"

"Don't ask."

"I believe I just did."

"Haven't I made enough confessions today?"

"What would you have to confess, O'Neil?"

"You mean other than the fact that I think he's screwing around on me?"

"Ouch," Joe said. "He couldn't be. He wouldn't dare."

"Oh, he'd dare, alright," Stevie said, nodding. "He did it to Susan, right?"

"That's 'cause Susan wasn't likely to shoot his ass for doing it," Joe replied, smiling tightly.

Stevie couldn't help but grin at that. "True, but apparently that's not much of a deterrent either."

"What happened?"

34

"He came home last night smelling like another woman," she said quickly, as if rushing through the statement would make its impact less.

"Did you ask him about it?"

"Duh, Sinclair," she replied, reminding him a lot of Midnight.

"What did he say?"

"He said that she hugged him when she dropped him off at the airport."

"And you don't believe him?"

Stevie thought about it for a long moment, then sighed, shrugging. "I don't know anymore, you know? I don't think he did anything, or he wouldn't have been so obvious with still smelling like her, or if he was, he would have just told me he did her. Denial for the sake of sparing feelings isn't exactly Collins' strong suit, ya know?"

Joe grinned, nodding. "Christian always does what he wants to do."

"Yes, he does."

"He'd be a fool to let you go," Joe said sincerely.

"You think so?" she asked, feeling the need for her own reassurances.

"Yeah, I do," he said, the conviction in his light blue eyes backing up his statement.

"Thanks," she said simply.

They spent the day in court. Stevie dropped Joe back by the department at 4:00 p.m., telling him she needed to go sign the papers for the house she was buying; she'd received the page while they were in court.

Joe made a point of asking about it the next day when he picked

35

her up out front. He was driving the Aston Martin he'd bought a couple of years before. Stevie all but drooled on the car. Joe found it endearing. They talked about the power of the car, and she admitted that she would kill to own one like it. Joe said he'd let her drive on the way home.

"You'd let me drive your car?" she asked, stunned.

"Sure, why not?" Joe said, glancing over at her.

"If it was my car, I wouldn't let anyone drive it," she said, grinning.

Joe laughed, pulling away from the curb.

"So," he began as he got onto the freeway after they'd gotten their coffee once again. "Did you sign your papers yesterday?"

"Yep, got it all taken care of."

"Now you two are buying this together, right?" he asked; that was the understanding everyone in the Gang had.

"Uh, no," she said. "My money, my deal, my house."

"But… we all thought…" Joe trailed off as he realized they'd all assumed a lot.

"I know what everyone thought," she said, shrugging. "I just didn't correct anyone. But, no, I'm buying this house on my own."

Joe looked over at her, narrowing his eyes, sensing that there was tension there. "Is he moving in with you?"

She glanced at him, and he could see that it was a sore subject. She shrugged. "I have no idea."

"Have you talked to him about it?"

"Nope," she said, sounding irritated. "He knows I'm buying it— I even took him over to show him the house. He hasn't mentioned a thing about taking up residence there with me."

36

"Is he aware that he's welcome to?" Joe asked solicitously.

"At the rate he's going, I don't know that he is welcome."

"Oh." Joe wondered if Stevie had any idea how much like Midnight she'd really become. He gave her a measuring look.

"What?" she asked, seeing it.

"You're a lot like Midnight was, do you realize that?"

"Am I?" she asked, surprised by what she perceived as a compliment.

"Yeah, you are."

"Cool," she said, grinning.

Joe laughed.

They spent the next two days in a companionable state. Joe found that he thoroughly enjoyed talking to her. She was young enough to keep him laughing, but mature enough and serious enough about the job to understand the gravity of what they were doing.

The last day of court, they left at lunchtime.

"Where do you want me to drop you off?" Stevie asked.

"Drop me?" he queried.

"Yeah, I have to run home for a few," she said, indicating the nasty run in her stockings.

Joe grinned. "Well, now that's something Midnight would never do."

"Oh, shut up!" Stevie said, laughing.

"Why don't I just go with you?" he asked.

"You're not hungry?"

"We can grab something on the way and eat there, if that's okay with you?" he said, curious about the place she shared with Christian. He'd never managed to get over there since they'd lived together.

"Fine with me," she said, getting into his car.

They arrived at her and Christian's apartment a while later. They'd stopped and gotten fast food, and took it inside to eat. Afterward, Stevie showed him around the apartment. It was a nice place.

"Okay, I'll be out in a minute," she said, holding up one finger.

After about ten minutes, Joe decided to check on her. He walked up to the doorway that led to her and Christian's bedroom. Stevie was just pulling on a second thigh-high stocking. She glanced up when she sensed him in the doorway. His eyes were on her legs; her skirt was hiked up high on her thighs, not obscenely so, but slightly higher than a miniskirt would be.

"Sorry it took me so long," she said, grinning. "Couldn't find anything."

"That looks like somethin'," Joe said, unable to take his eyes off her legs.

"Sinclair?" she queried, grinning widely at him. "You with me here?"

"Huh?" he said, dragging his eyes up to hers.

She smiled. "Problem?"

"Nope," he said, grinning again. "But damn, O'Neil, you have some serious legs."

"Serious?"

"Deadly."

She laughed as she got up off the bed, letting her skirt fall. Then she walked over to the bathroom sink.

"Now what are you doing?" he asked, leaning against the door-jamb.

"Fixing my face," she said as she reached into a drawer for a compact.

"There ain't nothin' wrong with your face either," he said, smiling.

She glanced over at him, a grin on her lips. "You flirting with me, Sinclair?"

"You still living with my cousin?"

"Currently. You still married?"

"Currently," he replied. "So I'd have to say that no, I'm not flirting with you at this time."

"Is that your official answer?" she asked, enjoying the game.

"Currently," he said, his light blue eyes twinkling. He was enjoying it as well.

"You'll let me know when it changes?"

"Definitely."

With that he walked back down the hall, leaving Stevie grinning to herself. She was sure he was just playing with her, but it still felt kind of nice to have her idol admire her.

***

Susan Endicott-Dibbins rushed to the emergency room, her heart in her throat. All she had been told was that her husband had been shot. There had been plenty of times when he'd been hurt—cut, bruised, even broken a rib—but never shot.

Spider met her at the ER desk, taking her in his arms instantly.

39

"He's okay, Susan, he's okay. It was just a graze."

He'd known how worried she'd be. He'd only just ascertained that his long-time partner and friend wasn't in any real danger. Dave had been unconscious when they'd brought him in, and there had been blood all over his face; it had been impossible to tell how serious his injuries were. He'd told Midnight what he'd known at the time, that Dave had been shot by one of the dealers he was working, so he'd known Susan would be frantic.

"Thank God," she sighed, even as Midnight did the same.

Midnight got on the phone and let everyone know Dave was okay. She couldn't get ahold of Joe, and found out why a few minutes later when he walked up. The Gang had just started arriving when Susan was allowed in to see Dave.

When she walked in, she saw the bandage on his head, and that he was sitting up against the pillows, his eyes closed. He opened his eyes immediately, holding his arms out to her. She climbed up onto the bed, moving into his arms. He held her against him, stroking her hair.

"I'm okay, babe," he said soothingly. "Just a scratch."

Susan was crying by this time, releasing some of the pent-up anxiety she'd experienced a few minutes before. "All Midnight said was that you'd been shot," she said, sounding devastated.

"I was, babe, but it was just a graze, no big deal."

She raised her head, looking up into his blue eyes. "David, you were shot in the head."

He gazed down at her for a long moment, then leaned forward and kissed her lips softly. "And I'm okay, honey. It wasn't my time."

"Oh, David..." she said, still feeling so relieved and shocked at the same time.

She knew that her husband of almost two years honestly believed that everyone had a predetermined destiny and that they couldn't change it. It didn't make it any easier to handle the idea of him being shot in the head—if the bullet had been just an inch lower... She hugged him closer as she stopped her thoughts. She had no idea what she'd do if she ever lost him.

Dave Dibbins was her life now. She loved everything about him, from his easygoing manner to his tough-guy muscle car, to his habit of saying the exact right thing when she needed it most, to his extremely dangerous and stressful job. That job kept him away from her for three or four days at a time, sometimes even a week, but when he was home for three or four days, he was all hers. He dedicated every waking moment to her, spending time holding her, kissing her, making love to her, talking to her about anything and everything and generally making her the happiest woman alive.

Dave held his wife to him, feeling bad that she had been so afraid for him and wanting to comfort her as best he could. She was the very balance in his life. He was an undercover narcotics officer, and he worked long hours, dealing with the scum of the earth. He moved among them, acting as they did, speaking as they did, and feeling their slime coat him for days on end. When he left behind his sleazy department-rented apartment, he went home to her. His proper English wife. She was the last person he would have ever imagined himself married to, but the only woman he could ever imagine wanting ever again. When he dragged himself in off the street, she took care of him, making sure he ate enough, rested enough, and relaxed. She made him forget everything but being with her and enjoying life.

41

There were hours in the middle of the night when he'd just hold her, feeling her warmth against him and thanking whatever powers that be that had brought her to him. They were almost a full generation apart, with sixteen years' difference in their ages, but there were rarely times when they didn't see things the same. In the year and nine months they'd been married, they'd never fought, not even once. Susan attributed that to him, citing his incredible ability to shut out the other side of his life, to leave the job at the sleazy apartment. Dave cited the fact that she was the sweetest, gentlest person he'd ever known, and he couldn't imagine being mad at her for a minute. They were a good match; every member of the Gang thought so. So did they.

"David…" Susan said hesitantly as she looked up at him again, still within the circle of his arms.

"Yes?" he asked, grinning as he recognized that she was about to ask him for something.

She bit her lip, her dark blue eyes shining up into his, and he knew that no matter what she was about to ask, he'd give it to her.

"I want you to take a vacation with me."

"A vacation?"

"Yes, that trip to London we never took," she said, reminding him of the two plane tickets he'd bought her the Christmas before.

"Ohh…" he said, his voice trailing off as he grimaced.

"What?" she asked softly.

"I don't know, babe…" he said, genuinely apologetic.

"Why not?" she asked, staring up into his eyes.

Dave closed his eyes, grimacing, making the members of the Gang hanging out in the doorway start to grin. It was obvious Dave

Dibbins, hardened narcotics officer, best in the business, couldn't resist his sweet little English wife.

"Ohh…" he groaned. "Don't look at me like that," he said, starting to grin, knowing he'd already lost.

"Like what?" she asked, her smile becoming ingenue in her attempt to look innocent.

Dave narrowed his eyes at her, his grin still present. "You know what."

"Please take me to London, David," she said softly, staring up into his eyes, her lips so close to his.

Dave sighed deeply, nodding. Susan laughed, hugging him.

"Not like you ever had a choice, man," Spider said from the doorway.

"Shut up," Dave said, laughing as he hugged his wife to him.

***

Kyle Masterson climbed into bed, sliding his arms around Rhiannon and pulling her back against him. He still wore his slacks and dress shirt; he'd only taken the time to kick off his shoes. Leaning down, he kissed her cheek.

"Rhi?" he whispered, not wanting to wake her but worried about her all the same. She'd been home with the flu for two days now, and she was rarely sick.

"Hmm?" she murmured, turning over to snuggle against him.

"How are you feeling, honey?"

She rubbed her eyes, reminding him of a little girl—especially when she looked up at him petulantly, like she was at that moment.

43

"I still feel like dirt."

"Ah, hon, I'm sorry," he said, leaning down to kiss her cheek again. Then his face grew serious. "I think you should go in and get checked."

Rhiannon, his wife of only six months, rested her head on his shoulder and shook it. "Why? It's the flu—they'll just tell me that I have the flu and there's no cure for it."

"Rhi," he said, touching her under the chin to make her look at him. "I want you to get checked, please?"

Rhiannon gazed at him for a full minute, searching his eyes. "This is important, Kyle," she surmised. "Why?"

His lips tugged in a partial smile; she did know him well.

"Barbara had been sick with the flu for months," he began, settling into the narrative tone he used when he talked about his deceased wife. "She was run-down, and tired all the time, and she felt achy. She finally went to the doctor. They ran tests, and that's when they discovered the cancer."

Rhiannon placed her hand on his cheek. "Oh, Kyle, I'm sorry," she whispered, then nodded. "I'll make the appointment first thing in the morning."

"Thank you," he said earnestly.

"I love you," she said, sorry that her being sick was bringing up bad memories for him.

"I love you too, Rhi. I just want to make sure you're okay."

"I know," she said, smiling up at him.

He leaned down and kissed her. She pulled back, giving him a mischievous smile. "You'll get my germs."

"I don't mind your germs," he replied, grinning and leaning down to kiss her again.

They were still kissing when there was a knock on their bedroom door.

Kyle sighed, then sat up. "Enter."

His older son, Nick, walked in. At fourteen, Nick Masterson looked very much like his father, though he had his mother's blue eyes. He was six feet tall already, and might still meet his father's height of six foot three before he was done becoming a man. His jet black hair was worn longer in the back, where it curled around his collar, much like his father's. He wasn't near as filled out as his dad, though. Kyle was an ex-Navy Seal who still maintained the regimen of working out on a daily basis. At forty-six, Kyle was stronger and more physically fit than many men half his age. Nick had the beginnings of a build, however, since he'd been working out with his father lately, deciding that being strong wouldn't hurt his chances with the girls.

"Dad?" Nick ventured softly, knowing that his stepmother was home sick and not wanting to wake her if she was sleeping—not so much out of concern for her, but because his dad would kick his ass if he disturbed Rhiannon.

"It's okay, Nick. What's up?" Kyle asked.

"Um," Nick said, walking over to the end of the bed, glancing at Rhiannon then back at his dad.

"Spit it out, Masterson," Kyle said, sounding like the Assistant Chief that he was.

"Well, I was kinda hoping you could talk to Chief Chevalier for me..."

Nick's dad still intimidated the hell out of him, no matter how

45

tall he got. Kyle had never lifted a hand to either of his sons, other than the occasional spanking when they were young. That didn't, however, eliminate the fear that if Kyle ever really lost his temper, he could damage his son pretty badly.

"About?" Kyle prompted.

"Well, you two are pretty close, right?"

"Close?" Kyle questioned, raising an eyebrow at the young man.

"Well, you know, you two were a thing…" Nick said, grinning, but stopped as he saw the dangerous look enter his father's eyes. *Okay, wrong play, Masterson,* he thought. "Anyway, you two are friends now, right?" he said hurriedly.

Kyle glanced at Rhiannon, who was endeavoring to hide her grin behind her hand.

"Yes, Chief Chevalier and I are friends. What's that got to do with you?"

"Well, I want to ask her daughter out," Nick blurted out.

Kyle's mouth dropped open. "Are you nuts?"

"Dad, have you *seen* that girl?"

"Yeah, I see her pretty much every day in the office, in her mother," Kyle said, then pinned his son with a look. "And I see her in her *dangerous, gun-carrying, overprotective father* too."

"I know, Dad, I know," Nick sighed, shaking his head. "I've seen him. But don't you see, if you could smooth it over with the chief, then her dad would have to say it's okay."

"Is that what you think?" Kyle asked, grinning. "You think that Rick just accepts whatever Midnight says?"

"Well…" Nick said, shrugging. "Yeah."

Kyle laughed, shaking his head. "Oh, Nicholas, you have a lot to learn about those two. You need to sit in on a few staff meetings when Rick doesn't agree with something Midnight wants to do. Fire-breathing dragons are less dangerous than he is. And no, he doesn't automatically approve anything Midnight agrees to."

"Shit." Nick looked crestfallen. "Oh, sorry," he said, catching his father's look.

Kyle didn't like either of his boys to act like anything other than gentlemen in front of women, even their stepmother. Even little Brenden, at age eight, spoke softly and gently around women. Kyle's influence on both boys was very noticeable. Though Brenden totally adored Rhiannon, so he was always sweet to her anyway.

"Besides," Kyle said, his tone changing, "how do you know that Mikeyla Debenshire wants to go out with the likes of you?"

"What?" Nick asked, surprised that his dad would say that.

"I mean, you're just some cop's kid—she's got money, power, beauty—" Kyle cut off with a yelp as Rhiannon poked him in the ribs.

"Kyle, stop it!" she said, giving him a narrowed look. "Nick, you don't listen to him. Mikeyla Debenshire would be lucky to go out with you."

Nick grinned, looking almost embarrassed at her praise. It was so hard not to like her sometimes. She always tried to help him when-ever she could, but he just felt that liking her meant he was betraying his mother. So he held himself back most of the time, not wanting to be too friendly. Rhiannon never pushed it, though, and he was grate-ful for that.

"So will ya, Dad?" he asked after a few long moments, not com-menting on what Rhiannon had said.

Kyle narrowed his eyes at his son, trying to decide if he should nail his ass for snubbing Rhiannon, but he knew Rhiannon felt uncomfortable when he put Nick on the spot about his rudeness. It was a fine line he walked every day between his oldest son and his wife. Rhiannon was always assuring him that she understood Nick's antagonism, that she knew it had everything to do with Barbara and nothing to do with herself. It still irritated Kyle that Rhiannon went out of her way to be nice to Nick and Nick just didn't reciprocate at all.

"I'll think about it," he said after a long pause. "Thing is, Nick, I don't know that you know how to treat a young lady of her caliber."

Kyle's look was pointed, and Nick knew his father was in effect nailing him to the wall for what he'd just done in ignoring Rhiannon. He sighed, shaking his head, and walked out of the room.

"Kyle…" Rhiannon began once Nick had closed the door.

"No, Rhian," Kyle said, making a cutting gesture with his hand. "I'm not going to let him get away with acting like that toward you and then do him a favor."

Rhiannon sighed, reaching up to touch his arm. "He's just trying to be loyal to Barbara. You can't fault him for that."

Kyle lay down next to her again, touching her face gently. "Rhi, if you weren't nice to him, I could understand it, yes, but you've busted your ass trying to be nice to him, and he acts like that. It irritates me."

"I know," Rhiannon said, searching his eyes. "But Nick needs to find his own way. You can't do it for him."

"Yeah, but I can make damned sure he knows I'm not happy about his attitude."

"He knows."

Rhiannon felt warmed by Kyle's insistence that his son treat her with respect, and also worried that she would cause an irreparable rift in an already damaged relationship. Kyle and Nick's relationship had been tenuous since Barbara's death from breast cancer over four years before. Nick had rebelled in an effort to deal with his anger over it, and Kyle, being a seasoned cop, had responded with swift, strict authority. Rhiannon had come into the middle of this minor war between father and son, and was determined to try and do everything she could to assist them.

Rhiannon herself knew how short life was. She too had lost someone she loved very much. Her husband of ten years, Jason, had been killed in a vehicle accident. Rhiannon had been shattered for three years, living a half-life of work and sad memories. It had been Kyle and his own sad experience with losing his wife that had brought her back to life. She and Kyle shared a very special bond, having helped each other back from the brink of the empty abyss their lives had become. She loved Kyle more than she thought she'd ever love any man again, and he loved her just as much. But with him she had inherited his two sons, and she was determined to do her best to help raise them.

"Are you going to talk to Midnight?" Rhiannon asked after a long time. Kyle was silent. "Kyle?"

"I don't know, Rhi," he said finally, sighing. "I mean, I wasn't kidding about Debenshire's protectiveness of Mikeyla. I don't know how he'd feel about Nick taking her out."

"How old is Mikeyla again?" Rhiannon asked, remembering the beautiful girl she'd met a number of times at the Debenshire home.

"I think she's thirteen now."

"And Nick is still fourteen."

49

"Yeah, but he'll be fifteen in three months."

"So he's still technically only a year older."

"Technically," Kyle said, grinning at the term.

"So why would it be bad for him to date Mikeyla?"

"Look," Kyle said, "I know my son, and I know he's got his hormones all in an uproar right now. If he's noticing Mikeyla it's because she's beautiful, and that can't be good."

"Kyle…" Rhiannon said, giving him a shocked look. "You don't trust your own son?"

"Rhi, I was a teenage boy once, okay?" he said, grinning rakishly. "I know what teenage boys think about twenty-four-seven."

"Sex, right?" Rhiannon clarified.

"Oh yeah."

"And you don't think he can control himself?"

"I think he's looking for more from the Debenshire girl than her parents will be able to accept her giving him."

Rhiannon smiled. "And I thought it was up to the girl to decide to say yes or no."

"Not when her parents are very intense cops it's not, honey. And if Debenshire even senses that Nick's up to no good with his girl, he'll probably kill him first and ask questions later."

Rhiannon bit her lip, holding back a grin, then sighed dramatically.

"A pair of star-crossed lovers take their life…"

"You're saying that he'll go for it anyway?" Kyle asked.

"I'm saying that if you think Mikeyla Debenshire hasn't noticed your extremely handsome son as he's noticed her, then you're deluding yourself, Masterson."

"And they'll see each other whether they have permission or not…"

"And he's done the right thing in asking you to smooth it over with Midnight."

"And I should reward that."

"And you should reward that."

He frowned at her, pursing his lips stubbornly. "Do I always have to be wrong?" he asked, starting to grin.

"Not always, just when it comes to defending your wife against your son," she said, leaning forward to kiss him on the lips.

"Can't help it—I love my wife," he said wistfully.

"And she loves you, and your recalcitrant son."

Kyle smiled at her, knowing that Barbara would resoundingly approve of this woman taking care of him and her two sons. He knew it beyond any shadow of a doubt; he just wished Nick would get it too.

The next day, Kyle ended up with the perfect opportunity to talk to both Midnight and Rick about his son's request. He and Midnight had gone down to the Pit for lunch, and he was just about to bring it up when Rick walked in and headed for their table.

"Ah-ha, I caught you two," Rick said, grinning as he reached for one of Midnight's french fries and sat next to her in the booth.

"Caught us having lunch?" Midnight replied, raising her eyebrow at him and swatting his hand as he reached for another french fry.

Rick laughed. "Yeah, I heard the chiefs didn't require sustenance."

51

"Ah," Kyle said, grinning. "You probably heard we could leap tall buildings in a single bound too, huh?"

"Somethin' like that."

Midnight and Kyle had quite recently scored an upgrade in pay for all officers and staff at the department, having done extensive research into what other big departments like theirs paid in comparable cities. The difference had been staggering, and Midnight had reasoned that she couldn't keep quality officers if they could make more money in other cities. Kyle had backed her up with all the statistics he'd come up with. The city council had voted unanimously to upgrade all staff pay by a surprising seven percent, to be raised another five percent the following year. The entire department was ecstatic, and it had earned more respect for the chief and Assistant Chief. Midnight and Kyle had been pretty pleased with the outcome.

"So what's up, Kyle?" Midnight asked.

"Well, it's of a more personal nature," Kyle began, still not sure what he was going to say. "I've had a request from my son."

"Okay…" Midnight said, thinking Nick had asked for a ride-along or something.

"He's asked me to clear it with you that he can ask your daughter out," Kyle said in a rush.

"He what?" Rick asked, his voice taking on a "You've got to be kidding" tone.

"He wants to take your daughter out—you know, as in a date," Kyle clarified, knowing Rick had understood perfectly the first time.

"Why?" Rick asked simply.

"Richard!" Midnight said, swatting him on the arm. "Have you *seen* your daughter recently?"

Rick looked at her, his face serious. "Yes, I have, and have you *seen* his son? I haven't seen a comer like that since Collins hit town."

Kyle grinned. Christian Collins was considered a player supreme by most of the Gang. Even if he was currently caught by Stevie O'Neil, who happened to be Kyle's sister-in-law. The complexities of the Gang could make a person crazy sometimes.

"Richard," Midnight began again, "Nick's never been anything but respectful to us."

"That's 'cause we carry *guns*, Midnight."

Midnight laughed, shaking her head ruefully. "You're hopeless, Debenshire."

"She's too young," Rick told Kyle.

"She's thirteen," Midnight put in.

"Nick's only fourteen," Kyle said.

"Nick's a guy," Rick said.

"You want your daughter to date girls?" Midnight asked, grinning.

"You know what I mean," Rick said, giving her a narrowed look.

"Yes, and you know our daughter has a good head on her shoulders, and Kyle's son has been taught by the best on respect for women," Midnight said, giving Kyle a wink.

Rick was silent, brooding. He knew he was going to lose this one.

"One date," he said finally.

"Richard…" Midnight began.

"One date," he repeated. "And if he lays one finger on her, I'll break it off."

"Gonna have her dusted for prints when she gets home, Debenshire?" Kyle asked, grinning now.

53

"Not a bad idea," Rick said, starting to grin too.

"Men!" Midnight said, with an exasperated sigh.

Nick was told that night that he had the go-ahead to ask Mikeyla Debenshire out. He picked up his phone with shaking hands. He'd feel like a total loser if, after all this, Mikeyla turned him down. She answered on the third ring, unaware of the huge amount of negotiating that had taken place so she could get this call.

"Hello?" she said, lying across her bed.

"Hi, Mikeyla, it's Nick Masterson," Nick said, already feeling stupid.

"Hi, Nick," Mikeyla replied, feeling flustered all of a sudden, but managing to hide it quite well. "What's up?"

"Uh…" Nick hesitated. "I was thinkin'…" he said, stammering. "Well, I mean, would you want to go out sometime?"

Mikeyla was silent for a moment, not believing this was happening. Nick Masterson was asking her out?! "With you?" she asked dumbly.

"Of course with me—who'd you think?" he said, sounding more like his confident self.

Mikeyla laughed. "Oh yeah, duh," she said, feeling nervous now. "Well, sure, yeah, I'd like to go out with you. When?" She winced, thinking she sounded too eager.

"How about Friday?" Nick said, thinking he sounded too eager.

"That sounds great," Mikeyla said, rolling over on her bed, sure she was going to go crazy before then.

"Okay. We could meet at Belmont Park if you want…" Nick said, trying to figure out how to sound cool when he couldn't drive yet and hoping that Mikeyla didn't think he was a total loser.

"That sounds fun!"

"Is seven o'clock okay?"

"Seven is great," Mikeyla said, feeling like an idiot.

"Okay, cool," Nick said. "I'll see ya in school tomorrow."

"Okay," Mikeyla said, dying to get off the phone so she could call everyone she knew. She was going out with Nick Masterson! *Oh my God!*

"Bye," Nick said.

"Bye."

Mikeyla spent the next two hours on the phone with all of her friends, telling them what had happened. Midnight walked by her room and heard her talking.

"Oh my God, Sandy, what am I going to wear? I don't have anything even decent, I'm going to have to beg my mom for some clothes money. Oh crap, what if her and Dad won't let me go? No, they'll know. No, Sandy, you forget, my mom and dad are cops— they'll know if I'm lying, or if I go somewhere other than where I said. My mom would have half the police force out after me, and my dad would kill Nick!"

Midnight made a point of walking back by the door, making sure her boot heels struck the hardwood floor hard enough that Mikeyla would know she was there. She stopped in the doorway.

"I gotta go, Sandy. I'll talk to you later," Mikeyla said into the phone, hanging up. She sat up on her bed. "Hi, Mom."

"Hi," Midnight said, leaning against the doorjamb and surveying her daughter's space. There were posters of music artists like Pink and No Doubt; Mikeyla also had a British flag on one wall, with a

55

picture of Rick, Joe, and the Black Knights in a frame below it. It had been a gift from Rick to his daughter when she'd asked about the gang he'd been part of in England. She'd been thrilled to see that side of her father. In deference to Midnight, Mikeyla also had a poster of a 1963 Corvette like the one Midnight drove. Midnight had no pictures of her gang, but had given Mikeyla a copy of the only picture she had of her younger brother, Thomas, who had died when he was sixteen. Mikeyla displayed it proudly, realizing that this boy would have been her uncle had he lived. She also knew that Midnight had been devastated by the loss of her brother, having gotten the whole story from Tom Ryan one night when he'd been over to visit.

Tom had known Midnight since his days as a patrol officer in Midnight's neighborhood, the "turf" Midnight's gang ran. It had been Tom who had found Midnight the night her brother had been killed, sitting on the street with her brother's head in her lap and his blood all over her jeans. It had been Tom who had seen Midnight through the hardest time in her life, and who'd supported her when she'd gone to college and the police academy to become the person she was now. Mikeyla was always finding new things out about her parents, and they never ceased to stun her with the depth of strength they seemed to draw from the tragedies in their lives. Although impossible for her to grasp fully at thirteen, Mikeyla did realize what incredible people her mother and father were.

"Guess what, Mom," Mikeyla said, her face alight with excitement.

"What?" Midnight asked, unable to keep from smiling. She'd missed this whole dating excitement in her own youth.

"Guess who asked me out."

"Who?" Midnight asked, pretending she didn't know, not wanting to spoil her daughter's high.

"Nick Masterson!" Mikeyla crowed. "Can you believe it?"

"Of course I can believe it, Keyl—he's got good taste," Midnight said, smiling.

Mikeyla bit her lip. "Do you think Dad will let me go out with him?" she asked, aware that her father was very leery of older boys around her, and Nick was almost fifteen.

Midnight looked thoughtful. "I think you should ask him."

"Oh God, Mom!" Mikeyla cried. "Can't you ask him for me?"

Midnight shook her head. "Mikeyla Marie, if you want to become an adult, you're going to have to learn to handle your own responsibilities."

Midnight knew that had Rick not already approved this date, she would have more than likely approached Rick for Mikeyla. She knew better than anyone how strongly her husband could react at first, before he had a chance to be reasoned with. Midnight wouldn't want to inflict Rick's caustic comments on their impressionable daughter.

Mikeyla sighed deeply, almost dramatically. "Okay, I'll ask him."

"Cheer up," Midnight said, grinning. "Maybe he'll be in a good mood when he gets home."

Mikeyla gave her mother a pointed look. "He's never in a good mood when he gets home."

"That's not true—he's been better lately," Midnight chided.

"Only because Angelica is taking care of all his paperwork lately," Mikeyla said, laughing, not realizing she was touching on a

57

sore subject.

"Yeah, well…" Midnight said, straightening up, her green eyes flashing a little bit. "Talk to him when he gets home," she said, and walked down the hall to her room.

She walked into her closet, taking off her jacket and hanging it up, then took off her holstered weapon, thinking about Angelica Muñoz. Angelica was a twenty-four-year-old ex–gang member who had set her sights on one Richard Debenshire early on, before she'd even met him. She'd seen him a few times, of course with his wife, but she obviously didn't care about that. When she'd gotten a chance to meet Rick she'd grabbed it, and ended up helping him take down one of the bigger gangs in town. After that she'd made a point of trying to be helpful to him. When he was drowning in paperwork, Angelica volunteered to help him out by staying late.

Rick had been surprised when Angelica started flirting with him. He'd told Midnight about it, and while she'd shrugged it off the first few times, over the last year Angelica's continued attention to Rick was starting to annoy her. Midnight knew that part of it was Joe's comment to her about being only two years younger than he was, and he was considering himself old at this point. She knew she shouldn't be letting things bother her, such as some young woman who thought she could take Rick from her. Midnight knew how much Rick loved her—she'd seen it in the footage from her funeral, in the devastation in his eyes. He'd also once again proven it when he'd stepped in front of a bullet intended for Midnight. A reporter had informed the world of Rick's intention, since he'd been in the hospital room when Midnight and Rick had discussed it. Rick's simple statement to Midnight had been, "I couldn't let him take you away

58

from me again," referring to Julio Martinez, who had been responsible for a previous attempt on Midnight's life that had been believed successful, long enough for Midnight's "remains" to be buried. Midnight had been found alive, but Martinez had escaped prison a year later and attempted to kill her again, and Rick had blocked him from doing so, literally. He had not been seriously wounded, fortunately, but the fact remained that Rick could have been giving up his life for Midnight. He loved her. Of that there was no doubt.

"So why am I letting the bitch bug me?" Midnight said out loud.

"I have no idea," came a reply from outside the closet.

Midnight grinned. She turned around and saw Rick standing in the doorway.

"Which bitch would that be, love?" he asked, quirking an eyebrow at her.

"Ahh…" Midnight stammered, then shook her head. "No one important."

Rick gave her a pointed look. "No one gets to you, so if this woman is, she's important. Who?"

Midnight narrowed her eyes at him. It was annoying, sometimes, that he knew her so well. She was, however, saved from answering by Mikeyla.

"Meeting in the closet?" their daughter asked from behind Rick.

Rick looked over his shoulder. "Maybe," he replied, grinning. He glanced back at Midnight, pinning her with a look that said, *We'll finish this later.* He turned and walked out of the closet; Midnight followed.

"Dad," Mikeyla said, "I need to ask you something."

"Okay." Rick nodded, moving to his dresser, removing his gun from his shoulder holster and taking out the ammunition magazine and the bullet from the chamber. He glanced over his shoulder at his daughter. "What is it?"

Mikeyla had been watching him unload, still fascinated by this side of her parents and realizing she really had two things she wanted to ask.

"Something I've been thinking about," she began, moving to sit on their bed, as her father shrugged out of his holster and hung it over the chair next to his dresser. He leaned against the dresser, looking at her, waiting for the rest. Midnight stood next to him, her expression showing her confusion at Mikeyla's tactic.

Rick spread his hands. "So what is it, Keyl?" He was clearly getting irritated at her vacillating.

"Well, can I come to work with you sometime?" she blurted out.

Rick looked perplexed for a moment. "Why?"

Mikeyla shrugged. "I just thought it might be cool to see what you guys do." She saw that her father's expression hadn't changed, so she continued, "I mean, it's not like you guys are accountants or bookkeepers. You chase after people and arrest them and stuff."

Rick glanced at Midnight and caught her grin. Then he looked back at Mikeyla, inclining his head. "You're right. Sure, if you want to come along with us during one of your breaks that would be fine."

"I want to see what you do too, Mom," Mikeyla said. "I mean, I might want to be Chief of Police someday too."

"Keyl, your mom can still chase them down with the best of them," Rick said, grinning. "She can just schmooze the city council too, when the occasion calls for it."

"Uh-huh," Midnight said, rolling her eyes.

60

"So, what, was that it?" Rick asked, sensing that his daughter wasn't done.

"Well, no," Mikeyla said, starting to fidget.

Rick's eyes went to Midnight's, and as if by telepathy he understood that he needed to be easier with this one.

"What is it, Keyl?" he asked, his voice softer now.

"Well, I got asked out, and I want to know if it's okay that I go," Mikeyla said cautiously.

"Asked out by who?" Rick said, glancing at Midnight, catching her slight grin and knowing they were talking about the same person.

"Nick Masterson."

Rick's lips twitched as he made it look like he was considering the idea. "Why do you want to go out with him?"

Mikeyla stared back at him for a long moment, realizing she should have known this wouldn't be easy at all. She sighed, thinking about it for a moment.

"I guess because he's always seemed different from the guys around here. Being from New York and all, he seems more mature. And he's been really cool when we get stuck together at the holiday stuff. He doesn't talk about all that dumb junk. And he's funny."

Rick raised an eyebrow at his daughter, giving her an appraising look. "Not 'cause he's the cutest boy in school?"

Mikeyla shrugged. "Of course I know he's cute, but if he had a dopey personality I wouldn't want to waste my time on him."

Midnight grinned, thinking her daughter definitely had a mind of her own. Rick glanced at his wife, thinking his daughter definitely had Midnight's spirit. He looked back at Mikeyla and nodded.

"Then yes, you can go out with him."

61

"Really?" Mikeyla asked, looking excited and relieved.

"Yes, really," Rick said, grinning. "Damn, you'd think you had Atilla the Hun for a father, or something!" he said, sounding disgruntled, even though he was still grinning.

Mikeyla got off the bed and hugged her father. "No, just a very protective cop for a father," she said, smiling. "Thanks, Daddy."

"You're welcome," Rick said, glad now that he'd agreed to her going on this date. He knew his overprotective nature tended to drive his daughter and his wife crazy. But he only had one little girl, and he wanted to know that she was safe at all times.

Mikeyla left then. Rick sat down on the bed to unlace his boots, glancing up at Midnight. She was standing at their bathroom mirror, washing off her makeup.

"Why was I reapproving something we'd already approved?" he asked.

Midnight glanced at him over her shoulder, shrugging. "I think it does her some good to have to ask you for stuff. It's good for her to see that you're not going to automatically say no all the time."

"And you knew I wouldn't say no this time," he said, getting off the bed and moving to stand behind her, watching her in the mirror.

"Right," Midnight confirmed, reaching for a towel to dry her face.

"So I gain points, and she gains confidence," he said, sliding his arms around her waist.

Midnight leaned back against him, smiling. "Right."

"Very good, Chief," he said, grinning as he lowered his head to kiss her neck.

"Thank you, Lieutenant," she said, her hands over his.

"You're welcome." He turned her around to face him, leaning down to kiss her lips.

They continued to kiss, and Rick promptly forgot to ask her about the mysterious woman "bugging" her. Midnight was grateful for that. She hated to talk about her insecurities, even with him.

CHAPTER 3

That same evening, Rhiannon greeted Kyle at the door. She looked like she felt better. She took his jacket from him, hanging it in the hall closet. Then she took his hand and led him to the back of the house, where the deck was. Kyle had just started getting a little nervous when she turned to him, and she had the most brilliant smile on her face.

"You went to the doctor," he said questioningly.

"Oh yeah," she said, nodding.

"And he said…"

"That I'm pregnant," Rhiannon replied simply.

"That you're what?" Kyle said, openmouthed.

Rhiannon smiled. "Pregnant, honey. With child," she said, reaching up to kiss him.

Kyle started to smile, hugging her close and literally picking her up off her feet.

"I love you," he said, unable to stop smiling.

"Good," she said as he set her back down. "'Cause I'm about to get all fat and ugly."

"Couldn't happen," he said with certainty.

"We'll see," she said, grinning.

"We need to tell the boys," Kyle said, sobering a little bit.

Rhiannon nodded.

64

Brenden was thrilled to find out that he was going to have a baby brother or sister. Nick, however, stared at them like they were insane.

"You're having a baby?" he repeated, looking at his father. "Dad, you're almost fifty."

"I'm aware of my age, Nicholas," Kyle replied coolly.

"You should be having grandkids at this point, not more kids of your own."

"Nicholas..." Kyle began ominously.

"Nick, look," Rhiannon put in, resting a calming hand on Kyle's arm. "I know this is a shock for you. It's a shock for me too, but—"

"Didn't you two use protection? I mean, God, everyone knows that! How stupid can you get?" Nick said, cutting Rhiannon off.

Kyle shot to his feet, his arm coming up, ready to slap his son into the next week, but Rhiannon reacted faster, jumping up and blocking the way.

"Kyle!" she yelled, holding her hands up. "Stop!"

Kyle pulled up short, looking down at her. Her eyes searched his face. He closed his eyes slowly, blowing his breath out and shaking his head. "I'm sorry," he whispered to her. He turned and walked out of the room.

"Oh, a new baby, what fun," Nick muttered bitterly behind Rhiannon.

She turned to him. "You know, Nick, it wouldn't hurt you to be less of a little bastard every now and then," she said, and with that walked out of the room to go and find Kyle, leaving Nick staring after her in surprise.

Rhiannon found Kyle out on the deck, staring into the darkness. She walked up behind him, sliding her arms around him, putting her cheek against his back. His hands covered hers, and she could feel his turmoil. They stood that way for a long time. Rhiannon wasn't sure what she could say to help him at this point. She knew he was getting closer and closer to violence with Nick, and she knew that it bothered him.

After a long while, he turned to her, taking her in his arms. She leaned against him, reaching up to clutch a handful of his shirt.

"I'm sorry this is so hard, Kyle," she said softly.

He was silent for a long moment, then shook his head. "It's not your fault, Rhian. It's mine. I let him get away with too much after Barbara died, and he's decided it's his right now to act any way he pleases."

"You were doing your own grieving. Besides, it's not like there's a manual out there for coping with a teenager when he loses his mother."

"I could have done more, spent more time with him…" Kyle said, trailing off as he shook his head.

"You did what you could, Kyle. You'll go crazy if you keep second-guessing yourself."

"I know," he said, then gestured to the house and the rebellious teen within. "There are days when I think I should just send him back to New York and let his uncle have him. Nick would be happy, and we'd have some peace."

Rhiannon stared up at him for a long moment. "Would Barbara want his uncle to finish raising him?"

Kyle gave her a sour look. "You know she wouldn't. Dirty pool, Templeton," he said, calling her by her first married name.

"Whatever it takes, Masterson," she replied sweetly. "Face it, no

66

matter how big of a pain in the ass he is, you love him, and you'd be miserable if you felt like you'd failed Barbara."

Kyle sighed. "I know, you're right." He leaned down and kissed her. "It happens a lot."

"I know," she replied, grinning.

***

Donovan sat in his English literature class, bored out of his mind. The only interesting thing about it was the instructor; she was very hot. Rosa Delario was indeed a beautiful older woman. With long black hair and dark, smoldering eyes, she looked like the classic Italian beauty. She wore dresses that were tight and high heels—the classic "hot for teacher" heels. Half the class, the male half, was in love. Donovan watched her with interest as she moved, flipping her hair over her shoulder as she talked. He had no idea what she was saying, but he knew he could watch her for a long time.

He and Jeanie hadn't gotten too far in the last two weeks. They'd gotten into a couple of arguments as to how the case should be handled. Finally, he'd told her to do her own damned thing and let him know if she had anything good. She'd told him to get the stick out of his ass. It was not a nice conversation. She'd slammed out of his house, not for the first time since they'd started working together. He'd stared after her, not moving. Eventually he'd sighed and got up to make himself a drink. That was the usual routine, a few really good belts so he could relax enough to sleep.

He was rethinking the evening that Jeanie had stormed out when he heard his name, and apparently it wasn't the first time, because her voice was raised.

67

"Donovan Curtis?" Rosa called again.

"Yes, ma'am?" he replied, his voice cracking effectively.

"See me after class," she said sternly.

"Yes, ma'am." *Great*, he thought, *sent to the dean's office week two on the case. Good job, Curtis.*

After class was over, he stayed in his chair as everyone else filed out. Rosa talked to a few students, and when the room was empty turned to him.

"Mr. Curtis," she said, moving to sit on the front of her desk, her dress hiked up to allow her to cross her legs. He caught a whiff of Opium perfume. "You seem to have a problem concentrating in my class."

"No, ma'am," he said. "I just... I had a fight with my girlfriend last night, and I was thinking about that."

"A fight?" she queried, her dark eyes staring into his.

"Yes, ma'am."

"Did you two break up?"

"Yeah, kinda," he said, looking embarrassed.

"Did she break up with you, Donovan?" she asked, leaning forward, a lot of cleavage showing.

"I..." he stammered. "Yes, she did."

"Why?" Rosa asked, pinning him with a look.

He shrugged. "She said I'm an asshole."

"Are you?"

"Ma'am?"

"Are you an asshole?"

"I, um, I don't think so, no," he replied, something in his mind

68

starting to wonder where this was going.

"Maybe you just need to be trained properly," Rosa said, nodding, as if to herself.

Donovan didn't reply, simply staring back at her. He fought the urge to grin like he normally would in a situation like this. Somehow he knew that would be the wrong thing to do. She seemed to want him to be the illiterate pupil. And something inside him wanted to be dumb for the moment.

"Yes, ma'am, maybe," he said, nodding.

Rosa looked thoughtful for a long moment. Then she stood, went around her desk, opened a drawer, and took out a card. She walked over and handed it to him.

"Be at my house tonight at seven o'clock. Don't be late, Mr. Curtis."

"No, ma'am, I won't," he said, his eyes on hers. He stood to leave, pocketing the card as he did.

Rosa Delario stared after him. He was a handsome boy, very handsome, with those beautiful teal-blue eyes. He would be easy to teach, and it might be fun. She didn't know if he had any spirit to him, though; he seemed too obedient already. Larry would say that was good, that he'd be easier to use that way, but she was growing tired of these boys lapping at her feet like silly puppies. She sighed heavily, picking up her papers and putting them in her briefcase.

That night, Donovan arrived at the house. It was a big, two-story place near campus. He was still debating with himself about the intelligence of getting involved here, but he figured as long as it didn't interfere with his case, he would be alright. Rosa's class was one of those that had been a chance, because one of the two kids busted had

69

been taking it. He'd gone for this one and Jeanie had taken the art history class, because he could stand art history even less than English lit. Taking a deep breath, he knocked on the door.

Rosa opened the door wearing a black dress with a plunging neckline. Her hair was loose and wild around her face. Donovan sensed danger in her, and for some reason it was drawing him in, instead of warning him away. She glanced at her watch and nodded.

"You're early. Good," she said. She led him to the study, and Donovan was stunned to see a man standing behind the bar. He looked the studious type, and after a long moment Donovan realized he was the university chemistry professor.

"Donovan Curtis, I'd like you to meet my husband, Larry."

Donovan was confused now. She was married? Then why had she invited him there? Even so, he stepped forward, extending his hand to the other man.

"Good to meet you, Donovan," Larry said, his pale, bony hand extended. "Would you like something to drink?"

"Uh, sure," Donovan said. "Beer?"

"Got draft on tap," Larry said, picking up a glass.

"Donovan," Rosa said, glancing at her husband as she put her arm around Donovan's shoulders, pressing close to him. "I want you to stay and have a few drinks with us. Is that okay?"

"Sure," Donovan said, shrugging, still not sure what the game was.

"Donovan's one of my students, Larry," she said to her husband as he handed her Donovan's beer.

"Oh, I see." Larry nodded. "Rosa takes a special interest in her students, Donovan, the ones that she feels need extra help. She loves

70

her teaching," he added proudly.

"Yes, I do," Rosa said, smiling. She gave Donovan a wink as she handed him the beer.

An hour later, Donovan had downed three beers and was feeling distinctly uncomfortable. What was he doing here? He was about to make his excuses to leave when the phone rang. Larry had to go to the lab; there had been a minor incident.

Larry kissed his wife on the cheek, telling her he'd be back soon. She smiled indulgently and told him to hurry. Larry left a few minutes later. Rosa's entire attitude changed then.

"These lab emergencies are so easy to arrange," she said, shrugging.

"You arranged that?" Donovan asked, surprised.

"Of course. You didn't really think I wanted him here this evening, did you?"

When he didn't answer, she laughed huskily, moving up to him, reaching a perfectly manicured hand up to slide through his hair, pressing her body against his. Donovan felt his body respond quickly, and with such force he was stunned by it. He leaned down to kiss her, but she pulled back, giving him a stern look.

"You will kiss me when I give you permission," she said, her tone all instructor to student.

Donovan stared down at her, unable to reply. His look reflected surprise.

"Let's go upstairs," she said, taking his empty glass from his hand and then taking his hand to lead him.

Donovan followed her, his mind a bit hazy from the beer. He

realized he hadn't eaten anything since that morning. *Great, Curtis. Get hammered before you get anywhere with her.*

She led him right into her bedroom. The room was done in a rose color and burgundy; it seemed to fit her pretty well. She stopped in front of her bed, covered with a deep burgundy velvet comforter. She turned and looked up at him, her dark eyes searching his.

"Unbutton your shirt, Donovan," she commanded.

He did as she'd told him, thinking somewhere in the back of his head, *What am I doing?* But his hands didn't respond to that, only to her command. Her eyes went to his chest as he pulled his shirt out of his jeans and unbuttoned it. Her nails grazed his skin as she ran them from his stomach up to his neck. He shuddered, his body once again reacting strongly. Donovan was sure he was going to explode when she leaned forward and put her mouth over one nipple, sucking at it. He inhaled sharply, making a hissing sound through his teeth when she bit down, his hands automatically going to her head to hold her there. She reached up, taking ahold of his wrists. Her nails bit painfully into his skin as she applied pressure.

"You will touch me only when I tell you to," she said when she had his hands down at his sides again. "Do you understand?"

Donovan searched her eyes for a long moment, knowing she was on some kind of dominatrix trip here. Finally he nodded.

In the end, she took him to dizzying heights. She put him under excruciating pressure, to the point where he was sure he couldn't wait any longer. But she ordered him to wait, and he did. In the end he was sure he was going to pass out from an orgasm that had him yelling. She had made him lie under her, not allowing him to make any aggressive moves of his own. She took no less than three orgasms from him, taking her pleasure from his body, before allowing him release. Afterward, she moved off him, pulling on a silk robe.

"Put your clothes on and go home," she said.

Donovan lay on the bed, looking at her in stunned silence.

She raised a black eyebrow at him. "Or do you want Larry to come home and catch you in my bed?"

Donovan shook his head and moved to get up. He was hit with a wave of dizziness, so he had to lie back for a minute. When he felt the wave pass, he slowly started to get up again. As he pulled on his jeans, he found that his hands were shaking, and he was feeling quite weak from the experience. Rosa watched him from her perch on the bed; she was smoking a cigarette by this time. When he was dressed, she walked over to him. She slid her hand into his hair, pulling his head down to her, kissing him deeply, making his body start to tingle once again. Then she pulled away, pushing him back and telling him to go home.

Donovan left the house feeling buzzed and drained at the same time.

The next morning he found that he still felt totally drained. He didn't move when the alarm went off. When it didn't stop, he reached over and yanked it out by the plug, tossing it across the room. Two hours later the phone rang. He picked it up.

"Yeah?" he said irritably.

"Donovan, where are you?" Jeanie asked.

"Sleeping," he muttered.

"No kidding, but you were supposed to be in class a half hour ago."

"Not coming in today," he said, already feeling himself drifting back to sleep.

73

"Donovan..."

"I'm not coming in, Jay. Get over it," he said, and hung up.

Jeanie stared at the phone in her hand, stunned that he'd actually just hung up on her. What the hell was with him this morning? For that matter, what the hell was with him this year? She shook her head, putting her phone back in her purse and heading to her next class. She had a few leads, and she wanted to see if she could get anywhere with them. To hell with Donovan Curtis and his attitude.

***

Everyone was full of congratulations for Kyle and Rhiannon. Stevie was thrilled to find out she was going to be an aunt. She hugged her sister tight.

"Congrats, sis," she said, smiling. "You've got it all now."

"Yep, and in a few days you'll have your own house," Rhiannon said, thrilled for Stevie.

"Thank the chief. This pay raise will really help a lot."

"Blue got a raise too, didn't he?"

"Yeah," Stevie said, but didn't elaborate. Rhiannon assumed she was buying the house with Christian too.

Things between her and Christian had become very tense suddenly. Two mornings before, the woman from Seattle had called at 6 a.m., waking them up. Christian had rolled over in bed and talked to her for twenty minutes. Stevie had finally gotten up and gone to take a shower. For the first time in a long time, Christian didn't join her. Things were tense after that. He told her the following day that he was going back to Seattle the following week. The week her house was

74

supposed to close, and she was going to move in. *Great*, she had thought, *right when I need help*. She had nodded, saying nothing, just finished her coffee and left the apartment. Since then they'd barely spoken. He worked late, and she was asleep by the time he came to bed. He fell asleep on his side and didn't touch her. She refused to think about it, refused to analyze it, moving forward and refusing to look back. Much like Midnight Chevalier had always done.

That afternoon, Stevie was headed to the range to do her quarterly re-qualification. Joe was meeting her there, since the last range master had left and no one had been hired to replace him. Joe was acting as range master for the department. It had been almost two weeks since she'd seen him. Even so, she was literally stunned into silence when she drove up and saw him get out of the Cadillac Escalade he was driving. He was dressed in jeans and a black shirt, with his usual shoulder holster and black leather boots. That wasn't the shock; the shock was that his hair, which usually fell five inches or so past his shoulders, was now cut to just above his shoulders. He also sported a goatee. Both made him look young and rakish; Stevie was sure she felt her heart stop.

She got out of her car and walked toward him as he leaned against the black Escalade.

"Wow," she said.

Joe grinned. "Me or the Escalade?" he asked, knowing her thing for cars.

Stevie laughed, shaking her head. "Definitely you. Your hair… God, you look great," she said, her voice indicating her shock.

Joe grinned sardonically. "I figured it was time for a change."

She smiled. "And what a change."

75

Joe inclined his head. "Glad you like it. I'm sure Midnight is going to yell at me."

"Why?" she asked as he led the way to the range entrance.

"Because if I've done it, Rick will think it's time, and she'll kill me and him if he cuts his hair."

Stevie laughed. "Terrible being a role model, isn't it?"

Joe glanced over his shoulder at her, and she winked. He laughed, shaking his head. "Shut up, O'Neil."

They got out onto the range a little while later. Not before Joe inspected and approved her weapon.

"Beretta Cougar?" he said, nodding approvingly.

"Yeah, got the knock-down of the .45, but it's smaller for my hands." Stevie grinned. "And I couldn't afford the H&K USP," she said, naming the gun he currently carried.

"They're not cheap."

"I know, about a grand with good night sights."

Joe nodded. She did know her guns. He was also happy to see that she kept her weapon very clean. She grinned when he noted that.

"What?" he asked.

"Oh, nothing," she said, still grinning.

"Come on…" he said, narrowing his light blue eyes at her.

"Did you ever read my file from the academy?" she asked, looking acutely embarrassed again.

"Generally…"

"I was an expert in marksmanship," she said, then gave him a sidelong glance as they walked out onto the range. "Know why?" When Joe shook his head, she said, "Because you were."

His brows furrowed. "Are you serious?"

76

"Hell, yes I am. Busted my ass practicing all the time. 'Cause I never knew when Joe Sinclair might notice."

Joe shook his head, unable to fathom anyone even caring what he thought.

A little while later she began her shoot. He found that her aim wasn't as dead-on as it could be, and noticed that she flinched every so often when she fired.

"O'Neil, is it your shoulder?" he asked, remembering it had been one of the places she'd been hit with the AK47 rounds.

She lowered her weapon, holding it down at her side, staring down the course at the targets, her lips tightening in disappointment.

"It's the shoulder, isn't it?" he asked.

After a long moment, she nodded unhappily. "My aim has been off ever since. I still hit the target, but not dead-on like I used to."

Joe nodded. "Ever work on shooting with your weak hand?"

"Only in the academy."

Joe looked thoughtful for a moment. "Okay, switch hands. Let's see how you do."

Stevie nodded, and did as instructed without an instant of doubt. She fired the first round and it hit the edge of the target. She shook her head, realigned her shot, and hit farther into the target, but still not well. Joe watched as she moved her neck around, and he was sure she was fighting the anger she felt at not being able to shoot well anymore.

He took a step up, putting his chest to her side and his left arm under hers, leaning in close so he could help her line up the shot. That was when he caught the scent of musk. It smelled so tantalizingly fa-

77

miliar, yet distinctly different. His body, so long without sex, responded to it instantly, and Joe had to literally draw in a quick breath to keep from pressing closer to her.

What he didn't notice was that Stevie was having a hell of a time concentrating as well. His hand under her wrist, the contact with her skin, had felt like he'd sent an electrical charge through her. She knew it was because she'd had so many fantasies about him and the range and just this kind of thing. But there was no comparison between fantasy and reality. Here was Joe Sinclair, standing right next to her, all male sexuality and strength. He was standing right there! Stevie squeezed her eyes shut for a second. *Yeah, O'Neil, standing right there and wondering why the hell you're not paying attention!*

Forcing herself to concentrate, she lined up her shot again and fired. This time she hit a little closer to center mass. She fired a few more times, every time coming very close to the center, but never quite there.

"Shit," she muttered, starting to feel a bit despondent over the poor showing she was making. This was *not* how the fantasy usually went.

"Let's try this," Joe said, his voice so close to her she shivered slightly.

She almost groaned out loud when he stepped in, putting his chest to her back, his arms going around her to hold her gun with her. His chin was just over her left shoulder, and then he moved a couple of inches closer and neither of them could think for a few moments. Neither realized what the other was going through. Joe was having a hard time not dropping his hands to her waist and pulling her back against him. Stevie was forcibly keeping herself from turning her head to put her face into his neck.

Joe helped her fire a few shots, both of them trying to act as normal as possible. Joe was telling himself what a dirty old man he'd become, and Stevie was telling herself to stop being a stupid little school girl with a huge crush on the teacher. When she was finally hitting center mass, Joe stepped back and let her finish off her magazine. He watched as she expertly released the empty clip, and with precision born of practice, pulled her fresh clip and loaded it into the weapon, pulling back the slide to chamber the first round. Taking her stance once again, she proceeded to fire in quick succession the fourteen rounds her clip held, hitting center mass every time.

"Damn…" Joe said, surprised at her flexibility.

She'd just shot an almost perfect score with her weak hand. Stevie O'Neil certainly adjusted quickly. As she lowered the weapon she looked over at him, smiling brilliantly.

"Acceptable?" she asked.

"Hell yes," Joe said, nodding in complete approval.

Stevie bit her lip, grinning. "Thanks, Joe," she said. "It never even occurred to me to use my weak hand. I haven't even shot like that since the academy, except for re-quals."

Joe nodded. "Well, you're damned good on either hand."

"Thanks," she said, unable to stop grinning. Joe Sinclair thought her shooting was good—how much better could this day get?

"I don't know 'bout you," Joe said, sighing, "but I need a beer. You game?"

Stevie smiled. "Definitely."

Joe nodded. They cleaned up the empty casings and then headed to his vehicle.

"So, you bought an Escalade, huh?" she asked as he opened the passenger door for her and helped her up into it.

Joe shrugged. "I needed something to haul all the gear I carry for the academy and for range master duties. The Aston isn't really designed for that."

"I guess not," she replied, grinning.

Joe went around and got in on the driver's side, catching her grin. "I know, I could have bought something cheaper, but…"

"But why not drive the best when you can afford it, right?" she asked, not sounding the least bit nasty.

Joe grinned, inclining his head. "Exactly."

He drove them down to the coast. They had a beer sitting out on the deck of a restaurant, looking out over the bay. Stevie noted that he tapped on his bottle of beer a lot with the ring on his right hand. His cell phone rang, and he answered.

"Sinclair," he said, still working on the gum he'd been chewing since they'd gotten into the Escalade earlier.

He listened, then shook his head. "That's not what I told them, Night," he said, sounding irritated. "I told them it was impossible to run the whole thing that night. I don't know why these fucking idiots insist on rushing everything through." He listened again, then made a face at something Midnight had said. "I'm not on edge, okay?" He rolled his eyes at her answer. "Yes, I was at the range, but—No, Night, I'm not, okay? Can we just move on?" he said, sounding very edgy indeed. He sighed, shaking his head. "Okay. Okay, yeah, I'll talk to you later." He hung up.

Stevie glanced over at him as he set the phone down. "On edge?" she asked, pinning him with a look.

Joe narrowed his eyes at her, then reached for his beer and took a long drink.

"You didn't answer me," Stevie said after a couple of minutes. "Why the edge?"

He raised his beer to her. "You are the reason for my edge, love." With that he drank the rest of it.

Stevie stared at him openmouthed for a long moment, then finished her beer in a long drink.

"Then tell me why we're here, instead of your hotel room," she said simply, her eyes never leaving his.

Joe's eyes widened in surprise, but then he stood up, took her hand, and led her through the restaurant. As he reached up to open the door of the Escalade for her, she turned to him. He looked down at her, and was caught off guard when she reached up to kiss him. Her lips were hesitant at first, but his hands at her waist and his body pressing hers against the car changed that quickly. Her kiss became confident, and searing. Joe groaned in the back of his throat, his lips responding to hers hungrily. Stevie pressed herself closer to him, and found that she didn't care where they were or who saw them.

Fortunately, Joe recalled that they were in a parking lot and pulled away, opening the door for her. Stevie got in, feeling her head spinning a bit. It had nothing to do with the shots of tequila she'd had either. She'd just gotten her first taste of Joe Sinclair, and suddenly every fantasy she'd had about the man paled in comparison.

The drive to the Hotel Intercontinental was achieved in record time, and within ten minutes they were at his room door, kissing before they even got through it. He kicked the door closed with a booted foot. She pressed him back against it, reaching up to pull his polo shirt out of his jeans, then proceeded to pull the shirt off him.

81

"Thirty-nine my ass," she said as she looked at his well-muscled chest in awe.

"Thirty-nine," he said, sliding his hands down her back to cup her butt. "And you have a very nice ass."

Stevie laughed, then leaned down to kiss his chest, eliciting a low moan from him. Spurred on by his reaction, she kissed across his chest, stopping at a nipple to circle her tongue around it. This had him pulling her closer to him and his finger lifting her lips to his again, and he kissed her, backing her toward the bedroom of the suite. Once there, he took his time, unbuttoning her shirt, kissing down her skin, inhaling the scent of musk once again and reveling in it. He realized with a start that Midnight wore musk, and it was probably the memory of their early days that had caused him to react that afternoon. He didn't stop to analyze it, just continued his exploration of her body. Once her shirt and jeans were off, he sat back, surveying her. She wore a leopard-print bra and black lace bikini panties.

"Goddamn, you are sexy," he breathed, moving to kiss her again.

Stevie was in heaven. She knew she couldn't and wouldn't think about what was happening. She'd wanted Joe Sinclair for too long. It was like suddenly getting a chance to sleep with the celebrity you'd always had on your walls. But he was real, and he was here, and he was making her body writhe with his strong, confident touch. In some ways he reminded her of Christian, but he was gentler, and definitely more vocal in his responses to her. Christian always played it cool, never really letting her know how much she was getting to him until he lost his control and took her. Joe would moan in response to her moans, his kiss becoming fevered and frenzied, then slowing down again as he regained his control.

Stevie didn't know where the idea of the legend of Joe ended and

82

her desire for him began, but she did know that she was dying to feel him inside her. To that end, she slid her fingers through his hair, urging him back up her body. She cried out, grasping his shoulders, as he moved up her against her and slid his body inside hers in one long stroke. Before she could even think to stop herself she was in the throes of an orgasm.

As her heartbeat became more normal again, she looked up at him and found that his eyes were closed. He opened them a moment later, staring down at her with their light blue intensity, and she swore she could literally feel the heat in them.

Joe had had to fight for control of his body, to keep himself from joining her instantly in her release, but he wanted this to last just a bit longer than that. He'd finally had to screw his eyes shut to keep from watching the erotic display of passion on her face as she came. He'd felt her still and opened his eyes, seeing her watching him. He smiled as he leaned down to kiss her again. Her hands slid down his arms, then back, and up and down his back. He started to move inside her again, lowering his head to kiss the hollow of her throat.

"God, you smell so good," he murmured in her ear, making her let out a low moan again.

He felt her begin to move with him, setting a counter to his rhythm, and he knew she was going to push him over the edge. He kissed her deeply again, trying to push back the thoughts of letting go. He moved his lips over her cheek, down to her ear.

"I've wanted you for too long..." he whispered huskily in her ear, by way of explanation for his lack of control, which he could feel slipping badly at that moment.

"I've wanted you forever," she replied in a voice so filled with heat and passion it sent him spiraling out of control.

83

Within moments they reached their release together. Her nails bit into his back as she grasped at him, her second orgasm made much more powerful by joining his.

A few minutes later, he lay still over her, keeping his weight off her with his arm and leg to her side. His face was pressed against her neck as he struggled to control his breathing.

"Jesus…" he breathed, unable to form a complete thought.

"And Mary and Joseph," Stevie replied, out of breath and grinning.

Joe chuckled, moving to kiss her neck softly.

"You've shattered all my fantasies, you know," she said after a long time.

"I have?" Joe said, sounding worried.

"Yeah, you're much better than I ever imagined you would be," Stevie was quick to tell him, realizing how her original statement had sounded.

Joe grinned. "That's it, stroke an old man's ego."

She pushed at his shoulder then, and he rolled to his back as she moved to lean over him on one elbow.

"Let's get one thing straight here, Sinclair," she said seriously. "I have no reason to lie to you."

His light blue eyes searched her face. "I know."

"And you're not old, goddamn it!"

"Thirty-nine."

"Bullshit."

"You want my ID?"

"I don't care what the damned thing says, Sinclair," she said, sliding her hand from his flat stomach, over his lean, lightly defined

84

six pack up his chest, her eyes following her hand, then trailing up to his eyes. "This is not the body of a thirty-nine-year-old man. You got it?"

Joe grinned. "Do you know how much like Midnight you sound sometimes?"

Stevie laughed. "No. A lot?"

"A lot."

"My goals have been met then," she said, grinning.

"You smell like her too."

"I do?" she queried, surprised.

"Yeah, what perfume do you wear?"

"White musk."

Joe nodded. "Midnight wears musk too—I'm not sure which one, but I know that scent anywhere."

Stevie nodded, looking like she'd just come to a conclusion. She moved to lie over him, pressing against him seductively as she looked down at him. "They say that the olfactory senses are the strongest memory trigger for human beings. You're getting off on me with your memories of the chief." Although what she said sounded harsh, he could see by the look on her face that she wasn't angry at the thought.

"Maybe," he said as he slid his hands up her back, moving them into her mass of fiery-red hair. "But I'm getting off on being with you just as much."

"Yeah?" she said, sounding young and unsure.

"Yeah, Stevie. You're an incredibly beautiful and far too sexy woman all on your own, whether you act or smell like Midnight or not."

85

She kissed him deeply. Lifting her head, she stared directly into his eyes. "You have no idea how good that makes me feel."

Joe reached up, touching her cheek, looking back into her eyes. "You have no idea how you've saved me," he whispered, pulling her down to kiss her again, then hugging her close to him.

They lay like that for almost an hour, her head on his shoulder, her face against his neck, as she'd wanted it to be earlier that afternoon. His hands smoothed over her back, touching her, caressing her, telling her without words how beautiful he thought she really was. In truth, it was mending his soul to know that a woman like her wanted him, and that maybe he wasn't so "old" just because chronologically he was almost forty. His father had been forty-eight when he died, and he had seemed old to Joe. But then, Joe had been twenty years old when his father had been killed.

Joe Sinclair Senior hadn't been a street cop either. He hadn't had the kind of life that his son had ended up leading. Joe Sinclair Senior had been a businessman. He hadn't worked out in the gym until his muscles screamed at him to stop. He'd sat behind a desk, making deals and running his publishing company. He didn't carry a gun for a living, but a briefcase. He didn't shoot a perfect three hundred score at the range every time; he shot a good golf game. Joseph Michael Sinclair was very different from his father, and he suddenly realized that it didn't really make him old.

Meanwhile, Stevie was marveling at the fact that he could lie like this. She was enjoying the comfort of just being there with him, but she couldn't help comparing it to how Christian was. Christian could lie with her for all of about ten minutes, then he was up, moving around, even if it was to get a cigarette. He always had so much extra energy; he was moving all the time. So this was different.

86

Raising her head, she glanced up at Joe. He was deep in thought. She watched him for a few moments, while he wasn't paying attention. It was impossible to believe that he was thirty-nine years old. There wasn't a wrinkle on his face; it was still smooth and tanned. His hair really did look good shorter. It was still long by cop standards, and still gave him a look of being untamed. It was actually more like Christian's hair now. She'd stared at his face so many times over the years, imagining what it would be like to know him like this. Now she knew, and it only served to interest her more.

Stevie knew she was pushing aside thoughts of Christian, and the fact that she had now cheated on him with his own cousin. It was not going to be easy to deal with. She wondered suddenly if Joe was thinking about Randy, and that he'd now officially cheated on her.

"Joe?" she said softly, bringing him out of his reverie.

His light blue eyes trained on her, then narrowed slightly, as if he were trying to discern what she was thinking.

"You cheated on him," he said quietly.

She nodded. "With his cousin, no less," she said, not looking pleased with herself about that.

Joe nodded.

"And you cheated on Randy," she said.

"With someone young enough to be my daughter."

"It doesn't matter."

"Why doesn't it matter?" he asked, his eyes searching hers.

"It's about who you are, Joe," Stevie said, moving to his side. "It's not about your age."

He shook his head slowly. "I don't know what it's about anymore."

87

Stevie stared down at him for a long moment. "Listen, Joe," she said, reaching down to touch his cheek. "You're in love with your wife." She shrugged. "I guess in a way I'm in love with your cousin. They're just not treating us right, right now. Okay, so maybe we over-compensated here," she said, grinning, "but it doesn't mean that this has to be something huge, does it?"

Joe looked at her for a long moment, knowing that she wanted him to reassure her, but he found he couldn't. "He'll probably want to kill me." He shook his head. "I don't know what Randy will do."

Stevie grimaced. "I didn't mean to cause you problems, Joe."

He gazed back at her for a long moment, then moved to put her under him. "You didn't cause me problems, Stevie. I wanted you, and knowing that you had, at least at some point, wanted me was too much for me to ignore." He kissed her lips. "I need you right now, more than you realize."

She looked up at him. "Well, I'm here," she whispered. "And very happily so."

He grinned, leaning down to kiss her again.

CHAPTER 4

Dave Dibbins was lying with his head against his wife's abdomen, his arms wrapped around her waist. He was asleep, his back bare, wearing only sweatpants, not used to the heat Susan's mother kept on during the day to combat the cold of an English winter. Susan was reading a book, with one hand absently stroking her husband's hair. She felt very happy to be home, even if it was a bit surreal. She was in her childhood bedroom with her husband. Her room was much as it had been when she was growing up. It was going to be interesting, sharing it with David, knowing the background he'd come from. They were from opposite sides of the spectrum, financially.

Even as she glanced down at him, Dave stirred and turned over, looking up at her.

"Hi," she said, smiling.

He grinned. "Guess I kinda passed out, huh?"

"You were tired, David," she said, her English accent still so elegant.

"I know," he said, reaching up tiredly to rub his eyes.

He had worked two weeks straight to tie up enough loose ends so he could take this vacation with his wife. It meant he hadn't slept while working undercover. He had expected to sleep on the plane, since the flight was about twelve hours. However, having never been on a plane before, he found he was too edgy to sleep. Susan had attempted to get him to relax, but Dave hadn't been able to. Once

89

they'd reached her mother's home, Dave's eyelids had been heavy. He had, in fact, fallen asleep in the car her mother had sent for them. Susan had taken him straight to her old room, finding his sweatpants and a shirt for him in their luggage and pulling him down on her bed so he could sleep. He'd sunk down onto the big, soft bed gratefully, wrapping his arms around her and falling asleep in the comfort of her warmth.

Sitting up, he leaned against the headboard of the Louis XIV bed. Susan moved to lie against him, setting her book on the bedside table. He pulled her into his arms. She dropped her head back against his left shoulder, looking up at him. He kissed her softly on the lips, then started looking around the room.

"Tell me about this place," he said, using the words she'd used when he'd taken her to his favorite place on the beach back in California.

Susan smiled, moving to sit between his legs and lean back against his chest. His arms were draped over his bent knees.

She pointed to the Lladró statues lining one corner shelf.

"I've collected them since I was little. My mother bought me the first one, that kitten there, with the orange stripes."

"What are they?" he asked.

"They're Lladrós. It's Spanish porcelain."

Dave nodded. "I've heard of them. I don't think I've ever seen one though."

"I've always liked cats, so I've always only collected those and the ones with cats in them."

"Cats, huh?"

"You don't like cats?"

Dave shrugged. "I've never had one."

"What about dogs?" she asked, realizing again how different his life had been compared to hers.

"Nope, couldn't really keep a dog in a trailer, babe. There wasn't enough room for the three of us, let alone any animals."

"So you never had a pet?" she asked, surprised.

Again he shrugged. "Never really had the time or the inclination."

"Wow," she said, shaking her head.

"What?" he asked, grinning.

"I just couldn't fathom not having pets. In fact…" she said, trailing off as she started to click her tongue. A few moments later two cats bounded into the room and up onto the bed. "These are my cats," she said, smiling warmly.

Both cats walked up to Susan, rubbing against her and purring. Dave just looked at them, not making any move to touch them. One was a long-haired tabby with black and beige stripes. The other was all white, with long hair and blue eyes.

"This," Susan said, pointing to the tabby, "is Guenevere. And that," she said, pointing to the white cat, which was now sniffing at Dave as he held out his hand, "is Magdalena."

Dave grinned, giving her a pointed look. "Maggie the Cat?"

"You know *Cat on a Hot Tin Roof*?" she asked, smiling widely.

"Yeah, somewhat," he said, his grin widening.

"What?" she said, putting her hands on her hips and giving him a haughty look. "How exactly do you know Maggie the Cat, David?"

Dave laughed.

91

"Don't make me hurt you, Dibbins," she said, smiling as she turned to him.

"Oh, hurt me."

She held her fist up to his face, and he kissed it, which made her laugh. He pulled her to him, kissing her softly, then drew her closer, deepening the kiss. His arms tightened around her as hers went around his waist. He touched her cheek, stroking it as his lips moved over hers.

Things were just getting heated when someone cleared their throat. Dave glanced up. He didn't recognize the woman standing in the doorway, but her eyes were all over him. Susan turned her head.

"Terry!" she exclaimed, moving out of Dave's arms and off the bed to hug the woman, whose eyes kept trailing back to him.

"David," Susan said, turning to him, "this is Theresa. She and I went to school together."

Dave nodded casually, his eyes connecting with Terry's again. "It's nice to meet you," he said, his tone polite but not very warm. He already had the woman pegged for a predator.

"I heard you'd gotten married," Theresa said as Susan walked back over to the bed, sitting down next to Dave.

Dave's arm moved around her waist, his blue eyes on the other woman. Theresa sat on the end of the bed.

"You two look very happy," she said, her eyes moving over both of them.

Susan smiled, and Dave leaned back against the headboard, resting his left arm over his knee. Theresa took in the gold Celtic cross hanging around his neck and the lack of a wedding band. Her eyes widened when she saw the tattoo on his arm. She looked back to

Dave's face and found him grinning almost maliciously.

"What do you do for a living, David?" Theresa asked politely.

"It's Dave, and I'm a narc," he said coolly.

"A narc?" Theresa repeated. "What exactly is that?"

"A narcotics officer," Dave clarified.

"A police officer?"

"Yeah."

Theresa nodded, knowing that Dave was already on the defensive with her. It meant that he didn't trust her. She wondered at that. When she had walked up to the door, seeing them in such a passionate embrace had made her wonder who this man was. His hands had been moving over Susan in such a sensual way, she had been impelled to see who the man himself was. When she'd seen his sky blue eyes, she couldn't help but look at the rest, and the rest was very nice. Little Susan had done quite well for herself. He was definitely handsome—but a police officer? Well, she did know that Susan's uncle was a police officer. Not that Theresa minded blue-collar workers, since her family was nothing but, but Susan Endicott was far from blue-collar level. Theresa could only imagine the fight these two had had to get married.

"David, Theresa is working as an au pair here in London," Susan said, stepping into the uncomfortable silence.

She could tell that Dave was not as impressed with Theresa as men usually were. Theresa stood a statuesque five feet nine inches tall, with long brown hair highlighted with blonde and deep brown eyes with long, dark lashes. She had a model's thin body, but there was just enough curve there to be enticing. Susan had always felt plain next to her. But now Susan was definitely different than she had

93

been back at university. No longer the scared mouse, and quite a beauty.

"Yes, you should see this man's bathroom!" Theresa said, grinning. "I think it's bigger than the house I grew up in."

"My Lord…" Susan said, shaking her head.

Dave said nothing.

"Dave, your wife singlehandedly saved my academic career," Theresa said, smiling at Susan.

"She did?" Dave asked, sounding only mildly interested.

"Yes, I was too busy being excited about being at King's College. Susan was the one to take me into hand and make me study. I was forever trying to get her to loosen up, and she was forever trying to make me be more serious."

Dave nodded, glancing at Susan, who looked embarrassed.

"Anyway, I was wondering if the two of you would like to go out while you're here visiting," Theresa said, sensing that things were getting decidedly uncomfortable.

Susan looked at Dave. He shrugged, then nodded.

"Sure, that would be fun," Susan said, smiling.

"Are you sure?" Theresa said, looking at Dave.

"Yeah," Dave said simply.

"Alright." Theresa stood. "I'll call or come by sometime in the next couple of days to shore up plans. Fridays are the best at The Tube, so that would be the best night to go."

Susan nodded, remembering that The Tube was the club Theresa had always been trying to get her to go to when they were younger. She walked her to the door of her mother's home. Theresa turned to her.

94

"I'm afraid your husband doesn't like me much," she said.

Susan shook her head. "Terry, he's just tired. He didn't get much sleep in the two weeks before the trip, and then couldn't sleep on the plane either."

"Two weeks?"

"He does undercover work, which keeps him on his guard all the time. That tends to keep him from sleeping when he's doing it."

"Oh, that must be grueling," Theresa said, looking sympathetic. "Well, I hope that's why he seems so cool to me. He seems very reserved."

"He'll warm up," Susan assured her friend.

Once back in the bedroom, Susan went to Dave, who had lain back down. She lay on her side, running her fingers over his chest. His sky blue eyes met hers.

"Theresa doesn't think you like her much," Susan said.

Dave shrugged. "I don't know her."

Susan narrowed her eyes, realizing that he was being noncommittal. "Do you not like her, David?"

He stared up at the ceiling. "She just strikes me as a predator."

"A predator?"

"Yeah," he said, reaching up to touch her cheek. "The kind of woman that likes to go after other women's men."

"Do you think she's after you?" Susan asked, surprised.

"I don't know. I just got a vibe from her."

Susan nodded. His instincts about people were usually quite accurate. "Well, I wouldn't be surprised. Theresa was always a little boy crazy." She kissed his chest. "And you are quite handsome."

95

Dave's lips twisted in a sardonic grin. "I don't think it's me, babe. I think she just wants something that's yours."

"Well, you are mine," she said, smiling.

"Yes, I am."

"And you didn't find her attractive?"

He shrugged. "Yeah, she was attractive, but I have the woman I want," he said, leaning over to kiss her lips sensually.

"Well, men used to go after her all the time."

"When? Back in school?"

"Yes, no matter how interested they were in me, as soon as they met Theresa, they forgot all about me."

Dave looked down at her for a long moment. "Did you downplay your looks then too?"

"Downplay them?"

"Yeah, babe," Dave said, grinning. "Like when you first came to work for Joe and Randy."

"Oh," she said, biting her lip and grinning, never having seen it that way when she was at university. "Well, I was rather nondescript then too, yes."

Dave shrugged. "You were always beautiful, Susan. You just hid it really well then."

Susan nodded. "I never really did it consciously, I just thought that being a nanny meant being unremarkable."

Dave nodded. "Maybe for some upper-class, London-society family, Susan, but for a cop like Joe…" He shrugged. "He's not exactly standard in that area."

"True," Susan agreed. "But I always felt like I needed to be more stable and less dynamic for the children."

"Dynamic?" Dave echoed, grinning.

"Yes," Susan said. "My Lord, David, you all are such dynamic, compelling individuals, it's got to be exhausting to try and keep up with you, especially with children who grow up in that environment. Sometimes, I think they need some good old-fashioned normal people around them."

"And we're not normal?" Dave asked in mock offense.

"You, David, are far from normal, and God knows my aunt, uncle, and Joe aren't anywhere near average."

"Well, I'll give you those last three," he said, grinning. "But I'm normal."

"David, normal people work from nine until five. They come home, they eat dinner and watch TV, then go to bed. You are far from normal, my love," she said, smiling.

"So, you're saying because I deal with dealers, sleep with one eye open or not at all, because I come home every three days, make love to my wife, and surf as much as humanly possible, and because I basically relax for three to four days before I go back and work again— that makes me not normal?"

"Right."

He nodded, then shrugged. "Okay, I can live with that."

"Well, good," she said, smiling. "You are, however, a rather dynamic individual yourself, Mr. Dibbins."

"I am, huh?" he said, leaning down to kiss her deeply.

When their lips parted, she was breathing a little heavier. "Oh yes," she said, her deep blue eyes sparkling as they looked up into his.

"And you, Mrs. Dibbins, are quite beautiful," he said, feeling so lucky to have her at that moment.

With her beautiful sapphire eyes staring up at him, her smooth golden skin, her delicately boned face, her perfectly shaped mouth, which he kissed again and again… Everything about her made him feel like he was the luckiest man alive. He found it hard to believe fate had smiled on him so greatly when she'd given Susan to him.

As he kissed her, he pulled her closer. They kissed for what seemed like hours, then he slowly removed her dress, deepening his kiss hungrily. When they made love, they reached their release together. Susan buried her face in his neck, moaning softly as she fought to contain herself lest her mother hear them. Afterward they laughed at how quiet they'd been, both of them conscious of the fact that Deborah's room was only three doors down.

"I love you," Susan whispered against his neck as they drifted off to sleep together.

"And I love you," Dave said, brushing his lips back and forth on her cheek. "You have no idea how much."

Susan fell asleep in his arms feeling very loved.

***

Things were getting crazy, and Donovan knew it. He'd been with Rosa every night since that first night. They spent hours in bed, and while the sex was incredible, it drained him to the very core. Every morning was a fight to get out of bed; most mornings he just didn't make it. Jeanie was on edge, and he knew that she had a right to be. He wasn't doing his job.

Jeanie had no idea that Donovan was sleeping with one of the instructors, but she knew he wasn't himself. Even the distance between them couldn't hide that. He was on edge all the time; the slightest thing would set him off. She'd given up trying to contact him when he didn't show up to his classes—she knew that would piss him off. She wondered if he really just didn't want to work with her and was hoping she'd opt off the case if he was a big enough pain in the ass. At this point, she was considering it. Talking to Spider had come to mind, but she didn't want to seem like a whiner. So she waited to see what would happen.

Rosa was all-consuming for Donovan. He wondered if he was becoming obsessive, and he was ashamed to realize it had everything to do with the effect she had on his body. He knew literally nothing about her. From the minute he walked in the door until the moment she ordered him out, she was in charge. It was a relief to finally have a woman tell him what to do, what she wanted, what she wouldn't put up with. One night, however, Donovan felt the need to exert himself, wanting to dominate her for a change. While their bodies were intertwined, with her on top as usual, he moved to put her underneath him. Her hands, which had been holding on to him as he moved her, clenched, and talon-like fingernails bit into his skin.

"What do you think you're doing?" she asked, her voice a low growl.

"Being a man, for a change," he said, grinning.

"You'll be what I want, when I want," she said, digging her nails deeper into his back.

Donovan winced. "Relax," he said, searching her eyes.

Her response was to rake her nails down his back, leaving bloody trails. He gasped, moving away from her instantly. She moved after him, pushing him back on the bed. He sucked his breath in, making a hissing sound at the pain touching the sheets caused. She

99

moved back over him, taking her pleasure and giving him none. When she was done, she told him to leave.

He got up slowly from the bed, glancing back to see his blood on her sheets. He wondered how she'd explain that to her husband, who was conveniently absent a lot these days. That thought dragged at him as he dressed. He left her house without a word; nor did she speak to him.

On the drive home, he got a call. It was Randy.

"Hey, Randy, what's up?"

"I wanted to tell you before you heard it some other way."

"What?" he asked, narrowing his eyes.

He already knew about Joe leaving her; he wasn't real happy with that, but realized he probably didn't know the whole story either.

"Joe's having an affair," Randy said simply.

"He's what!" Donovan yelled.

"Donovan, calm down," Randy said, sounding frustratingly calm herself.

"Bullshit. What fucking right does he have?"

"Every right, Donovan," Randy said. "He left me, remember?"

"Is that why he left, Randy? Because he was with someone else?" Donovan asked, wanting some logical explanation, since Randy hadn't really explained why her husband of over thirteen years had left her.

"No, I don't think so. I think this just happened. There's more," she said, sounding hesitant now.

"Great," Donovan said, clenching his jaw, grinding his teeth together. "Let's hear it."

"He's with Stevie O'Neil," Randy said softly.

"He's…" Donovan started. "You mean, he's having an affair with his cousin's girlfriend?"

"Yes."

"She's younger than me!"

"I know, Donovan," Randy said, again sounding far too calm.

"And you're divorcing the bastard when?"

"I'm not."

"Are you fucking nuts?"

"No," Randy said. "I see this as payback."

"Payback?" Donovan rolled his eyes. "You mean for Dickerson?"

"Yes."

"That was like twelve fucking years ago, Randy. I think the statute of limitations is up on that one," he said, letting his anger run free.

"Donovan, it's my choice," Randy said softly, surprised at his obvious fury.

"Yeah, and it's a dumb fucking choice. You're gonna let him fuck anyone he wants now, because you made a mistake twelve years ago? That's bullshit, and you know it."

"He left. What am I supposed to do?"

"Divorce his ass, and take half of everything he owns."

Randy was silent.

Donovan sighed, knowing he wasn't helping her at all right now, but his own situation was making it impossible for him to be sympathetic. "Look, I gotta go. I'll call you tomorrow," he said, still sounding irritated.

101

"Okay, Donny," she said, using her pet name for him. "Be safe."

"Yeah," he said, hanging up the phone.

When he drove up to his house a few minutes later, he noted that Jeanie's car was there.

"Fuck."

He was home earlier than normal, since things had gone so awry with Rosa, but he definitely didn't feel like dealing with Jeanie tonight. Anger was swirling in him. He was mad at himself for getting involved in this situation, mad at Rosa for insisting on this dominatrix routine; he was sure he'd have scars from her nails tonight. It was a ridiculous situation—he knew it, and he needed to get out of it, and fast. Now this shit with Joe. Who did the guy think he was? That he could fuck anyone he wanted over and they couldn't do anything about it? And there was Randy playing the stupid victim. He couldn't believe it!

He walked into the house, his features dark; Jeanie saw it instantly. She stood up from the couch, watching him warily. She'd never seen Donovan looking so outright furious.

"What happened?" she asked, not sure what would put Donovan in such a state.

Instead of answering her, he went to his liquor cabinet and pulled out a bottle of Jägermeister. He spun off the cap and took a few long swallows.

"Donovan?" she said, surprised.

"What, Jay?" he snarled.

"Jesus…" she said, taking an involuntary step back. "What's wrong?"

He grinned, a very nasty, angry-looking grin. "You mean besides the fact that my brother-in-law is fucking someone young enough to be his daughter? Or the fact that he's screwing my sister over while he's doing it?"

"Damn…" Jeanie said. "Joe's having an affair?"

"Yeah, Jay, Joe's having an affair."

"You know, Donovan, you can drop the attitude with me, okay?" she said, narrowing her eyes.

"No, Jay, I can't," he said. "I can't drop the attitude with you, 'cause then you think you're back in, and I won't let you do that."

"In?"

"Yeah, in with me, in my heart, in my bed."

Jeanie stared back at him, stunned that he was being so nasty to her, and that he was actually sounding cocky. Then she gave a wry laugh, shaking her head.

"I don't think I want to be 'in' with you anymore, Donovan," she said, turning to leave.

His hand on her arm stopped her. When she looked up, he was grinning sarcastically.

"You don't, huh? Why's that?"

Jeanie pulled her arm out of his grasp and gave him a dirty look. "Because you aren't the man I was in love with anymore, that's why."

"Oh yes I am. I'm just not so easy anymore."

"Well, neither am I," she said, turning to walk away from him.

She cried out when he grabbed a handful of her hair.

"Let's just see about that," he growled.

With that he pulled her back to him, his lips coming down on hers fiercely. He was kissing her, pulling her body to his, but there

103

was no tenderness, and not even any passion in the kiss, just anger and hate. Jeanie put her hands to his chest, trying to shove away from him, but he held her fast. One hand still grasped her long hair, the other pressed into her back, his fingers digging into her skin painfully. For a moment she panicked, but then her training kicked in; she'd spent some time with Midnight Chevalier and had learned a few things about good old-fashioned street fighting.

She relaxed in his embrace, allowing him to think she was giving in. Predictably, he sensed her surrender and loosened his hold on her hair and back. That's when she kneed him in the groin, which got her released. She stepped back and threw a punch with all her might, catching him on the jaw and sending him stumbling backward. Turning, she stalked out of the house.

Once in her car she sat shaking. She couldn't believe Donovan, who had never been rough with her in any way, shape, or form, had just done that. Looking down at her knuckles, she saw that they were bleeding. *Good*, she thought viciously. *I hope it hurts like hell in the morning.*

***

Rhiannon had found that she was eight weeks pregnant when she went for her first appointment with the OB-GYN doctor. The doctor was extremely nice, telling her what other symptoms she could expect. Rhiannon was feeling better; she knew it was simply knowing that all the nausea and fatigue would amount to a baby in the end. Kyle was ecstatic, as was Brenden, but Nick continued to be negative about the baby. He said he didn't care what he had to do, he had no intention of being a babysitter for them or watching them try to do it at their ages. Again, Kyle had had to leave the room to keep from striking his son. Things weren't getting any better there.

Brenden had climbed into bed with them one night, feeling the tension in the house and not liking it. Rhiannon felt bad for him. She knew he wasn't used to all this fighting. It warmed her heart when his little hand reached up to touch her cheek. She opened her eyes to find him staring up at her.

"Is my baby sister going to be pretty like you?" he asked.

Rhiannon glanced at Kyle, and he smiled, winking at her.

Rhiannon looked back down at Brenden. "I think it would be really nice if your baby sister or brother looked like your daddy too. Maybe he or she could have black hair like his and green eyes like mine. What do you think?"

Brenden nodded. "That would be okay."

Rhiannon smiled. "Good, then that's what we'll ask for, okay?"

"Okay," Brenden agreed, smiling too.

Rhiannon was happy at least one of the Masterson boys was okay with this baby thing.

***

Joe and Stevie hid out in his hotel room the entire weekend. She made one perfunctory call to Christian, leaving a message on the answering machine that she'd be gone for a couple of days. She left no details. They spent the weekend watching TV, ordering room service, and having sex. They both knew they were breaking all the rules, and very likely would be paying for it come the end of the weekend, but neither of them talked about it. Joe turned off his cell phone and told the front desk to hold all his calls. He was very surprised that Midnight herself didn't turn up at the hotel. He was hoping that meant she hadn't tried to get ahold of him. He knew he was lighting candles in the wind with that hope.

Sunday evening, they lay together on the bed, watching the sun go down into the bay. Joe lay behind her on his side, her back to him. One of his arms was around her waist, the other under her neck, snaked up around to hold her shoulder. Her fingers stroked his arm absently. Both of them were quiet for a long time.

"So what are we gonna do?" he asked quietly as the sun slipped below the horizon.

Stevie was silent for a moment, then shrugged. "I don't know," she said softly.

"He's gonna be pissed," Joe said.

"Oh yeah..." Stevie nodded. "He leaves for Seattle in the morning."

"Ouch," Joe said, aware that she was avoiding the situation. "When are you supposed to get the keys to the house?"

"Tomorrow," she said, her lips tightening at the fact that Christian had been avoiding the whole thing with the house too.

Joe nodded, blowing his breath out slowly.

"This isn't going to be easy, is it?" she said after a long silence.

"Nope."

"Any chance no one knows?" she asked hopefully.

"Nope," he said again, leaning down to kiss her ear softly.

"Shit," she said, making him grin.

"Well said."

He looked over at the night stand, where his cell phone sat, and sighed deeply. "Guess the responsible thing would be to turn that back on, huh?"

Stevie grinned. "Probably."

Joe picked up his phone and turned it back on. He had at least a dozen missed calls.

"Bloody hell," he muttered.

He scrolled through the messages, and could almost sense Midnight's irritation rise as he saw that she'd called him six times. The other calls were from various members, and the last was from Randy. So he knew they'd been worried. He also knew how Midnight's mind worked.

He nodded. "Yep, Midnight knows, and I'm betting she knows who I was with too."

"How?" Stevie asked.

"'Cause my partner doesn't do things halfway. She would have called the hotel to find out if I was here. Then she would have basically threatened someone into checking on me, like the room service people. Then she would have gotten a description of who I was with. Trust me, Midnight knows."

Stevie shook her head. It didn't pay to try and put one over on the Chief of Police, even if you weren't doing it on purpose.

"Are you going to call her?"

"Why?" he asked. "She knows I'm fine."

"Yeah, but..." Stevie grimaced. "Would you rather deal with the impending tirade in person or on the phone?"

"Good point," he said, grinning in spite of the tension already starting in his stomach.

He picked up his phone again and dialed. Rick answered.

"Hey, man, Night there?" Joe said.

"She's here," Rick said coolly.

Joe narrowed his eyes, sensing that he was just getting the tip of the iceberg in Rick's tone.

"Well, can I talk to her?" he asked, not apologetic in the least.

"I guess," Rick said, and put the phone down without another word.

Midnight came on a minute later. "Yes?" she said, as if taking any other call.

"Night, it's me, but you know that already," Joe said, his tone chilling a few degrees.

"Yeah, I know," Midnight said, her tone equally cool.

"You called?"

"Yeah, but since you didn't bother to reply, I took care of it."

Joe flinched. He knew he'd been shirking his responsibilities this weekend, and if he were with any other department he'd probably be on report at this point. In fact, he wasn't altogether sure he wasn't.

"What did I miss?" he asked, his tone not reflecting his chagrin.

"Oh, just the usual *vice* bullshit, nothing major," she said airily, making sure to emphasize that it was his job, not hers.

"I see," Joe said, maintaining a businesslike tone.

"Oh, by the way, call your *wife*. She's worried about you," Midnight said. Her tone could have cut through diamonds.

"I'll do that," Joe said, overly sweetly. "Thanks for your concern." With that he hung up, tossing the phone on the bed in disgust.

"What did she say?" Stevie asked.

"She told me to call my *wife*, that she was worried," he said, his eyes shooting sparks.

"Ouch," she said, using the word he'd used earlier to describe her situation with Christian.

"Yeah..." he said, smiling tightly.

His phone rang then. He blew his breath out, shaking his head as he reached for it.

"Yeah?"

"Are you nuts, man?" came Rick's voice.

"What?" Joe asked, his tone all captain.

"Bad enough you fuckin' blow off your job, but you're fucking your cousin's girlfriend? Have you totally fucking lost it? She's young enough to be your bloody daughter."

"Yeah, exactly what business is it of yours anyway?" Joe countered, losing his temper a bit.

Stevie watched, seeing the anger in his eyes and sensing the tension in him.

"We're your friends, Joe," Rick said condescendingly.

"Yeah, right up until I do something you don't fucking approve of."

"You looking for our approval, man? To do what? To screw your cousin over, cheat on your wife, and fuck a kid?"

"Go to hell, Debenshire, and take your opinion with you," Joe said, hanging up.

He was mad now. He stood up, yanking on his jeans and buttoning the first three buttons, leaving the other three undone. He began pacing back and forth, his hands clenching into fists. Stevie sat up. She could see naked anger on his face.

"Joe..." she said cautiously.

"What?"

109

Stevie stared back at him, her eyes widening a bit at his tone, making him stop pacing and look at her. He blew his breath out slowly.

"I'm sorry," he said. "It's not you, okay?"

"Well, it is me," she said, shrugging. "They're pissed because you're with me and not with Randy."

"Yeah, but I'm not mad at you, okay?" Joe sat on the bed, touching her cheek.

"I know," she said, nodding. "But it might just be easier for you if I leave."

"Will it?" he asked, his light blue eyes searching hers. "Or will it be easier for them?"

Stevie didn't answer; he was right.

"This is going to get rough," she said.

"Yeah, it is," he said, pulling her into his arms and holding her there.

The next day, Joe was sure he couldn't be farther in Siberia if he tried. It started out with his insisting she drive with him that morning.

"We need to present a united front, or they'll think we believe they're right," he said.

She couldn't argue with that, so she went with him.

When they got to work, Joe pulled into the lot, parking in his reserved spot. He got out and opened the door for her. She glanced around. She could almost feel every eye on them. Even in a department as big as theirs, news traveled fast. Joe reached into the back, pulling out his gear bag and shouldering it. He was striking in all black, with his shield clipped to his belt. Stevie had bought a shirt down in the lobby of the hotel, and wore it with her jeans; they'd been cleaned and pressed and sent back to the room.

To her surprise, Joe took her hand as he walked toward the building. She glanced up at him, and even though he didn't look back at her, she caught the grin as it curled at his lips. Yes, he was doing this on purpose. They got to the elevator without incident, but on the next floor, Spider got on. He nodded to Joe, his eyes skipped over Stevie, and then he pointedly turned his back to them both. Joe looked down at Stevie and shook his head slowly, then stared straight ahead. Joe and Stevie were on the same floor as Spider, so they all got out together. Once again, Joe took her hand, leading her to his office, instead of letting her go to her office in Spider's area.

Once inside, he kicked the door closed and moved to lean against his desk.

"You ready for this?" he asked.

"Will I ever be?"

"Probably not."

"Probably not."

He grinned. "Busy for lunch?"

"If they haven't lynched me by then, you mean?" she asked, batting her eyelashes at him.

"Yeah, if," he said, grinning.

"I think I could do that," she said, shaking her head and rolling her eyes.

"Good," he said, and went to sit down at his desk. "Noon, don't be late," he added, winking at her.

She laughed as she walked out of his office. This was not something she'd ever imagined having to deal with. Sleeping with a married man, and a living legend in the department no less. And now she was going to face the firing squad.

When she got back to her area, she went to her cubicle and turned on her computer.

"O'Neil," Spider said from behind her.

She turned, seeing him standing at the doorway to his office.

"Yes, sir?" she asked, knowing now was the time to be all business.

"In my office," he said commandingly. It wasn't usually Spider's style.

Stevie stood up, aware that she was about to get chewed on. She walked into his office and stood at his desk.

"Close the door," he said, taking a seat.

"Yes, sir," she said, then closed the door and returned to the desk.

"Sit down, O'Neil."

She sat without a word. Her eyes were trained on a spot just above his head.

"What's the status on the Yreka case?"

Stevie's eyes dropped to his for a moment, narrowing slightly. Her look told him she knew this had nothing to do with a case and everything to do with her dalliance with Joe Sinclair. Her eyes went back to the spot above his head.

"The case is proceeding. I have a meeting with Juno next week."

"Why not this week?"

"Because he's out of town this week," she said, her lips curling ever so slightly at his attempt to find fault with her work.

"And the Stinson case?"

Stevie's grin was wintery, until she schooled her features. "The Stinson case is completed. The report should be done by the end of the day."

"What did we get?"

"We got three arrests, two AKs, 20K in cash, and three pounds of high-grade meth," she rattled off.

Spider looked unhappy, which he shouldn't, considering such a good outcome. Stevie met his eyes directly, and there was no mistaking her contempt for his tactics. She raised an auburn eyebrow at him, as if saying, *Gonna keep this up?*

Spider looked disgusted with himself for a moment, then sighed. "Okay, O'Neil, make sure that report is on my desk tonight before you leave."

"You got it, Lieutenant," she said, her tone saying, *I already knew that.* She left his office, leaving the door open.

Later in the morning, she went downstairs for coffee. She saw Midnight with Kyle. Her eyes connected with Midnight's across the room. Neither woman looked away. Stevie canted her head to the side, her face an open challenge for Midnight to say something. Kyle said something to Midnight, making her break the stare, but not before Stevie saw her eyes widen at the challenge.

When Midnight glanced back, she saw that Stevie hadn't looked away, but she did when Midnight looked at her the second time, shaking her head in disapproval.

Taking her coffee, Stevie left the cafeteria before Midnight had a chance to walk over to her.

Kyle, of course, had been informed as to what was going on.

113

He'd made a point of not saying anything—Stevie was his sister-in-law, after all—but he did get on the phone to Rhiannon to warn her of the latest trouble her sister was in.

"Oh, Jesus…" was Rhiannon's reaction, as she realized what being set against the Gang would mean for Stevie. She knew her sister well enough to know she'd never back down.

"Tell me about it," Kyle said, sounding supremely unhappy.

In the cafeteria, he'd made a point of dragging Midnight's attention back to him before the chief had a chance to stride across the room to physically take Stevie on for what she believed was a slight against her "family." Midnight had been vehement about what was going on with Joe and Stevie.

"He's not thinking with the right head," she'd said derogatorily.

Kyle hadn't said anything, refusing to speak against Stevie but not willing to point out to Midnight that she was only assuming things. He knew that Midnight needed to calm down before she'd see reason.

Joe and Stevie had lunch. He took her to the Pit, and Stevie just shook her head, knowing he was challenging everyone with his actions.

Tom Ryan was in on that particular day, and he blundered into the whole situation, purely by accident. He walked up to the table, clapping Joe on the shoulder, asking how he was. Then he turned to Stevie.

"Tom, you've met Stevie O'Neil, right?" Joe asked.

Tom nodded. "You're dating Blue, right?"

Joe grinned, shaking his head as Stevie attempted to form a response. "She was, Tom, but now she's dating me."

Stevie stared at him, her eyes widening, trying not to laugh at the expression on Tom's face.

"But, Joe, you're…" Tom started to say, trailing off as he realized he might be saying too much.

"Married," Joe supplied. "Yes, Tom, I know, but I moved out a few weeks ago."

"Oh," was Tom's only response. He walked away, shaking his head.

"Jesus, are you nuts!" Stevie said, slapping him on the arm as he grinned unrepentantly.

Tiny and his wife, Jess, walked in then. Tiny looked at Joe, his eyes holding the other man's for a long moment, then shook his head, disappointed. Joe just stared back at him, refusing to lower his eyes. Jess' glance bounced from Joe to Stevie, then back to Joe, looking like she was trying to understand, but it was obvious she really didn't at all. She followed Tiny to a table in the back.

Kyle came in a bit later, fortunately without Midnight. Little did they know that Tom had called Midnight to inform her who Joe was with. Midnight had made a point of not going to the Pit for lunch that day, ordering her food from Kyle, who would take it back with him. He walked over to their booth, his eyes going to Joe.

"Joe," Kyle said, nodding.

"Masters," Joe replied, inclining his head slightly.

"Stevie," Kyle said, his eyes searching hers. "How are you?"

Stevie looked back at him for a moment, his gaze reminding her so much of how Jason used to look at her when she'd screwed up. She felt tears sting the back of her eyes. This was harder than she'd thought it would be. Instead of answering, she nodded, swallowing a

115

few times to get rid of the sudden lump in her throat.

"Kyle," Tom said, walking up with bags in his hand, looking as if he was rescuing him. "Here's your order."

"Thanks, Tom. What do I owe you?"

"I'll put it on your tab," Tom said, moving away again.

Kyle's eyes trailed back to Joe and Stevie. "Well, I better get this back."

"Yeah…" Joe said, his tone indicating disdain. Stevie said nothing.

After lunch, Joe walked her back to her cubicle. He stared back at Spider as the lieutenant watched them from his office.

Leaning down, Joe whispered, "Hang in there, O'Neil."

She nodded, giving him a tight little smile.

Later that afternoon, Stevie was at the copy machine, making copies of her report for Spider.

"So, did it hurt, O'Neil?" came a voice from behind her.

Glancing over her shoulder, she saw Bill Harris in the doorway.

"What, Harris?"

She was still cautious around the man who two years before had attempted to scare her when she'd received a promotion he thought he should have gotten. Spider had been the one to stop Harris then, along with Christian. Would they help her now? Or would they let Harris do what he wanted?

"Did it hurt?" he repeated conversationally.

"Did what hurt, Harris?" she asked, sighing.

"That fall from grace. Heard the thud all the way down here," Harris said, his grin gleeful.

"What bothers you more, Harris?" she asked, leaning casually against the copier, her emerald eyes sparkling in amusement. "The fact that I can make it with a captain in this department, or the fact that you can't even make it to sergeant with this department?"

"You fucking little bitch," Harris said, coming off the doorjamb and walking toward her.

"Ah, ah, ah," Stevie said, wagging her finger at him as she stood her ground. "Remember what happened last time you tried that, Harris. I hear the beach is nice this time of year."

"Cunt," he growled, standing half a foot from her.

"One you'll never get even close to," she replied, looking up at him, her voice confident. Inside she was shaking, but she'd be damned if she'd let him see it.

"Who'd want to?" he replied.

Stevie looked back at him. "At least one captain I know." She knew she was pushing it, but she was mad now.

"Yeah, well, don't get comfortable, O'Neil."

"Don't you have a patrol car to check out, Harris?" she asked condescendingly, her smile sweet.

"Bitch."

"You say that like it's a bad thing," Stevie replied, turning to pick up her copy job, and winked at him as she walked out. When she got back to her cubicle, she sat down heavily, her heart pounding. She knew she was walking a high wire with this. If Joe dumped her and went back to his wife, she would be the odd man out, and her career in this department could be over. It shook her confidence in what she was doing with Joe.

She was still sitting there when Joe walked up.

"You ready?" he asked, then glanced at her face. It was still pale.

"Hey…" he said, kneeling down in front of her. "What happened?" he asked, his light blue eyes filled with concern as they searched her face.

Stevie shook her head. "Nothing I shouldn't have expected," she said, her voice still shaky.

"Christ…" Joe said, sounding annoyed. He stood, extending his hand. "Come on, let's get out of here."

She nodded, taking his hand and allowing him to pull her up. She picked up the report that she'd made copies of. As she and Joe walked by Spider's office, Spider glanced up from the documents he was reading. Stevie stepped inside, her hand still in Joe's as he watched Spider. Her eyes connected with Spider's as she dropped the report in his in-basket. She went back over to Joe. He put his arm around her, and they turned together and walked toward the elevators. Spider stared after them, shaking his head. He had to give O'Neil credit—she wasn't caving under the pressure.

Out in the parking lot, Stevie mentioned that she needed to go pick up her keys to the house. Joe nodded.

"Where do you need to go?" he asked.

"I didn't mean you had to take me, Joe."

"I know," he said, grinning. "Where do you need to go?"

"To the house. It's at 1210 Pacific Beach Drive."

He nodded, getting in and starting up the Escalade.

On their way, they talked about what all they'd dealt with that day. Stevie even told him about the scene with Harris.

"He talks to you like that again," Joe said, his tone all captain, "you let me know. I'll have his ass on report."

"Midnight would probably side with him at this point."

Joe sighed, shaking his head. "Then I'll just kick his ass, how 'bout that?"

Stevie grinned. "That sounds good. Can I watch?"

"Of course," he replied, grinning too.

As he drove, he put his hand on her leg. She looked down and noticed that his signet ring, which he usually wore on his right ring finger, was now on his middle finger. She took his hand, touching the ring.

"Didn't you usually wear this on your ring finger?" she asked, knowing the answer.

She remembered many times over the years when she'd looked at that ring on his hand in the few pictures she had of him. She knew where he wore it, because for a few years it *wasn't* a wedding band.

Joe glanced over at her, then nodded. "Yeah," he said, shrugging. "Got too loose."

"You've lost that much weight?" Stevie asked, aghast at the thought.

"Guess so," he said, looking out the window as he drove.

It was then that Stevie realized how much stress he was really under with all of this. She wondered at his ability to hold it all together despite all that.

When Joe pulled up to the house Stevie had directed him to, he saw the real estate agent standing out front. He looked at the house; it was small, but seemed nice enough. It was the classic bungalow type, with a red-tile roof and whitewashed walls.

Joe and Stevie got out of the car and walked over to the agent. He was a small, wormy-looking guy whose eyes were too close together. He had been very helpful, as he was reportedly the area specialist and she'd wanted to buy near the beach. She'd just barely been able to qualify for this house, and the down payment and closing costs had taken just about every penny she had.

Steve Simms looked at Stevie expectantly.

"Keys?" she said, wondering why he was looking at her like that.

"Cashier's check?" Simms replied, smiling.

"What?" Stevie asked, feeling her stomach turn over.

"You didn't get my message?" Simms asked. When she shook her head, looking pale, he said, "I left you a message at your apartment. There is a last-minute prorated insurance amount you need to pay before I can give you the keys."

"How much?" Stevie asked, her voice reflecting the crestfallen look on her face.

"A thousand five hundred and seventy-three dollars."

Stevie shook her head. "I don't have that—I won't have that till I get paid again. Shit! What about the loan—can I roll it into the loan?" she asked. They'd have to re-draw the documents, which would keep her out of her house for another three or four days, but at least she'd still get it.

But Simms was shaking his head. "Proration amounts have to be paid up front. The mortgage company wants protection."

"I'll pay it," Joe said.

Stevie turned to him. "No, Joe, you can't."

"Why not?"

"You can't," she said shaking her head.

"Yes, he can," Simms said, thinking that she meant it legally.

"No, shut up," Stevie said, glancing at him.

120

Joe took Stevie's arm and led her back over to the Escalade.

"Stevie, do you want this house?"

"Yes, but—"

"No buts," he said, making a cutting gesture. "Let me do this."

Stevie shook her head, stunned.

"Please, Stevie, let me do this."

She thought about it. If she didn't pay this she was going to lose the house. She'd barely gotten it the first time, and the rates were threatening to go up any day now; she might be priced right out of the market.

"Okay," she said, leaning up to kiss him. "But I'm going to pay you back."

Joe grinned. "You already have."

"Bullshit."

"Come on, let's hit an ATM," he said, looking over at Simms. "Hang tight, we'll be right back."

An hour later, Stevie had the keys to her house. She unlocked the door and stepped inside, wanting to show it to Joe. He appreciated the hardwood floors, and they talked about what all she'd need to do in terms of work. When she showed him the master bedroom, she turned to him as he looked out into the small backyard, which was in dire need of a gardener.

"Joe," she began, looking up at his profile. He turned to her, his light blue eyes practically glowing in his tanned face. "I want to thank you," she said softly. "For the money that I had to come up with. I mean…"

Joe shook his head. "Don't worry about it, Stevie."

"I will," she said. "And I will pay you back."

Joe just shrugged, then looked down at her. "Got help to move in?"

Stevie laughed, shaking her head. "Not really. I seem to be on the opposite side of the world from the men in my life right now."

"Not this one."

"Yeah, but…"

"But what?" he asked, grinning. "I'm too old?"

She swatted his arm. "Stop that!"

Joe laughed, grabbing her by the waist. "Let me help," he said earnestly.

"Just remember you asked," she said, wagging a finger at him.

"I'll remember."

On the way back to the hotel, Joe put his cell phone on hands-free and dialed a number.

"Chevalier," came the answer.

Stevie's eyes widened.

"Yeah, Chief, Captain Joe Sinclair here."

"Yeah?" came Midnight's icy reply.

"I'm formally requesting two days off, starting tomorrow," Joe said, undaunted by Midnight's tone.

"That's not enough notice, Captain," Midnight said briskly. "Request denied."

"Fine, fire me then, 'cause I won't be there," Joe replied, and hung up.

"Joe!" Stevie said, stunned.

He shrugged. "Fuck her. I'm not playing this game with her. Regardless of what she thinks, she has no right to make this personal."

Stevie couldn't argue with that.

Joe's phone rang a few minutes later.

"Sinclair," he answered crisply on the hands-free.

"Joe, it's Kyle. What's going on, man?" Kyle asked, concerned.

Midnight had just stormed into his office and told him to start the paperwork to terminate one Captain Joseph Michael Sinclair the Fourth immediately. Then she'd slammed back out of the office. Kyle had sat staring openmouthed at his door. Was she nuts? Or was she serious?

Joe sighed. "I requested two days off. Midnight blew a gasket."

"She just told me to terminate you."

"So do it," Joe replied simply.

"Joe, you know I'm not gonna listen to her when she's like this, but Jesus Christ, what the hell is going on? I've never seen you two act like this."

Joe laughed, a self-deprecating sound. "That's 'cause we haven't acted like this for about thirteen years."

"Well, could ya knock it off. It's playing hell with the hinges on my office door," Kyle said, grinning.

Joe laughed at that, as did Stevie.

"Look, she's gonna kick my ass, but I'm approving the time off. Do whatever you need to do," Kyle said.

"I'm helping your sister-in-law move," Joe supplied.

"Oh, well, take three days then. She has a lot of crap."

"Hey!" Stevie said indignantly.

The three of them chuckled.

"Thanks, Kyle," Joe said seriously.

123

"No prob. Just come to me for a while, till all this stuff blows over, okay?"

"Yeah…" Joe said, sounding depressed suddenly.

They hung up then, just as Joe drove into the hotel parking garage.

They went up to the room. Joe kicked off his boots, as did Stevie. He moved onto the bed, pulling her down with him. They lay there, he on his back, she on her side. His arm was around her shoulders, her hand on his chest. Neither of them spoke for a long time, each lost in their own thoughts. Finally she reached up and touched his cheek.

"You know, Joe, if it would be easier for me to step aside…"

"No," he said simply.

Touching her on the chin, he guided her face up to his, kissing her softly on the lips. He pulled back, looking her in the eyes. "Do you want to be here with me?"

"Yes."

"Then be here with me, and to hell with the rest of them," he said, pulling her to him to kiss her again.

They made love a little while later. She found that he was more tender with her this time, as if he knew that she needed him to understand how hard this was on her too.

CHAPTER 5

In London, Susan got up one morning and told Dave she was going over to her father's office to talk with him. Dave guessed easily that she was going there to test his attitude toward her husband. He said nothing, knowing that Susan felt like she needed to protect him from her father's snobbish attitude. Dave didn't feel he needed protection, but he knew it would make Susan feel better to do things this way, so he told her he'd just hang out at the house and catch up on his TV.

Two hours after she'd left, Dave decided to get up and take a shower. The room they were staying in was basically a small master suite. It had a bathroom with a tub and a walk-in shower that was separated from the sleeping area by an open archway. He was just finishing his shower when the keen sixth sense that had saved his life any number of times starting tingling. Someone was in the room. He turned the shower off. His back was to the doorway.

"What are you doing here, Terry?" he asked without turning around.

Glancing over his shoulder, he caught her surprised look. She recovered quickly, moving to hand him a towel as he turned to get out of the shower. She passed him the towel, but not, however, before her eyes traveled down his body. When they made it back up to his eyes, she noted no surprise in them. She did, however, encounter the look that many criminals encountered. A look somewhere between warning and disdain.

He took the proffered towel, drying off quickly and wrapping it around his waist. He didn't bother to glance at her the entire time, sensing she was watching him.

"How did you know I was here?" she asked after a long few moments.

Dave grabbed a second towel, drying his hair and glancing at her in the mirror.

"In the business I'm in, it pays to have a bit of extra sensory perception. I felt you here."

"How did you know it was me?" she asked, hiding her surprise. He'd felt her there? And he'd known it was her—he'd called her by name.

Dave grinned. "I knew it wasn't my wife. She smells like jasmine; I'd know her anywhere. I also knew it wasn't Deborah, since she smells like Opium, and Liz smells like a cross between peaches and pears." He pinned her with a look, staring at her in the mirror. He turned around, leaning on the vanity. "You smell like sex." The way he said it, it wasn't a compliment.

Terry stepped closer, looking up at him seductively with her deep brown eyes. "Are you saying that's a bad thing?"

Dave moved his head back from her warily, his sky blue eyes connecting with hers and narrowing.

"It's not my thing," he said simply.

"Sex is everyone's thing, Dave."

Her eyes lowered from his, to travel over his chest, stopping at the thin scar at his shoulder. She reached up, touching the scar, raising her eyes to his again, to find him watching her with pursed lips.

"What is this?" she asked.

126

"Gun shot," he replied, moving to stand, making her back up, almost warily after what he'd just said.

"You were shot?"

"It happens in the business I'm in," he replied, moving past her to the large walk-in closet.

He stepped inside, tossing aside the towel, and pulled on a pair of faded jeans. When he walked back out into the room, she was waiting for him. He closed the door, and when he turned back around she was right there.

"Susan can't be enough for you," she said, staring up at him searchingly.

"Susan is all I need."

"Maybe you don't realize what you need," she said, reaching up and pulling him down to her, kissing his lips hungrily.

Dave pulled his head back, his hands held out to his sides and away from his body.

"Let me make this perfectly clear to you, Terry. I am very deeply in love with my wife. I know exactly what I want, and I married her." His tone was very serious. "Now, I'm telling you, step back off me, or I'm going to forget that I don't hit women."

Terry's eyes widened. She stepped back and leaned against the vanity, much as Dave had minutes before.

"You love Susan that much?" she asked, an odd tone to her voice.

"Which part didn't you get?" he said, canting his head to the side.

A slow grin started on Terry's face, and she nodded. "Good, then you're the man she should be married to."

127

"Excuse me?"

"Susan is a wonderful woman. She deserves a man that will love her above all others."

"So you're saying that was a test?" he said disbelievingly.

Terry shrugged. "I can't say that I wouldn't take you if I thought I'd have a chance, but yes, basically it was a test. Susan is my friend, and she's always had problems with men—or should I say, boys—who don't appreciate the wonderful person she is. I'm glad to see she didn't marry one."

Dave stared at her, his eyes still showing doubt.

"Dave, I'm not fool enough to try and seduce my friend's husband in her own mother's house. I can't say I didn't enjoy the view though," she said, winking rakishly. "Susan is very definitely a lucky woman."

Dave began to grin, shaking his head.

"Where is she, anyway?" Terry asked.

"Went to see her father," he said, moving back to the mirror and combing his hair.

"Oh, Lord, that man!"

"You've met him?"

"Oh yes," Terry said. "He's a top-notch snob."

"Well, I think my wife is trying to smooth the way before I get to meet him."

Terry nodded. "That sounds like her. She is forever trying to get her father's approval."

"Well, she's not bound to get it with the likes of me," he replied, not sounding at all remorseful.

"Deborah likes you though, right?"

"Yeah," he said, grinning. "I think so."

Terry laughed. "Then you've won the better half."

Susan walked in then. "David, I—" she began. "Oh, hi, Terry," she said, and hugged her friend then went over to her husband.

She kissed his chest softly, then turned her face up to his. He kissed her lips. Her hands moved up into his hair, pulling him closer as she deepened the kiss. His hands slid around to her back, drawing her into him. Terry looked on, thinking again that Susan was a very lucky woman.

When their lips parted, Susan looked up into his eyes. Dave saw a sparkle he wasn't sure he understood, but he grinned down at her anyway. She turned to Terry, putting her back to Dave, who pulled her against him with an arm around her chest, holding her shoulder. He leaned one hip against the vanity.

"So, Terry, what are you doing here?" Susan asked innocently.

"I came to see you two," Terry said, gesturing at them. "I wanted to shore up plans for Friday. We're still going out, aren't we?" She looked at Dave, as if asking if he forgave her.

Susan glanced back at her husband. He looked down at her, then shrugged. "Sounds good to me."

"Great," Terry said, smiling brilliantly. "Shall we have dinner before we hit the club? Say, seven?"

"Sounds alright," Susan said, nodding. Dave nodded too. "We'll pick you up," Susan told Terry.

"Great. I think we should cab it from my place, though. I intend to get very drunk, and I want you two to be able to have fun too."

Dave laughed, as did Susan.

They finished their plans, then Terry left. Dave sat on the bed, intending to ask Susan what had happened with her father. She walked over to him. Hiking up her dress, she straddled his lap. She kissed him deeply, pushing him back on the bed as she did.

When she pulled back, she looked down at him, her eyes searching his.

"You are the most wonderful man in the entire world," she said, her tone slightly awestruck.

"Why is that?" he asked mildly.

"Because you are," she said, smiling down at him.

Dave narrowed his eyes slightly, as if reading her mind. "You heard all of that, didn't you?"

Susan looked embarrassed. "I walked up and heard you say, 'You smell like sex.' I'm sorry, David, I just wasn't sure who you were talking to, and then I..." She shrugged, biting her lip. "I guess I wanted to know how you'd react."

"And you heard how I reacted," he replied mildly.

Susan marveled once again at the difference between Dave and the man she'd always thought she'd marry, Christian Collins. Christian would have been furious that she'd spied on him. Dave didn't even seem disturbed.

"Yes, I did," she said, smiling down at him. "And that's what makes you the most wonderful man in the world."

He kissed her. "No, it makes me in love with you."

"No one has ever loved me like you do, David."

"That's why I'm yours, Susan."

"Yes, you are," she said, smiling brilliantly. "And I love you so much."

"Show me," he said, his sky blue eyes staring up into hers.

She spent the next two hours doing just that. Since no one was home, they were able to be as loud as they wanted. In the end, Dave had to kiss her to quiet her down just a bit. She laughed afterward, lying against his chest.

"Why did you silence me?" she asked in mock offense.

"I didn't want the neighbors calling the cops," he said, grinning.

"David, the neighbors are an entire city block away."

"I know."

Susan laughed, leaning down to kiss his chest. They spent the rest of the afternoon relaxing and talking about nonsensical things. Dave never did get around to asking her about her father, which was just as well, since Susan had decided she didn't want her husband and her father anywhere near each other. Wilson Endicott had spent an entire hour telling his daughter what a silly fool she was, that David E. Dibbins would take every penny of her inheritance and leave her. That he was a gold-digger and a cradle-robber. Susan had finally told her father that he was nothing more than a cold, angry man with an adding machine for a heart. She'd slammed out of his office. Wilson Endicott had been stunned. His daughter had never raised her voice to him. This David Dibbins was having a very bad influence on her.

Friday night, Dave and Susan went out with Theresa. Dave found out quickly that Theresa often called Susan "Susie"; it seemed to be a pet thing with them. Dave found it amusing. He'd never thought of Susan as a Susie; she was too sophisticated for that. He followed them into the restaurant for dinner, always at their back, his habit of protecting Susan showing.

During the meal, he was regaled with tales of how wild Terry was. He was also warned that they both intended to get drunk and fully expected Dave to as well. He smiled indulgently, watching his wife act like a silly schoolgirl with her old school chum. At one point, Susan went off to the bathroom, and Terry leaned in close to talk to Dave.

"We're not scaring you, are we?" she asked.

"I deal with scarier people on school playgrounds," Dave replied, grinning.

"Oh my…" Terry said, her eyes widening as she began to chuckle. "We need a drink," she decided then, hailing the waiter. "What do you drink, Dave?" she asked, winking at him.

"Jack Daniels."

"We'll have a bottle of Jack Daniels and two straws," Terry said, winking rakishly at the waiter and tossing a couple of £50 notes on his tray.

Dave watched the waiter's face light up as he inclined his head and hurried off to get the bottle.

"That looks like it was a lot of money…?"

"It was," Terry answered with a grin.

"Nice."

"Have I impressed you?" Terry asked, looking as if she'd truly like to.

"Money doesn't impress me," Dave said mildly.

"What does?" Terry asked, looking up at him intently.

A slow smile spread over his face as he said, "My wife."

"Blast!" Terry said, laughing.

Dave grinned. Maybe he did have her pegged wrong. She had been quite funny all night. And quick to back off when he mentioned his wife. She didn't seem intent on grabbing him; she just liked flirting with him outrageously.

Susan arrived at the same time as the bottle of Jack Daniels.

"What is this?" she asked, giving Terry a suspicious look. "Are you trying to get my husband drunk?"

"Of course," Terry replied, winking at Dave.

He shook his head, grinning. Susan slid back into the booth next to him.

"Miss me?" she asked sweetly.

"Always," he said, leaning down to kiss her.

"Oh, good Lord, you two, not in the bloody restaurant!" Terry said, rolling her eyes.

"Shut up," Dave and Susan said together. The three of them laughed.

Thus was the beginning of their night. Dave and Terry drank the bottle of Jack Daniels, even getting Susan to try a few sips. The faces she made sent Dave and Terry into gales of laughter, causing Susan to laugh too.

They moved on to a bar, where Dave ordered Susan a drink called an Oatmeal Cookie. It was sweet, and he was sure she'd like it. Sure enough, she drank three of them before they left that bar. Moving on to another place, this one a nightclub with dancing, Dave took up a place at the bar, close to the dance floor. Susan and Terry took to dancing for him. By this time they were all well on their way to being drunk, Dave being the least so, since he had a higher drinking capacity than the ladies. Even so, he was feeling very buzzed and continued to drink, allowing himself to drop his guard, something he almost never did.

A slow song started, and Susan motioned to him to come join her. He walked over, leaning down to kiss her deeply. She looked incredible. She had gotten a little brave with her outfit, wearing a form-fitting black jersey dress that fell to about three inches above her knees, with slits that went all the way up to just below the top of her thigh. She wore silken hose and black heels, and her hair was loose, as she knew Dave liked it, and Terry had insisted she wear dark eyeliner and mascara, and that she absolutely had to wear a dark lipstick as well. The effect was stunning. Susan was always beautiful to him, but made up as she was, she was so devastatingly sexy that he couldn't take his eyes off her all evening.

Terry seemed to have an effect on Susan, making her more carefree and wild than she usually was. Dave liked to see her enjoying herself. She was a beautiful woman, and she had every right to show that off. She wore his ring on her finger, so he felt quite confident of himself, even if every guy in the place was drooling at the provocative picture she presented.

Susan wrapped her arms around him, swaying with the music. He knew she was drunk, but he also knew he could handle anything that happened, if he needed to, even if he was headed for drunk himself. He had confidence that came from years of protecting himself. Pulling her closer, he kissed her again. He felt rather than saw people watching them. And he didn't care. He was there with his wife, and enjoying himself for a change. To hell with what anyone thought.

Dave was dressed in jeans, black boots, and a black long-sleeved shirt. With his long fade and long, lean form, he looked pretty good to many of the women dancing around them. His open grin and handsome face attracted them, as did his obvious confidence without any sign of arrogance. Many a heart fell when he walked over to the beautiful blonde in the black dress. That's when they noticed the wedding rings, and more hopes died. Terry, however, didn't care about any of that. She was having fun, and she wasn't about to stop.

Dave felt Terry move up behind him, her hands on his back. He looked down at Susan to see if she noticed, and saw that she was glancing over his shoulder and smiling at Terry. He felt Terry's hands slide up his back and into his hair, and closed his eyes as her nails skimmed his scalp. Susan's hands, which had been around his neck, slid down his chest. Dave opened his eyes and saw her staring up at him. He grinned at her, leaning down to kiss her again. The kiss deepened as Terry's hands slid to his chest and downward. Both Dave and Susan were surprised as her hands moved to Susan's hips, pulling her in closer to Dave. Dave took one hand from Susan's back, reaching behind him, to touch Terry's back, pulling her closer. He felt Terry's hand on his hips then. Susan was caressing his chest, her nails tracing over his shirt.

Dave knew they were making a spectacle of themselves, but the alcohol in his veins didn't allow him to care. He'd seen much more sexual dancing since entering the club; he didn't realize, however, that people were watching them because of the attractive people that they were doing what they were doing.

When the song ended, the three of them headed over to the bar. Suddenly they seemed like celebrities, and people were buying them drinks left and right. Dave finally had to switch to straight Coke to keep from getting too drunk. Every so often, though, the Coke would contain Jack Daniels, and the bartender would wink at him. He was sitting on a stool, watching the crowd dance, when Susan moved to stand between his legs. He put his arms around her waist, pulling her back against him, kissing the side of her head. She turned her head, looking up at him. He leaned down to kiss her, and she turned her body to face him. He moved his hands to her waist, then slid them up her back, holding her to him. Things were getting a bit heated when he heard a voice right next to his ear.

"Easy now, kids," Terry said.

He turned his head to look at her. "Quiet, you," he said, grinning.

Terry laughed, shaking her head.

They danced and drank long into the night, into the wee hours of the morning when the bar closed. In the cab on the way to Terry's flat—since she lived in London proper, and Susan's mother would probably have heart failure seeing her daughter so drunk—Terry started drifting off to sleep. When they reached the flat, Dave had to carry her up the three flights of stairs.

"Flat, my ass," Dave grouched, grinning all the same.

Once Terry was safely put to bed, Dave and Susan went to the guest bedroom. They began kissing and removing each other's clothing, making love feverishly, the night's adventures having put them both on an expectant edge.

They talked afterward, facing each other.

"You had a good time tonight," Susan said softly.

Dave kissed her. "Yes, I did," he agreed. "Did you?"

"Oh yes," she said, smiling. "I'm glad that you were able to relax."

Dave shrugged. "It's easy to do in a whole other country."

Susan nodded, realizing suddenly that that had been the difference.

"At home you're on your guard too much to relax this much,"

136

she said, sliding her hand over his arm lovingly.

"Exactly." He touched her on the chin. "I do want you to realize something, though."

"What's that, David?" she asked, staring up into his eyes.

"I don't want you to feel like you have to do stuff like we did tonight to keep me interested. Okay?" His voice was sincere, and his eyes searched hers.

Susan nodded.

"I'm not Christian, babe. I have the woman I want for the rest of my life. And you're all the adventure I need, okay?"

"Okay," she replied softly, then grinned. "You did enjoy that with Terry, though, didn't you, dancing like that?"

He grinned. "I'm human, right?"

"Very definitely," she said seductively.

Dave laughed softly, then leaned down to kiss her. "I love you."

"And I love you, David," she replied, staring directly into his eyes.

They fell asleep lying in each other's arms, facing each other, the sheets barely covering them from the waist down.

As it turned out, they spent a number of evenings together after that. They enjoyed each other's company, and since Dave was fully aware that Terry understood his dedication to his wife, he was able to let his guard down with her as well. She also found that she liked his protective nature toward Susan, and even toward her while they were out. He would intercede whenever a man got too grabby with her, and Terry appreciated that. She hated to see them go home, and told them she'd love to come to California to visit. Susan agreed eagerly. Dave nodded, grinning. On the plane on the way back, Susan leaned her head against her husband's shoulder, feeling so happy. She almost hated going back home, because she knew she'd probably lose her husband for a few days again to his job. She'd enjoyed having him all to herself for two weeks.

As luck would have it, however, he ended up working on a case with Stevie. There had been a report of drug sales at a local private elementary school. Coincidentally, the school Joe and Randy's children went to. So the day after Dave got back from London, he found himself in Stevie's car, watching the activity around the school as people dropped off their children.

"We're watching for a black Cabriolet, right?" Stevie said, sitting casually in the driver's seat of her Trans Am, glancing over at him through her sunglasses.

"Right," Dave said, leaning back against the passenger's door. "So, you gonna tell me what I missed?" he said casually.

Stevie gave him a sharp look. "Don't you start with me too, Dibbs. I don't need it right now," she said, sounding weary.

"Hey…" he said, hurt. "I'm not gonna give you shit, Steve. I just thought you might want to talk about it."

Stevie looked out through the windshield, scanning the area casually, then sighed deeply. "It just happened," she said after a long silence. "I mean, I've wanted him forever, but I never really figured I'd ever get with him, ya know?"

Dave nodded, looking noncommittal.

"Anyway, so he was all messed up over this stuff with Randy. I was just being honest, telling him how I thought she was crazy. That led to me having diarrhea of the mouth and blabbing to him about how I've always wanted him. I wasn't making a play for him, Dave."

138

"I know," he said, sounding sincere. "And you probably were helping his ailing ego in the process anyway."

"Well, I just can't stand the idea of him thinking he's old. Jesus, the man looks better than some of the guys I've seen half his age."

She shrugged. "But the whole Gang is totally against us, and they're putting the pressure on him, and I think it's bugging him a lot."

"Steve," Dave said, "Joe's pretty damned tough. He can handle whatever they dish."

"The other day, he asked for two days off to help me move. Midnight denied it. He told her to fire him. She actually went to Kyle and told him to terminate Joe," Stevie said, her voice indicating her shock at the vehemence with which Midnight and Joe had fought.

"Hmm…" Dave said, narrowing his eyes. "Sounds like there's more going on here than just the surface stuff."

"That's what I'm thinking too," Stevie said. "But I'll be damned if I know what it is."

Dave nodded, still deep in thought. "Things will work out the way they're meant to, Steve, you know that," he said, reverting to his usual philosophy on life.

"I know," she said petulantly. "I just hope they don't manage to kill each other in the meantime."

Dave grinned at her tone.

"So, how was your vacation?" she asked, sounding overly cheery with the change of subject.

Dave nodded. "It was good."

Stevie gave him a pointed look. "Good?"

"Yeah, good," he said, smiling.

"And that's all I'm gonna get?" she asked, looking affronted.

"What do you want?" he replied, scanning the area once again.

"Details, man, details!" she said, shaking her head as if he should know that.

"Sorry," he said. "I could tell ya, but then I'd have to kill ya," he added, his sky blue eyes sparkling mischievously.

"Oh, I see…" Stevie said, nodding. "Get all the gory details out of me, then clam up. I see how you are, Dibbins. Fine, just fine…"

Dave laughed, even as his eyes fastened on the black Cabriolet that had just parked outside the school yard. He saw Stevie's head turn just slightly, so he knew she'd seen it too, but she promptly checked her hair in the mirror.

"You got him?" she asked, not looking away from the mirror, still checking her makeup for all intents and purposes.

"Yep," Dave said, flipping open the laptop he had on his lap.

"He's not getting out, but there's a kid approaching," Stevie said as she heard Dave tapping away on the keys.

"And why aren't you running the plate, Ms. Computer Geek's Girl?" he asked.

"I'm not dating the geek anymore, remember?" she replied mildly. "I'm dating the range master now."

"And I'm doing the computer geek stuff why?"

"'Cause I'm doing the driving, Dibbins. Deal with it," she said, grinning. "Got that plate yet, old man?"

"Bite me, kid," he said, grinning back at her. "Got it."

"Good," she said, watching as the kid, no more than ten years old, took the drugs the man handed him, gave the man money, and walked on.

"Shaunassey, you got him?" Stevie said, talking into the wire she had on her.

"Got him," came the reply in their ears. They both nodded.

"Just observing now, right?" she said to Dave, as he watched the kid being approached by a plain-clothes officer dressed as a crossing guard.

"Yep, for now."

"And there's your girl," Stevie said as the older-model black Jaguar came into view. Susan was bringing the kids to school.

"Uh-huh…" he said, smiling warmly.

"Jesus, that's disgusting," she said, rolling her eyes and shaking her head.

"What is?" he said as he winked at his wife as she drove by, glancing in his direction as if at any other car on the side of the road.

"You," Stevie said, reaching over to poke him in the ribs. "You're so disgustingly in love with your wife it gives me a toothache just to be in the same car with ya."

"Jealous?" Dave asked, grinning widely.

"Hell yes!" she said, grinning right back at him.

"So, what's up with Blue, or shouldn't I ask?"

"Dave, I'm doing his cousin—what do you think?" she deadpanned.

"True, but does he know yet?"

"I'm sure he does by now…"

Christian did indeed know. He'd received a call from Erin Wednesday night. He'd already suspected something was very definitely

141

wrong with his and Stevie's relationship, considering she'd disappeared the weekend before he left for Seattle. He'd figured she was pissed about him leaving when she was about to close on her house, but he had no idea how bad things were about to get.

He answered his cell phone, sitting with his laptop in his hotel room.

"Blue, it's me," Erin said.

"Heya, Erin, what's up?" he asked, grinning. She was a nice kid. Far too sweet and innocent for his tastes, but very earnest in her friendship. He couldn't help but like her.

"I wanted to call you…" she said, sounding hesitant in a way that reminded him of Susan.

"What is it, Rin?" he asked, shortening her name as he often did with people he liked.

"Well, I thought you should hear it from me, before you hear it some other way…"

"Hear what?" he asked, his stomach knotting instantly. He knew he wasn't going to like what he was about to hear.

"Stevie's seeing Joe," Erin said quickly, as if hurrying would make it hurt less.

It didn't.

Christian felt like he'd been slammed in the stomach with a sledgehammer. He forgot to breathe for a minute. Finally he expelled his pent-up breath in a single word.

"Fuck."

It was a reflection of how much he was hurt by this revelation, and Erin felt it over four hundred miles away.

"Blue?" she said, when he didn't say anything else.

142

"I'm here," he said, sounding like he was in shock. In truth he was; this was not something he'd ever expected.

"Are you okay?" she asked, knowing it was a stupid question. Of course he wasn't okay.

Christian was silent for a long moment as he felt the relief of fury flood through his veins, replacing the pain quickly.

"I'll fucking kill him," was all he said.

Erin had never heard him speak with such venom before, and she shivered. She nodded, not able to think of an appropriate response.

A few moments later he said, "Thanks for the heads up, Erin. I'll take care of it."

He said it as if she'd just told him about a problem in the office. It made her nervous. They hung up a few minutes later.

Erin went to bed that night wondering if she'd done the right thing at all. She found out the next day.

***

Joe was sitting in his office, working on the monthly overtime allotments, hunched over his desk, pen in hand, when he heard his door open. He looked up and saw Christian standing in the doorway. Joe could sense the barely contained fury in the younger man's stance. There was no mistaking that Christian was there with a debt to settle. Light blue eyes connected with light blue eyes so much alike. Joe's eyes dropped from Christian's, a knowing grimace creasing his brow, as he slowly put his pen down. He sat back in his chair, his forearms on the arms, his fingers working as his eyes narrowed at nothing in particular. He was considering his options, but he knew this was the penance for his indulgence. Knowing it was due didn't make it any easier to handle.

Finally nodding, he stood up. Walking to his door, he gestured for Christian to precede him. Christian nodded, turning to walk out of the area. Joe followed, his face set in a calm mask. Christian headed out of the building from the back, toward the motor pool. Joe had known that was where they'd end up, where the security cameras didn't film. He stopped, waiting. Christian turned around, his eyes searching Joe's face.

"Why?" Christian asked simply.

Joe looked back at his cousin, his eyes showing the remorse that he didn't speak. "It just happened," he said calmly, not making any excuses.

Christian's lips tightened as he pressed them together. He nodded, his light blue eyes narrowing. Without warning he gave a yell and charged at Joe, catching him in the midsection and knocking him to the ground, swinging as they hit the floor together. Joe had the breath knocked out of him as Christian's fist slammed into his side, but he knew he needed to get out from under Christian and quickly. Grabbing two handfuls of Christian's shirt, Joe literally threw him off.

Joe was on his feet again in an instant. Christian took a moment longer to get up, but Joe only stood waiting for it. Christian took a swing, connecting with Joe's jaw, making his head snap to the side. Joe hit back, knocking Christian back a foot. After they'd hit each other a number of times, they both stood gasping for breath. Christian leaned against a car, Joe standing hunched forward, his hands on his knees.

"All this time," Christian spat angrily between breaths, "I knew there'd come a payment."

"What?" Joe asked, looking confused.

"For letting me into your *family*," Christian said, saying the word like it was an insult.

Joe shook his head. "Stevie's not a payment," he said, narrowing his eyes dangerously.

"Well, paid up like a whore, didn't she?"

"You bastard," Joe said, launching himself at Christian, this time knocking the younger man to the ground and holding his advantage, punching Christian in the face. Christian rallied, and they rolled, each trying to gain the advantage again.

Suddenly strong hands were dragging them apart. It took Dave and Tiny to haul Joe off Christian, and Rick and Kyle to hold Christian back. Stevie and Rhiannon moved to intercede, going toward Joe. Erin went to Christian's side; Midnight was already there.

"You had to fucking have it all, didn't you?" Christian growled.

"You had her, but you needed to fuck someone else," Joe threw back.

Christian struggled against Rick and Kyle's hold on him. "You don't fucking know what you're talking about."

"Like hell I don't!" Joe bellowed, trying to throw off Dave and Tiny.

"Joe!" Stevie yelled, stepping in front of him. "Don't!" She stared up into his eyes, pleading with him. "Please…"

Joe looked down at her. He could see she was shaking. He didn't realize she'd witnessed almost the entire fight. Dave had seen Joe and Christian walk out and had jumped up, stopping to grab Stevie on the way. Spider had gotten on the phone to Midnight; Kyle had been in her office, as had Rick. Tiny had happened to be driving into the motor pool at the time, and had jumped out of his car to help stop the fight as the others got there.

After a long moment, Joe nodded. Dave and Tiny let him go. Kyle and Rick let Christian go, but everyone stayed close just in case tempers flared again.

Christian spit out blood on the ground, his light blue eyes narrowed at Joe, then looked at Stevie in unveiled hatred. Joe reached up and wiped the blood off his mouth with the back of his hand, his eyes never leaving Christian, his guard up.

"You want her," Christian said, spitting out blood. "Take her and get the fuck out of my life."

"Done," Joe replied simply. Putting his arm around Stevie, he turned and walked back toward the building.

Once inside, Joe leaned heavily against the wall, his arm above his head.

"Joe…" Stevie said, reaching up to touch his side. He flinched. "Jesus, you're really hurt…"

"I'm alright," he said, sounding anything but, his heart hurting just as much as his body did at that point.

He started coughing then, and groaning.

"Come on, let's at least get you to your office," Stevie said, worried that Christian would come in at any moment. She didn't want him to know how much damage he'd done to Joe. She wondered, too, how much damage Joe had done to Christian. Christian had been spitting out blood; she didn't know if that was just a split lip, or if it was worse.

Erin was wondering the same thing.

"Maybe you should go to the doctor," she said as she tried to clean the cuts on Christian's face. He jerked away from her for the third time, gasping.

"No."

"Blue…"

"Erin, I'm fine," he said tersely.

"You look anything but fine, Collins. You should go," Midnight said, sitting on his desk.

"I don't need to go to the fucking hospital," he said, his anger starting to ignite again.

"Easy…" Rick warned from where he leaned against the wall beside Midnight. He didn't like Christian directing any of that fire at his wife.

Christian held up his hands in surrender. "Look, I'm fine, okay? Can we just forget it?"

Midnight looked at Rick. He shrugged, and she sighed. "Fine, okay," she said, hopping off his desk.

Meanwhile, Joe was getting double-teamed by both O'Neil sisters and Kyle.

"Joe, if there's internal damage…" Stevie said, not for the first time.

"I'm bloody fine," he said, not for the first time either.

"Yeah, that's why you're breathing that way," Kyle observed.

"He's right," Rhiannon put in. "You're breathing like it hurts."

"It does fucking hurt," Joe said. "Have you ever taken a fist to the gut? It hurts like hell."

He touched a cut on his cheek, looked at his finger, and saw his blood. "He hits pretty fuckin' hard. Must get that from my side of the family," he said, grinning.

When no one else even cracked a smile, he rolled his eyes. "For Christ's sake, lighten up, people. Frankly, I'd forgotten what my own blood tasted like."

Stevie narrowed her eyes at him, but looked at her sister, shrugging.

"Back to your lives, citizens," Joe said, making a shooing gesture. "Show's over, nothing to see here."

Rhiannon and Kyle left. Stevie turned to look at him.

"Are you sure you're okay?" she asked, her eyes searching his.

"I'll live," he said seriously.

She looked back at him, her face drawn and unhappy. He pulled her into his arms.

"It'll be okay," he said quietly, not at all sure he was right anymore. Then he kissed her on the top of the head.

She went back to work a little while later, still shaken by what she'd seen. It had been a vicious fight, and she hated that it had been over her. She was worried about Joe, and worried about Christian. She called Erin a little while later, asking her to meet her in the cafeteria. Erin did, and Stevie asked her how Christian was.

"He's hurting a lot," Erin said.

Stevie nodded. "I thought he would be. So's Joe."

Erin shook her head. "Why can't these guys just shoot craps or something?"

Stevie shook her head in response. "Men like these always settle everything with fire."

"And kill each other in the process."

"Sometimes," Stevie said, feeling worse.

"Stevie," Erin said, putting her hand over Stevie's. "You couldn't have stopped them, you know."

"I know," Stevie said. "But I could have stayed the hell away from Joe Sinclair."

Erin shook her head. "There's a reason this all happened, we just don't know what it is yet."

Stevie narrowed her eyes. "You been hanging out with Dave?" she asked suspiciously.

"No," Erin said, baffled. "Why?"

"He thinks like that too," Stevie said. "Irritates the shit out of me," she added, grinning.

Erin laughed.

"Thanks, Erin," Stevie said.

"For what?"

"For looking out for Christian for me, and for letting me know how he's doing."

"You're welcome," Erin said, then she looked at Stevie seriously. "You still love him, don't you?"

"I never stopped," Stevie said, then shrugged. "Things just got all screwed up in a hurry with us. They always do."

"I'm sorry," Erin said, looking like she really was.

"Yeah," Stevie said sadly. "Me too."

That night, Joe ended up staying at Stevie's house. She wouldn't let him go back to the hotel for fear he was hurt worse than he was admitting. Joe started self-medication that evening, running through two full bottles of tequila while Stevie kept a watchful eye on him, even drinking with him. She was feeling a lot of effects from that day too. In effect she'd just had to face the consequences of her actions as well. Christian hated her now, or wanted to, which for Christian was as good as actually doing it. She had known that sleeping with Joe would end her relationship with Christian. While part of her mourned the loss, the independent part of her said, *Good, I'm glad he's gone.* Unfortunately, the part that was aching was not so easily ignored, and seeing Joe absolutely morose over the fight with his cousin didn't help in the slightest. Not only had she ruined her relationship with Christian, but she'd ruined Joe's too. That thought made her take an extra-long swig of tequila. She felt the alcohol move through her veins, the numbing effects finally starting to take hold.

Stevie and Joe slept late into the next morning, calling off shift.

Christian didn't show back up to work either. Like his cousin, he'd started self-medicating that night, drinking shot after shot of tequila. He did so at his favorite bar, having taken a cab there knowing he was going to drink heavily. Tara, his long-time friend and one-time lover, kept a close eye on him. She saw the dark bruises on his face as well as the split lip and cheek. Shaking her head, she'd pulled out the Herradura that London, as she called him, preferred. He tossed his credit card on the bar, and she kept pouring all night, sensing that he needed this. She'd seen him in this state often enough.

When the bar closed, Tara got help from one of the other bartenders to get Christian to her car. She took him back to her apartment, a place he often hid out in when he was feeling low and wanted to get away from his world. The next morning he refused the food she offered, throwing up and then walking down to the corner store

150

for more tequila. Tara's daughter was in school, so Christian was able to hang out on her fire escape and drink all day long; that was what he did.

Two days later he went back to the apartment he shared with Stevie. He'd stopped there the day he'd gotten back from Seattle long enough to change clothes and drop his suitcase; he hadn't wanted to spend a night alone in the apartment without Stevie in it. The first night back in the apartment was brutal. He drank until he passed out, and when he woke he started drinking again. At one point he got up to throw up, and looked in the bathroom mirror at himself. Light blue eyes, bloodshot and unhappy, stared back at him. The same thought went through his head that had been screaming at him for the last four days: *The one I wanted to keep, I couldn't.* The thought ricocheted through his mind, culminating in a yell as he drove his fist into the mirror. As he pulled his hand back, he noted the blood dripping off it, and watched it curiously for a few minutes then walked back to his bed, lying down and picking up the tequila again. Blood ran down his hand as he drank. It dripped on the sheets, but he didn't notice. He didn't care. Later that morning he passed out again.

***

Rick came home one evening that week and heard the shower running. He didn't realize he'd walked in on his wife's infrequent habit of standing in the shower to cry out all her frustrations.

"I'm home," he called out, not wanting to startle her.

The last time he'd scared her, she'd been ready to kill him with her bare hands, thinking he was an intruder.

Midnight's head snapped up, and she ran her face under the

151

shower so he couldn't see the tears. She didn't miss his gasp a moment later. When she looked up at him, he wasn't looking at her, but at the floor of the shower. She glanced down and noticed the red tint to the water.

"Relax," she said. "It's not blood."

"Okay…" he said cautiously. "What is it?"

"Hair color."

"What?" he asked, sure he hadn't heard her right.

"Hair color," Midnight said, her tone disgusted. "To hide the gray Ming found today."

Rick stared at her for a long moment. "She found gray?"

"Yeah," Midnight said, turning her back to him as she finished rinsing herself off.

A few minutes later she stepped out of the shower. She found him lying on their bed.

"Is your hair a different color now?" he asked.

"No, it should be about the same, just no more gray," she said, still sounding disgusted.

Rick nodded. He watched as she wrapped a towel around herself and then dried her hair. He continued to watch as she used the blow-dryer to finish the job. When she was done he sat up.

"C'mere," he said.

She walked over to the bed. He took her hand and pulled her down to him. She straddled his outstretched legs. He gazed up at her hair, reaching up to touch it, smoothing his hands over it, then looked into her eyes.

"You are still the most beautiful woman I've ever met."

"Even if I'm old?" she asked, depressed.

"Midnight, you are not old."

She looked back at him, her expression telling him she felt it.

"Okay, so we're both old and decrepit, and we should just go off and die together," he said, the beginnings of a grin on his lips.

"Shut up, it's not funny," she said, looking even more pouty now.

He held back his grin. "I know. It's a bitch, getting old."

"Debenshire!" she said, slapping his arm.

"Hey!" he said, laughing. "You said you were getting old."

"You aren't ever supposed to agree with me on that," she said, narrowing her eyes at him.

"Oh, I'm sorry." He looked appropriately contrite. "I didn't get the memo."

"You're gonna make me hurt you, aren't you, Lieutenant?"

"Oh, please, Chief, please," he said, grinning as he stared up into her eyes. He sat up, pulling her closer to him. His lips took possession of hers, kissing her deeply as he removed the towel. Fortunately neither of the kids were home; Marie had taken Ricky to the park and Mikeyla was studying at a friend's house. His hands moved over her, touching her in familiar places, reminding her how well he knew her body and what she liked. They spent a long two hours that night making love, proving to each other that they were not old, that they still had a lot of passion for each other, and that there was no limit to how many orgasms one woman could have.

Rick fell asleep next to her, his arm over her possessively. Midnight smiled to herself. He was hers; he'd always be hers, no matter what.

Rick and Kyle were preparing to go to the Organized Crime and Criminal Intelligence Conference held yearly in Sacramento by the Bureau of Investigation. Midnight was disturbed to learn that Angelica had talked Rick into letting her attend the conference too. Midnight denied the application for conference registration fees for Angelica. Rick appeared in Midnight's office a little while after she'd set it in her out-basket.

"Okay," he said, walking in without knocking, since her door was open. "I'm game. What's up?"

Midnight looked up from the report she was writing. "With?"

Rick held up the conference request.

"Oh," she said.

Rick lowered his head, looking at her from behind a veil of brown curls. It was something he did when he knew she was being evasive. After a moment, he nodded, then turned to close her door. He walked around her desk and leaned against it.

"Okay, what's goin' on, babe?" he asked, searching her face.

Midnight shrugged, glancing up at him but not holding his eyes. "I just don't think she needs to go. I think it's excessive."

"Excessive?" Rick repeated, knowing she was hiding behind budgetary terms to keep from telling him what was really wrong.

"Yeah," she said, still refusing to look at him.

Rick knelt down next to her chair, reaching up to touch her chin, bringing her face around to his. "What's really goin' on, Night?"

Midnight pressed her lips together in agitation. She'd known she'd have this conversation with him if she disapproved Angelica's request. She never denied a request for training or information. She figured the more the officers knew, the better equipped they were to do their job. But this wasn't business; it was personal. And Rick could sense it. Damn him for knowing her so well!

"Hey…" he said, smoothing his thumb over her cheek. "Look at me."

Her eyes met his finally, and in them he could see irritation and some trepidation.

"Okay, talk. What's wrong?" he said, standing and pulling her up with him.

She dropped her head to rest against his chest, her forehead pressed there. "I just don't want her up there with you, okay?"

"Why?"

Midnight's head came up in a flash. "Because she's young, beautiful, and after you—that's why." Her tone said that he should have known that.

Part of him did know it, but he hadn't wanted to assume that was her reasoning. He nodded slowly, then pinned her with a look.

"Do you trust me?" he asked.

Midnight swallowed, then nodded slowly.

"Then you should know that nothing will happen up there."

"Rick," she said with a sigh, "I trust you, but I don't trust her."

"Yeah, but she can't do anything without my cooperation, can she?"

"No…" Midnight said, trailing off with an unspoken "but."

"No," Rick repeated. "She can't do anything, Midnight." He slid one hand behind her neck, tilting her face up to his with his thumb at her jaw. "I love you. I don't want any woman but you. Okay?"

Midnight nodded, not looking pleased with the whole thing.

"Nothing will happen," he said.

155

"Right."

"Midnight…"

"I know, I know, okay?" she said, petulant now. "I just don't have to like it, do I?"

Rick grinned. "No, you don't have to like it, babe."

"Good, 'cause I'm not going to," she said, giving him a sour look even as she started to grin too.

He leaned down, kissing her softly. "There's the woman I know and love."

"Yeah, underneath all the green makeup," she said, curling her lip in self-disgust.

"S'okay, I like it when you get jealous," he said, grinning. "Means you still love me."

"Is that what it means?" she asked, smiling now.

"Yeah," he replied, smiling too.

"I see."

***

Things within the Gang were decidedly tense. Dave had come out against them on their attitude about Joe and Stevie, citing that the Gang had no right to judge something they didn't understand. That either way, Joe deserved their support, since he'd supported all of them often enough. While Joe appreciated Dave's attitude, it didn't lessen the nagging depression that had been weighing on him since the fight with Christian.

Stevie felt it, and did everything she could to keep Joe's mind off what was happening. Many nights were spent simply holding him after he'd drunk himself into a stupor. She started dragging him to the gym again, and she started going again herself, having gotten out of the habit in the last few weeks. It seemed to give him an outlet for all the frustration he was feeling. He drank less, and at least fell into bed exhausted rather than passed-out drunk. They split their time between his hotel room and her house.

One Saturday morning he'd come over to find her in her backyard, pulling weeds.

When she glanced up at him, he was raising an eyebrow at her.

"Therapy," she said, shrugging. He grinned and walked into the house. A few minutes later he came back out wearing a T-shirt and shorts, and started pulling weeds right next to her. She glanced over at him, her look appraising.

"Guess I need therapy too," he said simply.

She grinned. They worked for hours, and he finally took his shirt off when it got too hot.

Stevie looked up as he tossed it aside. "Let me guess," she said. "You're tired of pulling weeds and figure distracting me will get you out of it?"

"Huh?" he said, his brow furrowed in obvious confusion.

Stevie reached up, running her nails lightly down his chest, her look seductive.

"Ohh…" he said, grinning. "Yeah, that's it."

She laughed. "I knew it, ya bum!"

They spent the rest of the day working hard, and then enjoyed a long, leisurely shower and a session in bed afterward. Weekends were easier, since they weren't at the office, where they had to withstand attitude and looks from the Gang and other members of the department who believed whatever the Gang did.

***

Christian Collins spent his evening much as he had for the last couple of weeks. He got home from work, he poured himself a drink. He worked on the computer, he poured himself another drink. He took a Vicodin for the pain in his ribs, he poured another drink. He read the label on the bottle that said not to take it with alcohol, he poured himself a shot and took the pill with it. He didn't look at his feelings; he didn't think about anything. He'd continue working on the program he'd been creating, drinking until he was numb. Once he was numb, he'd work feverishly until midnight, and then he'd pour a large glass of tequila and drink it down, passing out gratefully an hour or so later.

He'd started avoiding the office, because Erin was hassling him about how much weight he was losing, how haggard he looked, how tired he looked. She made the mistake once of pushing it by calling him at home. He'd promptly told her to leave him "the fuck" alone. When he was sober he felt bad about saying that to her; she was a nice kid, and she was just trying to help. But before he could string the thought together to call her and apologize, he was well on his way to being drunk again, and he never did. She didn't call back.

One more woman out of his life.

On Monday morning, Kyle, Rick, and Angelica left for the conference. By Wednesday Midnight was snapping at everyone. Every time she talked to Rick she was just sure she was missing something. She

158

asked if Angelica had kept her distance. Rick said she had, but Midnight could tell he was telling her what she wanted to hear. It irritated her no end. She trusted her husband, but she knew men were easier to seduce than women, and a very pretty, sultry Latina intent on getting a man in bed was probably the most dangerous there was. Angelica was definitely the sultry type. Midnight was on edge, and everyone knew it.

In Sacramento, Rick was endlessly amused by the reports he was getting about his wife's behavior. Manny had called to complain that Midnight had yelled at him about a report that had been on her desk for a full day.

"I can't deal with her, man, get your ass back here!" Manny wailed.

Rick chuckled. "Dealing with stressful situations builds character, Manny."

"Yeah, I got your character, Debenshire. Get back here and lay your wife so she'll get off everyone's back."

"Careful, Manny..." Rick warned, still grinning in spite of himself.

He liked that Midnight missed him. He even liked that she was jealous of Angel. She had nothing to be jealous of; Rick knew that, and that was why it was easy to be amused. He had indeed lied when he'd told Midnight that Angel hadn't tried anything; she had, one night even showing up and asking if she could take a shower in his room, since hers wasn't working right.

Rick had grinned. "Let me see what I can do," he'd said, going to her room next door.

In the end it became obvious she'd unscrewed the shower head

159

to make the water spray everywhere. Rick ended up wet for the adventure, but he didn't end up seduced. He was quite flattered that Angelica thought she wanted him, but not so flattered that he even considered taking her up on the countless offers.

During a lunch break one day, they were waiting for Kyle to join them out at the pool, where everyone was eating. A woman clad in a very scanty black bikini walked by Rick, winking at him. He smiled, inclining his head to her. She continued on her way.

"See?" Angel said, sounding triumphant. "You look!"

Rick grinned. "Angel, there's a difference between looking and touching. I'm not blind."

"So, who's to know you touched?" she asked slyly.

Rick just looked back at her, as if to say, *You've got to be kidding.*

Kyle joined them then, saving Rick from having to answer. Not that he would have. Angel was constantly trying to hint to him that if he slept with her, Midnight would never know. Thing was, he wasn't interested in sleeping with her, or anyone else but his wife. It was disgusting that such a hardcore player as he had once been could be so thoroughly caught, but Midnight had caught him, and he never intended to give her reason to let him go.

"Everything okay on the home front?" Rick asked Kyle, aware that he had just been calling home.

"Yeah, same as always. Nick's being an asshole, and Brenden doesn't want to eat anything but hamburgers for dinner."

Rick laughed. "Yup, Ricky's thing is french fries now. He'll eat anything as long as it has fries with it."

"Nick used to have a ketchup fetish—everything had to have ketchup on it," Kyle said, shaking his head. "Barb had to buy the stuff by the vat."

Rick grinned. He noted that Kyle could mention his dead wife now without getting choked up. He knew that had everything to do with Rhiannon, with meeting her and bonding with her as she mourned the death of her husband. Everyone was fairly sure it had been destiny, since Rhiannon's husband and Kyle's wife had died on the same day.

Angelica rolled her eyes, bored by the talk about children. Two guys as good-looking as these two were, and all they could talk about was their kids! It was just ridiculous! Two years before, when she'd come to FORS with information about the leader of Dos Fuegos, she'd been intent on meeting Rick Debenshire. She'd seen him on TV when he was burying his thought-to-be-dead wife. Even in his obvious grief, he'd been gorgeous. Her boyfriend at the time had made fun of the big bad puto of a cop being all sad, but Angelica had been fixated on him from then on. She wanted him, and Angelica always got what she wanted.

Well, she didn't always get what she wanted, but she was determined to get to Rick. It had become a challenge now. She'd heard about his and Midnight's passionate relationship and wanted to experience Rick's passion first-hand. She was sure Midnight just held his reins tight, and that was why he hadn't taken her up on her many flirtations. She was hoping this trip to Sacramento, away from the watchful eyes of the chief, would allow him to loosen up a bit. Three days and he hadn't loosened up, but Angel was determined to win this time. Wife or no wife.

***

Nick was sitting in his room, playing on his computer, when he heard

161

something. He wasn't sure what it was, but it had sounded like a thud. Thinking it might be Brenden, and knowing that Rhiannon had gone in to lie down, saying she was really tired that night, Nick got up to check. He walked out into the hallway and listened. He didn't hear anything. Brenden had gone to bed an hour before; maybe he'd just turned over and kicked the wall or something. Nick shrugged. Just as he was turning to go back into his room, he heard Rhiannon yell his name. The sound of it made the hair on the back of his neck stand up.

He ran down the hall and threw open the door to his dad and Rhiannon's bedroom.

"Rhiannon?" he said, turning on the light. He could hear her gasping.

She was lying on the floor, writhing in pain, holding her stomach.

"Rhiannon!" he yelled, striding over to her and dropping to his knees. "What is it, what's wrong?" he asked stridently as he looked to see if she was hurt. That was when he saw the blood on her sweatpants, where there shouldn't be blood in her condition. "Oh shit..." he said, feeling his heart starting to pound.

Rhiannon groaned between gritted teeth, gasping for breath a moment later. "Nick... Nick..." she said, over and over in a pained whisper.

"It's okay," he said, taking her hand as he reached for the phone. "I'm here, okay? I'm here." He called for an ambulance, explaining that his stepmother was pregnant and she was bleeding, and that his father was out of town. They said they'd send an ambulance right away. He set the phone down for a minute, reaching out to try and

162

comfort her. "It'll be okay," he said, not sure he was right, but knowing it was the right thing to say.

"Call… your… dad…" she said between breaths.

"I will. I have to go get the numbers off the fridge. Will you be okay?" he asked, worried.

Rhiannon nodded, even as she grimaced in pain again. Nick ran down the hallway and into the kitchen, snatching the list of cell numbers off the fridge. Kyle had left the list of everyone in the Gang, but Nick was most concerned about two numbers. His dad's and Stevie's.

On his way back to the bedroom he stopped in Brenden's room and shook his younger brother awake.

"Get up, Bren, I need your help with something," Nick said, making his voice cheery.

"What?" Brenden said, sitting up sleepily.

"I need you to go watch for the fireman," Nick said, widening his eyes excitedly.

"Fireman?" Brenden echoed. "Is there a fire?"

"No," Nick said. "But we need the fireman here to check on Rhiannon. She's not feeling well, and the fireman can make her feel better, okay?"

"She's sick?" Brenden asked, worried.

"She'll be okay, Bren. She just needs a shot or something," Nick said, wrinkling up his nose.

"Shots are yucky," Brenden said, shaking his head.

"Yeah, but Rhiannon's brave—she won't cry," Nick said. "Now I need you to put your robe on and go wait out on the steps for the fireman, and bring them to Rhiannon and dad's bedroom when they get here, okay? Can you do that for me?"

163

"Of course!" Brenden said, excited about the prospect of helping out and meeting a real fireman.

"I knew I could count on you," Nick said, smiling.

He went back into Rhiannon and Kyle's bedroom, glancing back to see that Brenden was headed to the front door. He picked up the phone. Sitting down on the floor next to Rhiannon, he touched her arm.

"I'm back, okay? I'm right here."

Rhiannon took his hand, holding it tight. He could see she'd been crying, but she was doing her best to look like she hadn't. He set the phone back down, stuffing the sheet of paper into his jeans pocket. He moved around to Rhiannon's head, taking it gently in his hands and moving it onto his lap. She looked up at him through pain-filled eyes. He smiled down at her.

"You're gonna be okay," he said, sounding so much like his father at that moment, Rhiannon's eyes filled with tears. "It's okay," he said, reaching down to take her hand again. "I've seen girls cry before."

Rhiannon laughed lightly, even as her tears spilled over and down the sides of her head.

A few minutes later the paramedics got there. Nick moved back to let them work. He went to take Brenden back to his room, putting clothes on him hurriedly.

"We're taking her to the hospital—you coming with?" the paramedic asked.

"Can my brother come too?" Nick asked.

"There's no adult to take him?"

"My dad's out of town."

"Yeah, okay, sure."

"Come on, Bren, you get to ride in a real ambulance," Nick said excitedly.

Brenden followed happily, pulling on his jacket.

Once at the hospital, Nick and Brenden had to wait outside. Nick asked where he could use a phone. He was directed to a payphone. Holding Brenden's hand, Nick pulled out all his change and started dialing. He called his father, who didn't answer, so he left a message saying that Rhiannon was in the hospital and she'd been bleeding. Then he called Stevie, who also didn't answer, and then he decided to call Midnight as well, leaving them brief messages. He hoped Stevie or Midnight could get there soon.

Midnight called back first. He told her what had happened, and she said to hang tight, that she'd be there as fast as she could. Stevie called right after that, sounding tired.

"Stevie, it's Nick, Kyle's son. Rhiannon's in the hospital—we're at Mercy."

"Shit," Stevie said, sitting up in bed and glancing down at Joe, who moved to sit up too. "Is she okay?"

"I don't know. Can you get here?"

"Yeah, I'll be there as fast as I can."

Stevie hung up even as she was getting out of bed and pulling on her clothes.

"What happened?" Joe asked, doing the same.

"Rhiannon's in the hospital. I don't know what happened."

Within minutes they were in Joe's car. They pulled up just as Midnight did. She shot Joe a dirty look as he strode past the front of her car, holding Stevie's hand. Stevie caught the look and just shook

165

her head, more worried about her sister at that point.

Within an hour most of the rest of the Gang was assembled. Nick had explained what had happened at the house a number of times by then. The only ones missing were Donovan and Jeanie, who were on a case, and Kyle and Rick, since they were still in Sacramento. Midnight had finally been able to get through to Rick, who got ahold of Kyle; they were flying back as fast as they could get a flight.

When the doctor emerged, he asked for Nick. Nick stood, and Stevie went to stand next to him. Joe followed. The rest of the Gang ranged out behind them, but pointedly away from Joe and Stevie, and Joe continued to receive vile looks from Midnight.

"How is she?" Nick asked, sounding truly concerned.

"She's going to be fine," the doctor said, surprised that there were so many people there. "Unfortunately, she has miscarried. She lost the baby," he said, looking appropriately sedate. "We've managed to control the bleeding, and she's resting comfortably now. You can go in to see her, but I only want one person in there at a time. She needs to rest."

"Nick, you go first," Stevie said, feeling a bit dazed.

Nick nodded, following the doctor.

Inside the room, Nick sat down in the chair next to the bed. Rhiannon's eyes were closed. When the doctor left, she heard the door close and opened her eyes, looking at Nick sadly.

"Thank you," she said softly. "For getting me here. Where's Brenden?"

"He's outside with one of the nurses. He's okay," he said, looking at her worriedly. "The doc says you're gonna be fine."

Rhiannon nodded, trying to smile but not doing too well. She looked away as the tears started again.

"Hey…" Nick said, standing up and looking down at her.

Rhiannon shook her head, even as tears rolled down her cheeks. Nick wasn't sure what to do. Finally he just took her hand, squeezing it gently. Rhiannon glanced at him, her eyes showing her surprise. Nick smiled encouragingly and she nodded in response, closing her eyes.

A little while later, the doctor came into the room. He gave her an update on her condition. She nodded, holding back tears when he confirmed that she'd lost the baby.

"What did I do wrong?" she asked quietly.

"Nothing," the doctor said.

"Then what happened?" she asked, feeling helpless.

"Maybe too much stress, too much tension, or just nature—it's hard to say."

Rhiannon nodded, looking away. She missed the stricken look on Nick's face. The doctor left a little while later.

"Nick," Rhiannon said softly. "Can you just tell everyone that I don't want to see anyone right now?"

"Sure," he said, starting to walk out of the room.

"Nick?"

"Yeah?"

"Thanks," she said, smiling wanly.

He nodded, and left.

Meanwhile, in the waiting room, Joe had had it with Midnight's looks.

"Joe, wait," Stevie said, making a grab for his arm. But he

shrugged it off, standing up and walking over toward Midnight.

She turned to him as if she'd been waiting for the confrontation. Indeed, she had. Her nerves were drawn to near breaking at this point, since Angelica had answered the phone in Rick's hotel room. She was in need of an outlet—unfortunately, Joe was the easiest target.

"You have a problem?" he asked acidly.

"Yeah, I do." Midnight nodded, staring back up at him with narrowed eyes. "What are you doing here with her?" she said, indicating Stevie, who had come to stand a few feet back from Joe, watching the confrontation worriedly.

Joe looked back at Midnight for a long moment, as if not comprehending what she'd asked.

"Well, since it's her sister that's here in the hospital, I figured she might need some support," he said, as if speaking to a dull-witted child.

"Sorry we had to drag you two out of bed," Midnight snapped, having taken in his disheveled state.

Joe's eyes narrowed dangerously. "Who the fuck do you think you are?"

"I used to be your best friend," she shot back.

"Yeah, you used to," Joe said, his lips tightening.

Midnight glanced past him at Stevie. "But I've apparently been replaced by a younger model," she said acidly.

Joe's mouth dropped open in surprise for a moment. Then he closed it, laughing sarcastically. "No, last time I checked, I haven't fucked you in years." His light blue eyes burned into hers. "And now I remember why," he all but spat.

Midnight's hand lashed out like lightning, slapping him hard. Joe's head snapped back an inch or two, and he closed his eyes. When he opened them again they were as cold as ice. He inclined his head to Midnight as if thanking her for the slap. His eyes went to the rest of the Gang standing around behind her, all in varying degrees of shock at the scene they'd just witnessed. He shook his head and turned to Stevie, turning his back on all of them.

"I'll be outside if you need me," he said, pointing to the quad behind them.

Stevie nodded, looking as shocked as the rest of them. When Joe walked away, her head came up and she looked back at the Gang, her eyes skipping over all of them. She walked back over to the chairs where she and Joe had sat a few minutes before. She sat down, refusing to look at any of them again. Dave and Susan moved to sit with her a few minutes later.

Nick came out ten minutes after that, not noticing the tension among those waiting. He walked over to Stevie, telling her what Rhiannon had told him. Stevie nodded, asking Nick to tell her she'd come by the next morning. Nick nodded, and turned to walk away.

"Hey, Nick," Stevie said.

Nick turned back to her.

"Thanks for calling me. I appreciate it," she said softly.

Nick shrugged. "I figured you'd want to be here."

"Thanks," she said again. Nick walked away then, heading back toward Rhiannon's room. Stevie glanced at Dave.

"Want me to tell them?" he asked, realizing that she probably didn't want to have any more confrontations.

"No, I got it," Stevie said, looking over at Midnight and the rest of the Gang.

She walked toward Midnight. Dave and Susan followed her. As she reached Midnight, she felt a hand at her back; glancing behind, she saw that Joe had come in.

Midnight took in the three people backing Stevie up. She was already feeling ashamed of herself for losing it the way she had, but backpedaling wasn't Midnight Chevalier's style, so she said nothing as her eyes settled on Stevie.

"My sister said she doesn't want to see anyone right now," Stevie said evenly. "I'm sure she'd appreciate the gesture you all made in coming down though," she added, her eyes taking in everyone. "And I thank you too." The last was said with a great deal of sincerity that left many members of the Gang feeling rather abashed at their own behavior.

There was a lot of nodding.

"Let Rhian know that if she needs anything to tell me," Midnight said, her tone as nice as she could possibly make it.

"I will, thanks," Stevie said, staring directly back into Midnight's eyes.

Midnight had to admit, even to herself, that Stevie O'Neil definitely had a backbone to her. Not that she'd doubted it, but Stevie was standing up to the Gang in her own way, and doing it well. One had to hand it to her—she had guts.

The Gang dispersed little by little. It was only then that Stevie noticed that Christian had been there too. He said nothing to her, merely giving her a curt nod when their eyes connected. She stared back at him, refusing to break it first. Christian did, glancing at Joe, his eyes narrowing icily. He nodded to Dave, winked at Susan, then turned and left.

Stevie let out the breath she didn't realize she'd been holding, as did Susan. Susan had heard about the fight between Joe and Christian. She'd been aghast that they'd done each other so much damage. She'd been further stunned by the scene between Midnight and Joe a few minutes earlier. She'd never seen her aunt so on edge, and she'd been shocked by what Joe had said to her. Dave's only reaction had been to say, "Ohh…" when Joe had made the comment about not fucking Midnight in years. It was apparent that Dave had seen this kind of thing before. She asked him about it later that night.

They were in bed, Susan lying with her head on his chest, his arm around her shoulders.

"David?" she began, levering herself up to look at him. "It's obvious you've seen my aunt and Joe act like that before…"

"Oh yeah," he said, nodding. "It's been years though."

"What happened then?"

"Well, the last time Joe and your uncle got into it was when Midnight was in the hospital. Rick tackled Joe, thinking that he had gotten Midnight pregnant."

"What!" Susan cried.

Dave grinned, knowing how outrageous it would sound to her. "Oh yeah…" he said. "This was when Joe and Randy were split. Your aunt and uncle were on their way to divorce too, because your uncle was having an affair. Randy was having an affair with some other cop, and Joe climbed into a tequila bottle up in Sacramento. Apparently, Midnight went up there to drag him out, and things just happened…" He spread his hands, indicating how things just happen sometimes. "Anyway, right after your aunt got back from Sacramento was when she was attacked by the creep Randy was dating and left for dead. The doctors couldn't figure out why she was hemorrhaging so badly, and that was about the time Joe showed up, telling them, including your uncle Rick, that she was pregnant. Rick assumed it was Joe's and went after him."

"Good Lord," Susan said, shaking her head.

Dave shrugged. "We're a lively bunch."

"I never realized just how lively until I married you," she said, smiling.

"I'm glad I could introduce you to my world," he said. "But Joe and Midnight, and Midnight and Rick, and Rick and Joe, they fight all the time—it's just not usually that harsh. I don't think I've heard Joe talk to Midnight like that since before she married your uncle."

"Really?" Susan said, having been stunned to hear Joe talk the way he had that night. He was always very polite and proper around her.

"Oh yeah," Dave said, rolling his eyes. "They used to get into huge fights. They've always been fire and ice, those three."

Susan sighed, shaking her head. "Must be exhausting."

"Or exciting as hell," he said, grinning.

"Stop it," she said, sounding very proper.

He leaned down to kiss her, and they were done talking for a while.

Back at the hospital, Nick stayed outside the room for an hour, talking to a few of the nurses as he waited. He peeked into the room and saw that Rhiannon's eyes were closed. He walked in quietly, sitting down in the chair again. He felt like it was his responsibility to watch over her until his father could be there. Brenden was asleep on the big cushioned chair outside the room, under Nick's jacket; a nurse was keeping an eye on him.

Rhiannon stirred and opened her eyes, seeing Nick in the chair next to her bed.

He moved forward immediately, looking down at her. She looked so sad, he felt the strongest desire to make her feel better.

"You know," he said quietly, "I was talking to the nurses outside, and they said that this kind of thing happens a lot in the first trimester. That it's totally normal for a woman to go on to have a healthy baby the very next time."

Rhiannon smiled weakly at him, appreciating his effort to make her feel better. She reached down and touched his hand, which was on the bed right next to her. She squeezed it gently. "Thank you."

She felt the need to tell him how much it meant to her that he was being so nice and so brave right now. She had no idea what she would have done if he hadn't been there. She'd been unable to get up off the floor when she'd fallen off the bed trying to reach for the phone.

Nick nodded, hooking his foot around the chair and pulling it closer to the bed so he could sit down and hold her hand at the same time. They were silent for a long time. Rhiannon drifted in and out of consciousness, the painkillers they'd given her making her groggy. Nick was there every time she woke up. He asked her if she wanted something to drink, or was she hurting. Did she need anything? She asked about Kyle, and he told her that he would be there as soon as he possibly could be.

CHAPTER 6

As it turned out, Kyle didn't get to the hospital till the wee hours of the morning. He stopped at the nurses' station, telling them he was there for his wife. The nurses pointed out the room. Kyle walked in, not before seeing that Brenden was sleeping in the chair just outside. He looked toward the bed and was shocked at the sight. His wife lay there, his normally recalcitrant son in a chair next to the bed, his hand in Rhiannon's, his head down on the bed next to their clasped hands. He was asleep, as was Rhiannon. It was a poignant moment. Kyle stood absorbing it, steeling himself for whatever was to come. He was fairly sure Rhiannon had miscarried, and that was the reason for the blood his son had described. At this point, he was just grateful that she was okay. And it was obvious that the emergency had brought out the man in his son; he couldn't help but feel proud at that.

Kyle walked over to the opposite side of the bed and leaned down, kissing Rhiannon on the forehead softly. She opened her eyes instantly.

"I got here as soon as I could," he whispered.

Rhiannon smiled softly. "It's okay, I had a good surrogate," she said, her eyes indicating Nick.

Kyle looked down at him, smiling proudly. "He did good, huh?"

"Kyle, he was wonderful," she whispered.

Kyle searched her eyes. "I'm sorry I wasn't here."

174

"You couldn't have known. It's okay," she said gently, reaching up with her other hand to touch his cheek. "I'm okay," she said, even as her lip trembled slightly with emotion.

"Dad?" Nick said quietly as he lifted his head.

"Yeah, I'm here, finally."

"Good," Nick said. "We needed you."

"I know, son," Kyle said. "I'm sorry I couldn't be here sooner."

"It's okay, I know you got here as fast as you could," Nick said, moving to stand up. "I think we're okay," he said, looking down at Rhiannon, sounding so much like a man again.

"We're okay," Rhiannon agreed, smiling at him.

"I'm gonna go get something to drink," Nick said, stretching. "Dad, you want anything?"

"Coffee?"

Nick nodded. "Rhiannon? You want anything?"

"No, Nick, thanks, I'm okay."

Nick nodded again. "Okay, I'll be back," he said, and walked out of the room.

Kyle watched his son go. "Who replaced my son with a man?" he asked in wonder.

"I don't know," Rhiannon said, shaking her head. "But I'm glad he was there, Kyle."

"I am too. What happened?"

"I woke up feeling a little cramping. I got up thinking it was nothing, just having slept wrong or something. But when I tried to stand, it hurt. So I lay back down. I tried to reach for the phone, but it was too far, and I actually fell out of the bed trying to get it. I couldn't get back up—every time I tried, the cramps got worse. When

175

I saw the blood, I yelled for Nick," she said, touching Kyle's hand. "He came on the run, Kyle. He was so brave, he took charge of everything. He was great, he really was."

Kyle nodded. "I'm glad."

"Me too."

Kyle took off his jacket, laying it on the end of the bed, then sat down, shifting until he lay next to her. He put one arm over her head, reaching down to stroke her hair, taking her hand with his other. Rhiannon's eyes filled with tears. She turned her head, burying it against his shoulder as she cried.

"It's okay, hon, it's okay," he said softly. "There will be another baby. Just so long as you're okay. I love you."

"I love you, Kyle. I'm sorry," she said, her voice muffled because her face was still against his shirt.

"There's nothing to be sorry for, Rhian," he said gently. "Did the doctor say what caused it?"

Rhiannon hesitated for a moment, then shook her head. "They don't know what causes this. Nick told me that the nurses told him this kind of thing happens a lot in the first trimester."

Kyle nodded, leaning down to kiss her temple. "We're okay, babe, we're okay…" he said soothingly.

Rhiannon nodded, snuggling closer to him, wanting to draw from his strength. Kyle's arms went around her, holding her gently but with the strength she needed most at that moment. She fell asleep listening to the sound of his heartbeat. Nick came in a little while later and stood watching his father holding Rhiannon. It dragged at him that the doctor had said that stress and tension could have caused the miscarriage. Nick knew he'd been causing a lot of tension in the house with his attitude about the baby and Rhiannon in general. He was truly afraid that he was the reason she'd lost the baby. It made him sick.

Kyle looked up from where he lay.

"I hear you were very brave tonight," he said quietly, not wanting to wake Rhiannon.

"I just did what had to be done, Dad," Nick said, not willing to take any credit at this point.

"Rhiannon said you did more than that, Nick. She said you were really great," Kyle said, his eyes on his son. "Thank you for that," he added, so sincerely it brought tears to Nick's eyes.

"It's okay, Dad," he said, feeling choked up.

"Your mother would have been very proud of you tonight."

"You think so?" Nick asked, sounding suddenly like the young boy he'd been when Barbara had died.

"Yeah, I do. She wanted you raised to be a gentleman." Kyle grinned as he recited the words as Barbara had said them: "With the emphasis on 'gentle' and not 'man.'"

Nick laughed quietly. "I remember when she used to say that. I never got it till right now."

"Well, that's what she meant, son."

Nick nodded. "Is Rhian going to be okay?"

Kyle looked down at his wife, then back at his son. "She's dealt with a lot of death in her lifetime, but I think if she has us this time, she'll be okay, yeah."

"Will you try to have a baby still?"

"Nick, Rhian's only thirty-three—she's never had children, and she wants at least one of her own. So, yeah, I think we'll probably try again."

177

Nick nodded.

"Do you want to grab a cab and take Bren home?" Kyle asked.

"Nah," Nick said. "I'll just stay here with you guys, if that's okay?"

"Sure," Kyle said, surprised that his son wanted to stay at the hospital instead of going home to his comfortable bed. He was definitely growing up.

***

Donovan was having a hard time concentrating on the task at hand. He had a fairly nasty headache. Rosa finally got irritated.

"What is the problem?" she asked, her tone clipped.

"I'm sorry," Donovan said, sitting up as she moved off him. "I have a headache that just won't quit tonight."

Rosa nodded, as if in understanding. "The headaches are starting already…" she said, more to herself than to him.

"What?"

"I'm surprised," she said, sitting against the headboard and lighting a cigarette. "It usually takes a bit longer."

"What takes a bit longer?" Donovan asked, starting to get the strangest sensation that he was about to get nailed with a bomb.

"The withdrawals."

"Withdrawals from what?" Donovan asked, his face a mask of anger held in check as his tension mounted.

"From the X, sweetheart," she said so sweetly that he was sure he hadn't heard her right, or had mistook her meaning.

"The what?" he asked, his face disbelieving.

178

"The X," she repeated, then clarified when he obviously wasn't getting it. "You know, Ecstasy, Adam, XTC..." She shook her head at him like he was a fool.

"You've been giving me Ecstasy?" he asked, too stunned to believe what he was hearing. His headache was getting worse.

"Well, just a little bit," she said, smiling. "Enough to keep you coming back for more."

"You've got me hooked on a narcotic."

"Don't be silly. It's not a narcotic—I mean, not really. It's just a fun drug."

"Why?" he asked, ignoring her comment.

Ecstasy was indeed a drug; it was a fairly powerful amphetamine with hallucinogenic properties. Suddenly things started to click. The reason he'd been so tired lately, the mood swings, the constant need to be moving when he was awake, the sex... *Oh, Jesus...*

"Why?" he yelled.

"Relax, lover," she said, reaching out to touch his chest. "I can get you more. I just need you to do me a favor first."

"What kind of favor?" he asked, already knowing. *Fuck, fuck, fuck,* was all he could think. He'd been sleeping with his dealer this whole time, and he'd had no idea. *Great narc work, Curtis,* he thought snidely.

"Well, see, tenure doesn't quite pay like it used to, and since I like to be comfortable," she said, indicating the lavish bedroom around them, "I need supplements to my income." She pinned him with a look. "If you want more X, then you'll need to start selling for me."

"What do I have to sell?" he asked, making his voice sound more desperate. He was desperate, but it was desperation to get out of there and go shoot himself.

"Oh, some X, of course, some roofies, and a little bit of meth," she said, shrugging casually. "No big deal, just party stuff."

"Isn't that dangerous?" he asked, sounding like a kid and feeling like his head was about to explode.

"Oh, stop," she said. "We're not talking *Miami Vice* time here," she added, laughing ruefully.

"I don't know…" he said, shaking his head. "I don't want to get kicked out of school or nothing."

Her face became a cold mask. "Get up, get dressed, and get out. I'll give you three days. By that time you'll be begging me to sell. Get out!" she screeched.

Donovan got up, throwing on his clothes and doing as she bid.

When he got out to his car he was ready to throw up from the pounding in his head. He drove home as fast as he could, ending up throwing up in his driveway. He went into the house, took off his clothes, and took a cold shower to try and counter the heat his body was going through. He stood there feeling like an idiot. How could he have not known that she was spiking the drinks she gave him every night? Was he really that stupid?

No, he'd been that desperate for a woman who would tell him what she wanted from him. For someone else to take control of him for a change. The incredible sex he thought he was getting from Rosa had simply been a drug-induced fantasy. The scene with Jeanie flashed through his head, and he groaned. He'd managed to convince himself that Jeanie had overreacted. Had she? Or had he been so doped up on X he didn't remember what he'd done and said to her? How many nights had he driven home drugged? How many more

180

guys had she done this to? And it was no wonder none of them wanted to come forward. They'd been doing exactly what he'd been doing—thinking with his dick. He was thoroughly disgusted with himself. The pounding in his head got worse, causing him to throw up twice more, dry heaves since he had nothing left in his stomach. He crawled into his bed, shaking from head to toe and knowing it was only going to get worse. *Serves you right, Curtis,* his mind screamed at him. *Next time think with the other head.*

***

Rick climbed into bed behind his wife at 3:00 a.m. She turned over immediately, having been tossing and turning, waiting for him to get home.

"When did you get in?" she asked, reaching out to touch his cheek.

"'Bout two hours ago. I've been on the phone getting updates," he said, leaning down to kiss her softly.

"Updates?" she asked, furrowing her brow.

"Yeah," he said, a slight grin on his face. "I received a number of pages from the Gang as we were touching down... mostly pertaining to my wife."

"Oh," Midnight said, knowing the Gang had been freaked out about her confrontation with Joe.

"Yeah, oh," Rick said, still grinning. "What happened, babe?"

She shrugged casually. "We just got a little out of hand."

"A little?" he repeated, pinning her with a look. "You haven't slapped Joe in years, Night, and I know you wouldn't do that unless

181

he'd really pushed."

She grimaced. She'd been afraid the Gang would tell him what had happened; apparently they'd only told him the part about her becoming violent.

"I know, I know..." she said self-effacingly.

"What did he say?" Rick asked, having heard that Joe had said something to Midnight that had pissed her off.

His tone had taken on a warning quality. Midnight knew she was risking him going after Joe next time they met up by telling him, but if she didn't, someone else would.

"Well, I made a comment to him about dragging him and Stevie out of bed." Again she grimaced, knowing she'd been out of line. "And he got pissed, asking who I thought I was. I said I used to be his best friend before I was replaced with a younger model." She hesitated then, seeing Rick's look change. She knew he didn't like that she was now constantly thinking of herself as old, and he half blamed Joe and his issues with his age for that.

"Then what?" he asked when she didn't continue.

"Uh..." she said, still not sure if she should tell him.

Again his look was pointed, basically telling her that if she didn't tell him, he'd find out one way or the other. Sometimes it did not pay to have so many close friends who enjoyed regaling the most dramatic tales.

She sighed. "He said that last time he checked he hadn't fucked me in a long time, and now he remembered why." She said it in a rush, trying to get it out quickly.

Rick stared down at her openmouthed for a long moment. He closed his mouth, his jaw tightening as he clenched his teeth, his eyes narrowing.

"And you *only* slapped him?" he said. "If I'd been there, I would have decked his ass."

"I know," she said, already thanking her lucky stars he hadn't been there.

Joe and he would have gotten into it, and there would have been no one that could have pulled them apart. Joe and Midnight's previous relationship was well known by everyone, but Rick didn't like it brought up so graphically, especially not by Joe himself. He also didn't like anyone disrespecting Midnight, and he wouldn't stand for it in his presence. It was an endearing quality about him, kind of an old-fashioned, chivalrous quality in a very modern man. However, it could become a problem where someone as hot-tempered as Rick was concerned, considering his wife was Chief of Police.

Rick took a slow, deep breath, expelling it slowly. He shook his head. "I don't know what's going on with all of us. It's like everything's going to shit in a hurry." He sounded depressed by the thought.

"Are we?" Midnight asked, her tone such that he knew she was talking about the two of them.

"No, we're not, Night," he said, his look direct. "We're fine—it's everyone else that seems to be goin' crazy."

Midnight looked back at him for a long moment. "Why was she in your room, Rick?"

He dropped his head, knowing she'd been worried about it. A small part of him had hoped she'd just trust him and not ask, but he knew how Midnight was, and with his previous record, she needed to ask. When he raised his head, he looked her directly in the eye.

183

"She was in my room, I was in hers. We exchanged rooms because she said her air conditioning wasn't working well enough." He touched her on the chin with his index finger. "I texted you to tell you, Night. You never answered."

"You texted me?" she asked, looking mystified.

"Yeah," he said. "You never answered."

"When?"

"Around seven thirty."

She grimaced, closing her eyes, then opened one to look at him comically. "I got a notification but it failed to show me the text. Damn, I'm sorry. I should have asked you to clarify," she said, shaking her head.

"It's okay, babe. I just figured you were busy and would get back to me when you had a chance."

Midnight nodded, feeling a little foolish, but she wasn't ready to give up just yet. "She hit on you up there though, didn't she?"

Rick pursed his lips, then nodded. "Yeah, she did," he answered honestly. "But I blew her off, babe, okay?" He put his hand to her cheek, looking into her eyes searchingly. "You can trust me—you know that, right?"

Midnight sighed, nodding. "Rick, I told you, I do trust you—it's her I don't trust."

"Yeah, but I have to be willing for anything to happen, right?"

"True," she said. "But the fact that she just keeps at it is disrespecting me and us."

He grimaced. "I hadn't really thought about it that way," he said, realizing that for Midnight it was a major slight.

184

She really was still the gang leader she'd been in her youth. She didn't take insults lightly. Especially not when it came to her husband, someone she considered her territory without a doubt. They'd been through a lot of hard times together, and come through them. While it had made their marriage stronger, it had also given them more to protect. Midnight protected it zealously.

"Look," he said, pulling her closer to him, his lips nuzzling her temple. "You are the woman I love, and the only one I want. I've told her that, but you're right, she should have more respect for me and you. I'll talk to her again."

"No," Midnight said, looking up at him with the determined expression he'd seen so many times in the more than thirteen years they'd been married. "I'll talk to her."

"Night…" he said, his tone cautionary. "You can't go around threatening people anymore, ya know. You're a chief now."

"Who said I was going to threaten her?" Midnight asked sweetly, in a tone that Rick recognized as very definite sarcasm.

"Midnight," he said, narrowing his eyes. "Don't get into trouble over this. It's not worth that."

"You are."

"She's not, though, babe."

Midnight grinned, liking the sound of that. She kissed him, and they promptly forgot Angelica, and anything else but each other.

The following day, Mikeyla asked her mother for a ride to school. Midnight obliged, happy for a chance to talk to her daughter. Things had been so up in the air lately, they hadn't had time to talk much.

185

In Midnight's Corvette, the one Rick had replaced the year before at Christmas time, she looked over at her daughter. Mikeyla was dressed in hip-hugger jeans, a peasant blouse in blues, and low platform slides that all the girls were wearing these days. Her long copper-blond hair, a shade lighter than Midnight's, was pulled back from her face in two very retro-looking braids, with the rest flowing down to the middle of her back. She looked like the consummate hippy. Midnight couldn't help but think how beautiful her daughter was becoming; she and Rick were going to have to start meeting the boys at the door while wearing their guns and badges at this rate. That reminded her about the date with Nick Masterson that Mikeyla had gone on. Mikeyla had been quiet about it, and Midnight wondered at that.

"So," Midnight said, reaching over and turning Kylie Minogue down on the radio. "You never really said how the date with Nick went. Can I ask?"

Mikeyla shrugged, looking over at her mother. "It was okay."

"Just okay?"

"Yeah," Mikeyla said, making a face. "He was a bit of a guy, ya know?" She said it like it was a bad word.

Midnight chuckled. "Yeah, I know all about that—I work with a lot of them," she said, rolling her eyes. "So what happened that made him guy-like?"

Mikeyla sat back in her seat and started fiddling with a loose thread on the upholstery. "Well, he took me to a pizza place, which was kinda cool, since it wasn't a very crowded place. We talked about stuff, but nothing too heavy, just like school and stuff. Then we went to the batting cages." She said the last rolling her deep blue eyes.

"Uh-oh," Midnight said, grinning. "Batting cages?"

"Yeah," Mikeyla said, sounding a lot like her mother at that point.

"Oh." Midnight knew her daughter, and she wasn't even remotely interested in sports.

"It's just not my thing, you know?"

Midnight laughed. Her daughter definitely had a way with words. "Did you tell him that it wasn't your kind of thing?"

"Well, no, Mom, duh," Mikeyla said, rolling her eyes again.

"Well, duh, Mikeyla, if you don't tell him it's not your thing, you can't expect him to just know, can you?" Midnight fired right back.

"He should have figured that out. I mean, I sat there the whole time not saying a word."

"Well, it was a little late then, don't ya think?"

"It doesn't matter anyway," Mikeyla said, doing her best to look uncaring. "He hasn't talked to me since then, and I don't really care if he does."

Midnight nodded, not saying anything. She knew Mikeyla had been very excited about going out with Nick, and she also knew she was very disappointed that it hadn't gone well, but it wouldn't help to point that out to her now.

"Hey, Mom?" Mikeyla said after a few moments of silence.

"Yeah?" Midnight asked, glancing in her rearview mirror as she got on the freeway.

"Is it true that you dated Nick's dad?"

Midnight glanced over at her daughter, wanting to see if Mikeyla looked upset by the prospect; she didn't look like she was.

"Yes," she said. "I dated him a long time ago, before I ever even met your father."

187

Mikeyla nodded. "Yeah, that's what Nick thought too." Then she gave her mother a pointed look. "So Dad wasn't your first."

Midnight laughed, shaking her head. "Honey, I didn't meet your dad till I was older. So, no, he was far from my first."

"Who was your first then?"

Midnight hesitated, not sure why her daughter was asking these things, but she'd always been determined to be honest with Mikeyla, no matter what. She also didn't see any harm in telling her.

"My first was one of my professors in college."

"College?" Mikeyla asked, sounding stunned.

Midnight grinned, nodding.

"How old were you?" Mikeyla asked.

"I was nineteen."

"Wow," Mikeyla said, sounding surprised. "I thought you were a gang member and all that."

Midnight inclined her head. "I was, but that didn't mean I was loose."

"Yeah, but…" Mikeyla said, shaking her head. "I thought gang members were all wild and stuff."

Midnight grinned. "Don't ever stereotype a group of people so easily, Keyl. When I led my gang, I didn't trust anyone enough to let them get that close to me."

"I'm sorry, Mom, I didn't mean anything by that."

"It's okay, I'm just saying it's never safe to overgeneralize anyone."

Mikeyla nodded, mentally wrestling with all the different aspects of her parents.

"So, how come you waited?" she finally asked.

Midnight was silent for a moment, part of her worrying that her thirteen-year-old was so interested in sex, but also knowing that keeping everything a mystery would just make it more attractive to a young girl.

"I just needed to make sure I trusted the person I was that intimate with."

"Trusted?" Mikeyla echoed.

"Yeah. Sex isn't something you just do—it's a very big decision and not something anyone should just do... Do you know what I mean?"

"You mean, just because Sarah jumps off a bridge, doesn't mean I should too?" Mikeyla said, sounding very mature for her age.

Midnight chuckled. "Exactly!"

They were silent for a bit, until they got to Mikeyla's school and Midnight pulled into the parking lot, turning a lot of heads. Some were looking at the car; many were looking at the woman behind the wheel. Mikeyla noticed that, and glanced over at her mother.

Midnight was dressed in black slacks, dress boots, and a hunter green Oxford-style silk shirt. Her hair was pulled back from her face with a black clip. She wore light makeup, and still looked very young for her age.

"Hey, Mom?" Mikeyla said as she reached for her backpack.

"Yeah?"

"You and Dad have it, don't you?" Mikeyla said, sounding like she already knew the answer.

Midnight sighed. "Some would say we do. We definitely have it for each other."

Mikeyla nodded. "Yeah, all my friends think you two are really cool."

"Cool?"

"Yeah, you know how you two are always kissing and stuff. It's cool that you two are still so hot for each other."

Midnight laughed, shaking her head. "I guess that's a good thing, huh?"

"Yeah, it is," Mikeyla said, leaning over to kiss her on the cheek. "And Mom," she continued, "thanks for not telling me I had to wait till I was twenty-one and out the house before I was allowed to have sex."

"No, that would be your father's line," Midnight said, grinning.

"I know!" Mikeyla said, laughing as she got out of the car.

She waved as her mom drove away. She was happy she'd talked to her; things had been going around in her head for the last few weeks, and it felt good to ask about it. Her mom had surprised her, and she was glad. Smiling to herself, Mikeyla went to catch up with her friends, who were waiting at their usual table outside the cafeteria. She saw Nick Masterson on her way—he looked really tired.

Walking over, she stopped to look up at him.

"I heard about your stepmom," she said.

Nick nodded, looking unhappy.

"Are you okay?" Mikeyla asked, biting her lip.

"Yeah, I guess so," he said, sounding anything but. He shrugged then, sighing. "No, I'm not really."

"Do you want to go talk?" she asked, knowing she was probably being a pain and he was probably about to tell her to get lost.

"Don't you have to get to class?" he asked, looking surprised at what she'd offered.

"Yeah," she said, shrugging. "But I can blow it off."

"Well, if you want to…"

"Only if you want," she said, not wanting to make it seem like she was just trying to get him to be alone with her.

Nick hesitated, caught between the desire to seem cool and able to handle anything and his true need to talk to someone. Finally he blew his breath out.

"Yeah, I really could use someone to talk to," he said honestly.

"Cool, let's go out to the football field," she said, nodding toward it.

He nodded and followed her over. She sat on the grass, tossing her backpack down next to her. Nick followed suit. He wasn't sure what to say to her, though, so he hesitated again.

"So what actually happened last night?" Mikeyla asked, curious in spite of herself.

"Well, I heard this noise, and then Rhiannon yelled for me," he said, relieved to have her ask questions instead of having to start talking on his own. "When I got to her and my dad's room she was on the floor. When I looked at her she had blood, you know, where there shouldn't be any. I was scared shitless."

"Oh my God," Mikeyla said, putting her hand to her mouth. The image of her mother lying in her own blood years before was flashing through her mind.

"Yeah," Nick said, looking grim. "So I got the ambulance and they took her to the hospital."

"That was really brave of you," she said, remembering her mom saying that to her dad that morning—that Nick had been really brave about the whole thing.

191

Nick shrugged. "I just did what I thought I should do. Ya know?"

Mikeyla nodded.

"The thing is…" he said, trailing off as he hesitated again. He wasn't sure what he should admit to, and not even sure he wanted to hear himself say it.

"What?" she said, reaching out to touch his arm. Neither of them realized how much like her mother she looked at that moment.

"Well, the doctor told Rhiannon she lost the baby because of stress and tension," Nick said, grimacing.

"Okay…" Mikeyla said, not sure why that was a big deal. Her mother and father were stressed all the time. "Everyone is stressed these days, Nick."

"Yeah, but the thing is," he said, swallowing hard, "I think it's my fault."

"Why do you think that?" Mikeyla asked, shocked.

"Because I was being such an asshole about the baby," he said, sounding ashamed of himself. "I kept fighting with my dad about it, and Rhiannon was always trying to make peace between us. But I wouldn't let her, and I was mean to her too, and now she could have been really hurt… I mean, I don't know, but…" He trailed off as he took a gasping breath, feeling a huge lump in his throat.

Mikeyla watched him, shocked that he seemed literally near tears. Without bothering to think about it, she moved to kneel next to him, putting her arms around him. To her surprise he leaned against her. She thought he was probably crying—she could feel his shoulders shaking—but she didn't say anything. She'd seen much stronger men in her life cry. She'd watched her father fall apart a couple of years before when they thought Midnight was dead. This wasn't new territory for her to see, only new for her to be the one

192

doing the consoling.

After a long while, Nick reached up and wiped his face. Mikeyla discreetly turned her head so he would have a little privacy to compose himself. She knew guys hated to be seen crying. Even her father got mad when he got too emotional about something, usually cussing a blue streak whenever he got caught at it.

She sat back down on the ground, kicking off her slides and wiggling her toes in the cool grass as she glanced at him surreptitiously. He looked up at her then, and she was surprised again by how green his eyes were. He grinned in a self-deprecating way, but she could tell he was appreciative that she hadn't mentioned anything about his loss of control.

"What do you think Rhiannon and your dad will do now?" she asked.

"My dad says Rhiannon really wants at least one baby, because she's only thirty-three."

"You don't sound like you mind the idea now," Mikeyla pointed out.

He shrugged. "I don't think I really minded it so much then," he said candidly. "I just didn't want to like anything she did, ya know?"

"You mean Rhiannon?" Mikeyla asked, canting her head to the side.

Nick nodded. "Yeah."

"Why? Because of your mom?"

She'd heard about how Nick's mom had died of breast cancer the same day Rhiannon's husband had died in a car accident. She also knew that her parents and their friends felt that Rhiannon and Kyle had been destined to be together to heal each other because of that

193

fact.

Nick looked surprised that she knew about his mother; they'd never talked about it before. He nodded.

Mikeyla looked thoughtful for a minute. "Do you think that if you like Rhiannon you'll be backstabbing your mom?"

"I guess I feel like..." he began, trying to gather his thoughts. "Like my dad moved on 'cause he had to—you know, because of the sex and stuff. But that doesn't mean me and Bren have to have a new mom, right?"

Mikeyla thought about that. "No, it doesn't mean that," she said. "But do you think Rhiannon is trying to act like your mom?"

"No, she's not. I mean, she always tries to say stuff that's nice to me, but..."

"Does she maybe just want to be your friend?"

"Yeah, that's what she said one time, that she just wanted to be my friend." He shrugged. "But I just feel like she's just saying that so I won't not like her."

Mikeyla bit her lip in thought. "But now you feel bad about the way you were acting with your dad, that maybe that made her lose the baby."

"Yeah," Nick said, sounding confused by that answer.

"Why do you feel bad? I mean, if you don't like her anyway. Why would it matter?" Mikeyla asked, trying not to sound mean.

Nick thought about it for a minute. "I guess because she was so upset about it," he said. "And she was hurting so much last night, I just felt really bad."

Mikeyla nodded. "I think you like her more than you wanted to, Nick."

"Yeah…" he said, sounding disappointed in himself.

"When you were little," Mikeyla said, having just had a thought, "when your mom was alive, did she get sad when you were hurt?"

"Yeah," Nick said, looking at her like she was crazy for asking that.

"So do you think she'd want you to be hurting right now?"

Nick took a deep breath and sighed, shaking his head.

"So maybe it's hurting you more to not like Rhiannon than it would if you just let her be your friend and see what happens," Mikeyla said, proud of herself for coming up with a conclusion.

"Didn't I hear that your mom has a psychology degree?" he asked her after a few moments.

"Uh-huh," Mikeyla said, nodding.

He grinned. "Think it could be genetic?"

"Maybe," she said, laughing.

Nick laughed too. They went on to talk about other things for a while, until they heard the second bell ring. They'd already missed the start of their first class. Nick stood up and held out his hand. Mikeyla took it and he pulled her up. As she was wiggling her feet back into her shoes, he touched her under the chin. She looked up and saw that he was looking down at her seriously. Her breath caught in her throat as he leaned down toward her. He kissed her softly on the lips, making her heart stop, she was sure of it. He pulled back, looking down at her.

"Thanks, Keyl," he said seriously.

She smiled up at him. "You're welcome. Now, you want to walk me to study hall, since we're late?" she said, grinning at the last.

"I think that's fair," he said, laughing as he bent down to pick up

195

their backpacks.

Mikeyla was secretly thrilled when he carried her bag all the way to study hall for her. He even opened the door for her, and sat next to her when they got inside. She was glad she'd taken the chance to ask him if he'd needed to talk.

CHAPTER 7

Rhiannon got a call from the school that afternoon, telling her that her "son", Nick, hadn't been in his first-period class. She asked him about it that afternoon. When he got home from school, she was lying propped up in bed. The hospital had let her out, and Kyle had taken her home. He'd run out an hour before to pick up some things at the grocery store. That had been when the school called, fortunately.

Nick knocked lightly on Rhiannon and his dad's door.

"Come in," Rhiannon said.

Nick opened the door. "They did let you out, huh?" he asked, leaning against the doorjamb.

"Yeah," she said, smiling. She shrugged. "I guess I was wasting their space."

"You'll do better at home."

"Nick," Rhiannon said, a little hesitantly, "I wanted to let you know the school called today. They said you weren't in your first-period class."

"They did?" he said, surprised that the school had called about such a minor thing.

"Yes," Rhiannon said, her tone far from angry. "I got the call, though—your dad doesn't know."

"I did cut my first class," Nick admitted. "I was talking to

Mikeyla Debenshire."

"Really?" Rhiannon asked, a little surprised. "How did your date go, by the way?"

Nick grimaced, shaking his head. He walked into the room and sat on the bed. Rhiannon hid her surprise that he suddenly seemed willing to be around her.

"I don't know," he said. "I was sure she hated my guts till this morning."

"So what happened on the date?"

"Well, everything was cool till we got to the batting cages—then she got all distant."

"Uh, batting cages?" Rhiannon said, her expression somewhat horrified. When Nick nodded, she shook her head, her long ponytail swinging, making her look young. "Nick, Nick, Nick…" she said, grimacing comically.

"What?" he said, laughing now. "I thought it would be cool."

"Yeah, but did you even ask her if she was into sports?"

"I thought you girls wanted the guy to make all the decisions," Nick said seriously.

"Oh, brother," Rhiannon said, rolling her eyes. "Not if it means we have to spend time in a batting cage."

Nick looked embarrassed. "So you think it was that, huh?"

"Probably didn't help, Nick."

"But she was really cool to me today…" Nick said, sounding really confused.

"Well, that's hopeful then."

"Yeah…"

He looked at Rhiannon for a moment, as if seeing her for the first time. She really was a very pretty lady, with her emerald-like eyes, smooth, creamy skin and long, dark red hair.

"We talked about all the stuff with the baby and all," he said, finally wanting to be honest with her for a moment.

Rhiannon nodded, surprised that he was being so friendly. She wondered if something had changed in his heart. Hope started to take hold in her then; if she could make friends with Nick, she knew it would settle everything down in the house. Kyle's biggest problem with Nick lately was his attitude toward her.

"Rhiannon..." Nick reached out to touch her hands, which were folded over her belly. "I want to apologize to you," he said, surprising himself. "I've been really mean to you, and you didn't deserve it at all. I mean, you didn't do anything. I just..." He trailed off as he shrugged, looking away.

"You loved your mom very much, Nick," Rhiannon said softly. "That much is very evident to me. I'm really not trying to take her place in your life. I love your dad very much, and in marrying him, I became part of yours and Brenden's lives. That doesn't automatically mean that I'm your mom now. It doesn't even automatically make me qualified for the job." She hesitated, catching his eyes with her. "I'd like to be your friend, Nick. I'd like to be able to be here when you need someone older of the female gender to talk to. I'd like to hear about your girlfriends, your accomplishments, and even your failures if you need encouragement. But I'm not trying to be your mom—I don't think anyone could ever take her place. It sounds to me like she was the best at it." Her tone was very sincere, and Nick couldn't help but be moved.

He didn't say anything for a long moment. Then he stunned her by leaning forward to hug her carefully. Rhiannon hugged him back,

199

gratefully. Glancing up, she saw that Kyle was standing in the doorway, tears in his eyes. She smiled at him through the tears that misted her own eyes suddenly.

Nick sat back, looking at her, then sensing his father in the room, he glanced over his shoulder. Moving to stand up, Nick looked at him.

"Dad, I cut my first class today," he said, sounding more and more like a man every minute. "I was talking to Mikeyla Debenshire—she was helping me get a better handle on the stuff here at home. I'm sorry I cut class."

Kyle nodded, still looking affected by the scene he'd just come upon. "Thank you for telling me," he said, aware that Rhiannon probably wouldn't have. She seemed to be protecting Nick a lot lately.

"I owe you an apology too, Dad," Nick said. "For how I've been acting lately. But I want you to know I've got it straight now."

Kyle looked at his son for a long moment, wondering when and where the boy had grown up so fast. Stepping forward, he extended his hand. Nick took it, shaking it. Kyle pulled him forward and hugged him. Rhiannon looked on with fresh tears in her eyes. She knew she was being overly emotional right now, but she was also very glad to see the man she loved making up with his son. Nick left the room a little while later, and Kyle moved to sit down next to Rhiannon, pulling her into his arms gently.

"I love you," he said, his lips against her temple. "And I think you're wrong."

"Wrong?" Rhiannon asked, glancing up at him.

"Yeah, I do think you'd make a fantastic mom, and I think Nick will realize that eventually too."

Rhiannon shrugged. "As long as he lets me share in his life, Kyle,

200

and share it with you, then that's enough."

"I can hope for more, can't I?"

"Sure," she said, grinning.

"Thanks," he replied, tilting her face up to his, kissing her lips softly. They spent the rest of the afternoon talking. She told him about the situation between Nick and Mikeyla.

Later that evening, after Kyle had made dinner, they all sat down together to eat.

"Rhiannon?" Nick said, surprising her again by using her name.

"Yes?"

"What do you think I should do? I mean, to fix the thing with Keyl," he said, grimacing.

Rhiannon looked back at him for a moment. "I think you should call her up and tell her you just realized what a dork you were," she said, grinning. "And that you'd like to take her out again, and this time she gets to choose the activity."

"I can't believe you took her to the batting cages," Kyle said, giving his son a wry look.

"Shut up, Dad!" Nick said, grinning. Then he looked at Rhiannon. "She gets to pick the activity?"

"Yes, Nick, anything she wants."

"Anything?" Nick asked, sounding terrified.

"Yes, Nick, anything."

"You're gonna get stuck watching some fruit-loopy foreign film," Kyle teased.

"Kyle Michelangelo Masterson! Do not tease your son!" Rhiannon gasped, laughing.

"Yeah, Michelangelo, don't tease me," Nick said, grinning.

Kyle gave them both a dirty look, then turned to Brenden. "You still love me, right?"

"Yup," Brenden said, grinning widely.

"I'll pay ya later," Kyle said out of the side of his mouth, making Brenden laugh. Rhiannon and Nick joined in. It was a nice evening.

***

Jeanie was fed up. Donovan hadn't been doing his job on this case, and she'd had it. She was going to tell him she was asking to be reassigned, that he could just do the case himself, since he obviously didn't want her on it with him. She strode up to his door and hit the buzzer for the intercom. There was no answer. She knew he was there; the Mustang was in the driveway. She buzzed three more times. Finally, she punched in the code she knew by heart, cussing a stream of expletives as she did.

"Donovan!" she yelled as she walked in the door. "I know you're here," she called, looking around the house.

It was dark. She hadn't seen him in two days. He hadn't bothered to show up for classes again. It had been a week since the incident when she'd slugged him; she'd seen him once since then, and he'd looked at her like nothing had happened. She couldn't believe it—she'd expected at least an attempt at an apology, but nothing. He'd basically looked right through her. Asshole!

"Donovan?" she said, turning and walking down the hall to his bedroom.

The bathroom light was on, and she saw him huddled under the covers.

"Donovan?" She peered down at him. He looked terrible. There were dark circles under his eyes, and he was sweating, even though he was huddled under no fewer than two comforters and it was spring and at least sixty degrees out. "Jesus..." she whispered. "What's wrong with you?"

He didn't answer, closing his eyes slowly then opening them again.

"Donovan?" she said, reaching down to touch his cheek.

He jerked away from her. "Don't!" he exclaimed, holding his hands up defensively. "Don't touch me, Jay. God, please..." he said, shaking his head dazedly.

She looked at his hands. They were shaking like leaves in a stiff breeze.

"My God, what's wrong?" she gasped.

He shook his head, his face a mask of disgust.

"Donovan... you should be in a hospital," she said, thinking he was extremely sick.

"No," he said, his voice a hoarse croak. "No hospital, Jay, please..."

"Why?" she asked, afraid now. "What is it?"

"She's got me hooked on X," he said quickly, just as a cramp seared through his stomach, making him curl up into a ball, groaning loudly.

"Who?" Jeanie asked. "Donovan... God, how?"

He shook his head. "Please, Jay, no hospital, promise me. I can't... Midnight'll get hammered. I can't... I fucked up... Please... God..." He trailed off as he groaned again.

"Okay, okay," Jeanie said soothingly. She knelt next to the bed.

"Tell me what I can do. Let me help you."

"Shoot me," he said seriously.

"Not an option," she said, grinning in spite of herself. "Hold on, I'll be right back." She left the room for a few minutes, coming back with a washcloth, a bowl, and a bottle of water.

Jeanie spent the next two days going through everything with him. She held the cold rag to his forehead when he was hot, wrapped him in blankets when he was cold. Talked him down when he was hit with anxiety attacks, sure that he was going to die or that he was going to ruin the department. Fed him sips of water to keep him from dehydrating. Rubbed his back soothingly when he threw up for the hundredth time, noticing the red welts that looked like nail marks all the way down his back but not saying anything.

By the third day, he was able to sleep without constantly waking up in pain. Jeanie lay next to him, watching him, stroking his hair soothingly. From what she knew of Ecstasy, Donovan had gotten away lucky. She knew he could have died, that it could have sped his heart up to the point of an attack and he'd never have known what hit him. She didn't know how he'd gotten into this situation, but she knew that she needed to be here for him this time.

He'd been there for her when she'd needed him before, when she'd been beaten up by a suspect and hurt badly. Even though she'd literally left him to move four hundred miles away, for the job she'd been doing when she was hurt, Donovan had flown to San Francisco to see her in the hospital. He'd been the one to take her out of the hospital, and in the end the one to drive her all the way back to San Diego, at the expense of his own bad back, so she could go "home." He'd been there for her when she'd deserved it the least. This was payback, as far as she was concerned.

She drifted off to sleep thinking along those lines, and woke a few hours later to the feel of a hand on her cheek. She opened her eyes. They were lying facing each other on the bed. His teal-blue eyes, looking much less pained and bloodshot now, were staring into hers.

"How are you feeling?" she asked, trying desperately not to be affected by his nearness or the tenderness she saw in his eyes.

"Much better, thanks to you," he said quietly.

"I don't know that I really did anything."

"You were here, Jay," he said, his eyes not leaving hers, even when she looked away.

"You needed help," she said simply.

"And you stayed," he said, taking on a pained look. "Even when I deserved to be shot."

"For what?"

"For that night," he said. "I don't remember what I did, Jay, but for you to haul off and slug me like that, I must have been way out of line. I'm sorry."

"I kneed you too—you must not remember," she said, shaking her head. "But I understand why now, Donovan. You weren't yourself. And if I hadn't been so busy justifying it in my mind, I would have known something was wrong," she added, shaking her head ruefully.

"Jay, I should have known, and I didn't," he said, sounding annoyed at himself. "I can't believe I was so stupid."

"What happened? Who did this to you? And how?" she asked, her tone not the least bit accusatory.

"Rosa Delario," he said. "And she was real devious about it. She slipped it in my drink right before she laid me every night," he said, his tone so derisive that Jeanie had to grin.

"Oh my," she said, her eyes widening.

Donovan grinned in spite of the seriousness of what he'd just told her. "Shut up, Jay."

"Seriously, though, how would you have known?"

"Well, Jesus, I was a basket case the next day every time—that should have clued my narc mind in, shouldn't it?"

"Was it real, ah..." Jeanie bit her lip as she tried to come up with an appropriate term. "Well, ah, energetic sex?"

"Yeah, but..." Donovan said, shaking his head.

"So you figured she wore you out."

Jeanie was purposefully keeping the thought out of her mind that Donovan had been screwing another woman. This wasn't about that.

"Yeah," he said. "That's what I told myself, but..."

"But what?" she said. "We were sent after Rohypnol, not Ecstasy. Neither of those guys busted had X on them. And Rohypnol has a different effect—you wouldn't have been looking for symptoms of Ecstasy. Besides, what dealer gives out freebies on a nightly basis?"

"The ones that want their low-end dealers hooked so they have to sell to keep getting their dose."

"Jesus Christ," Jeanie said, shaking her head. "And who the hell would have ever thought of that one, Donovan? It's not exactly your mainstream hook to deal."

Donovan stared down at her, his lips pursed in thought. She did have a few valid points, but nothing excused that he'd been thinking with his dick.

"I was thinking with my dick," he said.

"You were being a young, virile man, Donovan. You didn't know she was a dealer. She wasn't even one of our suspects. You just took that class because it was one that one of the guys was in."

"Yeah…" he said, narrowing his eyes. "And the other was the chemistry class, put on by her husband."

"Chemist, eh?" she said, her eyes sparkling.

"Yup," he said. "And I'll just bet he's doing the cooking."

"You can bet he is," Jeanie said, nodding.

Donovan lay on his back, blowing his breath out in a sigh. "How the hell are they going to try this case?" he said, shaking his head. "I fucked up."

Jeanie leaned up on her elbow, looking down at him.

"You didn't fuck up, Donovan," she said firmly.

His raised eyebrow had her grinning. "Okay, so you may have made our case a little harder. Pardon the pun." That earned her a grin from him. "But," she said, putting her fingertip to his lips, "if you hadn't been attractive to her, we may have never broken this case. It's obvious she's very careful about keeping it all off campus. And we were chasing our tails everywhere else. So, this went the way it had to."

"Yeah…" he said, grimacing. "I knew she was gonna proposition me to sell, the whole time I was laying her." He rolled his eyes.

"Stop it, Donovan," Jeanie said. "You did what you did, which is no more than any normal, healthy, single man would have done when offered sex by a woman that beautiful."

"You think she's beautiful?"

207

"Yeah, in that Italian princess sort of way," she said, grinning.

"I think you're beautiful," he said unexpectedly, reaching up to touch her cheek.

"Smooth talker."

"Yeah, that's me," he said, brushing her hair back off her forehead.

"Donovan?" she said, her tone changing slightly.

"Yeah?"

"What happened to us?"

Donovan drew a deep breath, sighing and shaking his head. "I don't know, Jay. I just got to feeling… apathetic about everything."

"Why?"

"I guess because you and Erin were both saying, 'Whatever you want, Donovan.' I just felt like I was under all this pressure to decide, to make all the moves, to make the relationship or break it. Ya know?" He looked up at her, hoping he was making sense. "It was like you both turned into these pliable dolls I could play with or not. I got to where I felt like I was being an asshole no matter what I did."

"You weren't an asshole," Jeanie said. "I guess we were both so afraid to ask for too much, or we'd lose you totally." She shook her head ruefully. "And in the end, I guess we lost you anyway, didn't we?"

"I lost me," Donovan said. "I couldn't bring myself to trust you again, but I couldn't give my heart to Erin either."

"I can't speak for Erin, but I know I tried to be whatever you wanted when you wanted it. Frankly, it was tiring," she said, grinning.

"And it wasn't you, either," he said, pinning her with a look.

"I know."

"And you were the woman I wanted, the one I met and fell in love with."

"The one that's screwed you over more times than you can count?"

He grinned. "I can count to three, Jay."

"Can you?"

"Uh-huh," he said, putting his hand to her forehead and shoving her away from him playfully.

She jabbed him in the side with her finger, making him laugh. They wrestled back and forth for a couple of minutes, until it was obvious he was tired.

"Still feelin' it, huh?" she asked, concerned again.

"Yeah," he said, lying on his back, his hand on his chest.

He closed his eyes drowsily. Jeanie leaned up over him, stroking his hair.

"Is your head hurting at all? Do you want any meds?"

"God, no more drugs in my system right now, please," he said, rolling his eyes.

"Tylenol might help the headache, counter it a bit," she said, but he shook his head, leaning it into her hand as he closed his eyes.

She smiled down at him. He was a combination of sick little boy and devastatingly handsome, vulnerable man. He was hard to resist. She stroked his hair, brushing it back from his face. Without stopping to think, she leaned down and kissed his forehead. When she pulled back, his teal-blue eyes were on hers. Without a word she leaned down again, kissing his temple this time. She moved to his cheek, kissing it softly, brushing her lips back and forth across his jawline.

He reached up to touch her face, guiding her lips to his. They kissed softly a few times, his hand sliding back into her hair, caressing the back of her neck. When they parted, he trailed his lips along her jawline to her ear.

"Thank you," he said softly, making her smile.

She turned her head, looking down at him. "You're welcome," she said, leaning down to kiss him again.

The fire ignited then, unexpectedly. His hands slid over her, pulling her closer, his lips kissing hers deeply, his hands cupping her face, his mouth all but devouring hers. Jeanie pressed against him, her hands on his chest and shoulders, grasping at him. She moaned against his lips as he pulled her shirt out of her shorts, continuing to pull it up and off her, tossing it aside. He made quick work of removing her bra, moving to touch her breasts, caressing.

"Oh God, Donovan..." she gasped against his lips.

She touched his chest, his arms, sliding her hands down them, then back up to his shoulders. He kissed her neck, sucking at her skin. She moved her lips to his shoulder, kissing it, and moved downward. She got to his belly before his hands were dragging her up, her skin sliding along his, causing them both to moan and gasp. His lips claimed hers again as he pushed her shorts down, and she dragged at his sweats, pushing them out of the way.

"I need you, Jay," he groaned against her lips. "God, I need you so much."

"Please, Donovan, please..." she said, nodding.

He slid her down his body, impaling her. She gasped, kissing him deeply. They made love, taking as much enjoyment from each other as they'd ever had, climaxing together. Jeanie fell asleep in his arms that night, feeling very happy. Donovan fell asleep holding her,

210

feeling complete again.

"You wanted to see me, Chief?" Angelica asked, standing in the door-way to Midnight's office.

"No," Midnight said, standing up from her desk.

"No?" Angelica looked confused. There had been a handwritten note on her computer this morning: *Come see me,* signed *Midnight.* Who else would have written it?

"Come on," Midnight said, gesturing with her head for Angelica to follow her.

Angel followed. Midnight took the elevator down to the first floor and walked out to the parking lot, stopping at her Corvette and turning around, leaning on the front fender.

"I wanted to talk to you," she said.

"But you said…" Angel started, thinking the chief was losing it.

Midnight shook her head, 'No, *I* wanted to talk to you—Midnight Debenshire, not Chief Chevalier."

Angel nodded, knowing for sure now that this was about Rick. She had suspected that was the case. Midnight using her married name confirmed it. Her look at Midnight was wry—was the chief actually going to pull a power play? Angel didn't believe for a minute that Midnight wouldn't use her power as chief for her own personal issues.

"What do you know about me?" Midnight asked.

"What?" Angel replied, surprised.

"Come on, Muñoz," Midnight said, her tone slightly taunting. "What do you know about me? Who I am, what I do," she said, her voice quite calm.

Angel was more wary now. Was Midnight mad? She couldn't tell. Was she just good at hiding it?

"I know you're married to the LT," Angel said, addressing her top issue first. "I know you're the chief here," she added, sure that was what Midnight wanted her to say.

Midnight nodded. "Is that all you know?"

Angel shrugged. "Yeah," she said, not liking the tact Midnight was taking. It was definitely going to be a power play.

"What set did you run with?" Midnight asked.

"The Barrio Girls," Angel answered proudly.

Midnight nodded, looking unimpressed. "And when someone messed with OPP, what happened?" she asked, referring to the slang term "Other People's Property."

Angel's head came up. Midnight was going to threaten her?

"They got messed up," she said.

Midnight nodded again, her look pointed. "You ever hear of The Vettes?"

Angel's brows furrowed. "Yeah, old-time gang down in Sidro."

"Tough gang?"

"So I hear," Angel said, shrugging. "They don't run no more though."

Midnight nodded. "I know. That's 'cause I quit."

"What?" Angel said, looking a little pale suddenly. "You ran with The Vettes?"

"No, baby girl," Midnight said, her tone chilling a number of degrees. "I ran The Vettes."

Angelica was shocked. It took her a few minutes to recover her composure.

Midnight waited, knowing the girl would pull it back together but savoring the stunned look on her face anyway.

Finally, Angel shrugged with overconfidence. "That gang's been gone for years."

"Yes," Midnight said, her green eyes glittering with menace. "But I'm still here."

Again Angel was taken aback. She hadn't really ever dealt with Midnight directly; she could see now why she intimidated people. But Angel was confident she still had the upper hand here.

"So you're worried that I'm gonna take your man," she said, nodding sympathetically, her look cocky.

"Can't take what's not up for grabs."

"Oh, I think he wants to be," Angel said. "I mean, no offense, you look good and shit for your age, but you can't ever beat a little bit of new honey."

"Wanna bet?"

Angel actually had the temerity to laugh. "You really think you can take me?"

"You and ten of your friends, little girl," Midnight said without hesitation. "But I digress. You're obviously still under the impression my husband wants you." She shook her head in disbelief.

"Oh, he wants me, but I think he's afraid to do it 'cause you'd kick him out and take your money with you."

Midnight grinned. This girl really didn't know anything about them, did she? "Angel, just a little FYI here. Rick's the one that has the money, not me. So you're still not convinced that he's not interested?"

"Nope," Angel said breezily. "I think he's just afraid of you."

213

Midnight laughed outright at that. "Richard Joshua Debenshire isn't afraid of anyone, including me." Her gaze was assessing then. "But I can see you need some kind of proof. How about we make a deal?"

"What kind of deal?" Angel asked, surprised that Midnight was even still having this conversation. Why didn't she just threaten to fire her, or trump up charges on her if she didn't agree to leave Rick alone?

"It's simple, really," Midnight said, spreading her hands plaintively. "You make your best play, and if he doesn't go for it, you back off him."

"And if I don't?"

"I'll make you wish you had."

Midnight's confidence was unnerving. Angel considered her options, then started to grin as she nodded.

"Hope you're ready to lose your man," she crowed.

"Hope you're ready to lose period."

So it was that Midnight went back to her office, and Angel went to planning.

That night, Rick received a text as he was leaving the office. It was Angel:

I was hoping we could talk.

Rick replied: Okay, when and where?

My place, now. Angel smiled. This was going to be easier than she'd thought.

Alright.

214

Rick thought it was time they got some things straight. Her advances were getting on Midnight's nerves, and that was causing him tension with his wife. He didn't need the headache. Angel was helpful, but she wasn't irreplaceable; no one was. He had no idea Midnight had talked to her that afternoon, and no idea what he was walking into.

He got to Angelica's front door a half hour later. Angel answered wearing a black silk bathrobe that stopped at the tops of her thighs. Her legs were bare. Rick closed his eyes, shaking his head. Midnight would kill him if she knew he'd even stayed another second. But he was determined to get this done with.

"Angel..." he sighed.

"Just come in, Rick," she said, not daunted by his tone at all.

Rick stepped inside and she closed the door, brushing against him as she did. Rick pursed his lips in irritation, but she didn't see any emotion at all in his blue eyes; naturally, she assumed he was just playing it cool.

"Angel, haven't we done this already?" he asked, his tone hinging on anger.

"Well," Angel said, giving him her best baby girl pout, "we have, but you've never really seen what you'd be getting," she added, reaching to untie her bathrobe.

The robe slithered to the floor, and Angel stood in front of him totally naked. Rick didn't even bat an eyelash. He stared back at her, as disinterested as he'd ever been. Then his expression changed, making it clear to her that she'd just made a fool out of herself. Angelica was shocked. She had been so sure that if Rick saw her young, sexy body, he'd be panting for it. Every other man she'd allowed to have her had been. What was wrong with him?

215

Rick bent down, retrieving her robe and handing it to her pointedly.

"Now we're gonna talk," he said, his tone all lieutenant.

He took her arm and walked her over to the couch in the living room, standing by as she hurriedly pulled on her robe, tying it tightly. He sat down and waited for her to follow suit, which she did, looking very embarrassed.

"Angelica, let me make this perfectly clear," he said, his tone no-nonsense. "I am very deeply, insanely in love with my wife. No woman—young, old, short, tall, beautiful, or exotic—will ever interest me again. We've been married over thirteen years, and I still spend every minute of every day waiting to go home to be with her." He paused to make sure she was really listening this time.

Angelica nodded, not saying anything. He was confirming what Midnight had tried to tell her. Why hadn't she listened?

"Now, I know I haven't been stringent on telling you to back off, simply because I didn't feel that your flirtations were at all harmful. We work well together, and accomplish a lot. But it's been pointed out to me that your behavior is utter disrespect for not only me and my marriage but for my wife. Disrespect of my wife or my marriage will not be tolerated." He looked at her sternly, making sure she understood how serious he was. Again she nodded. "Now, you have a decision to make. Either you want to knock off the flirting and get back to working with me, or you want to quit the unit. If you quit, I'd be happy to give you a recommendation to another department. The Sheriff's Office has a good gang task force."

Angel stared back at him for a long moment, surprised by how he was handling this. Did these people not get how much power they had? Or did they just refuse to use it? Or were they that confident in

216

their relationship? Angel was gaining a new respect for Rick and Midnight with every moment.

"I'm sorry," she said, her eyes downcast. She shook her head, abashed. "Your wife told me you wouldn't go for it, but I didn't believe her."

"She what?" Rick asked, his English accent clear in his shock.

Angel glanced up, then bit her lip. "I talked to her today, and she said that I could make one last play for you, and if you didn't go for it, I had to back off."

Rick gave a sardonic bark of laughter, shaking his head. "I'll kill her," he said, more to himself than to Angel.

"She told me that if I didn't back off after that, she'd kick my ass," Angel said, curious now.

"I don't think I'd test her on that," Rick warned.

Angel shrugged, looking unconvinced of Midnight's fighting ability. "Anyway, she wins—I'll stop. I promise."

"Good."

Rick stood up, as did Angel. She walked him to the door, apologizing once again. Rick drove home thinking of how many ways he was going to beat the crap out of his wife for putting him in that situation.

Part of him felt pretty good though. He'd been presented with a major temptation, something most other guys would have gone for in a heartbeat. He hadn't even been slightly interested. Angelica was beautiful, that was for sure, but she wasn't Midnight. When one had the best, why try anything else?

At home, Rick found Midnight in their office, working on the computer. He walked up behind her chair and leaned down to kiss her neck.

"Mmm…" she murmured, glancing up at him.

He reached out and turned her chair around, kneeling in front of her.

"Forget to mention a conversation you had today?" he asked, staring up into her eyes.

"I, uh, might have," she said, grinning.

They had talked ten minutes before he'd left the office to head home, so he knew the conversation she'd had with Angelica had happened before that time.

"You could have warned me," he said, his tone mildly reproachful.

"Richard, if I'd warned you, she would have said that I was threatening you so you wouldn't go for it."

"Midnight, you knew I wouldn't."

She nodded. "Yeah, I was pretty sure you wouldn't. But all the same—"

"Pretty sure?" he said, cutting her off.

She shrugged slightly. "Rick, she's a twenty-two-year-old Latina with a fire in her pants for you. I wasn't sure what she was going to try, but I was fairly sure it was going to be an all-out play."

"And still you agreed to it."

"Rick," she said, looking him in the eye. "If you ever wanted anyone else, I wouldn't want you with me."

"Well, I don't want anyone else."

"Good," she said, starting to grin. "Then you can stay."

"Can I?" he asked, smiling.

"Maybe."

"How about I convince you?"

"How about you do," she said, glad the kids weren't home at that moment.

Rick leaned forward, capturing her lips with his. As he kissed her he pulled her to her feet. They kissed for a long few minutes, until finally he picked her up and carried her to their bedroom. He reminded her again how attractive he still found every inch of her body.

Later, at the dinner table, they were both grinning like kids. Mikeyla noticed and found it amusing. She was also glad they were in such good moods, since she'd had to explain to them both why she'd cut her first class. Midnight had told her she thought it was very grown up of her to help someone out like she had. Rick had grumbled about not cutting any more classes, but it had been obvious he was more concerned about who Mikeyla had been helping. It was becoming more and more obvious to Rick and Midnight that Mikeyla had a pretty big crush on Nick Masterson. Midnight found it endlessly amusing; Rick didn't.

***

Unbeknownst to anyone, Christian had stepped up his drinking the night after seeing Stevie and Joe together at the hospital. It had been bad enough knowing they were together, but seeing it was more than he could handle. He'd hung back, watching every move they made, feeling constantly like someone was driving a knife into his stomach. On the drive home from the hospital he put in Def Leppard's X, forwarding to the fifth track, "Long Long Way to Go"—the song that had been going around in his head for days now. He sang the words, feeling every one of them and dying to get drunk so he could forget them. The song spoke of the loss of love, and how it was going to take a long, long time before he could really say goodbye. He'd lost Stevie, and it seemed that there was no way to ever get back what he'd thrown away so blithely.

He knew Stevie wasn't someone he was likely to ever get over. Later that night he lay musing in his drunken state. He had had so many women want him, try to capture his heart and hold on to it. Susan had been the first to capture his heart, but she'd been unable to hold him. Stevie had not only captured his heart, but was still holding it for ransom as far as he was concerned. It was ironic that now the tables had finally been turned on him. He was in a situation where he was not in control of whether or not there was a relationship. It pulled at him, and he hated himself for being so weak.

What was the big deal about Stevie O'Neil? Just another woman in a long, long line. Why was she special? Moments after he'd thought that, the answer came to him. He was sure there was a little devil sitting on the headboard next to his head, whispering to him. *Because she matches you in every way. She has the fire and heat you're looking for. She gives back everything you give to her, good or bad. And she won't take your shit.* The last thought made him laugh sardonically, shaking his head.

No, Stevie didn't take his shit. If she thought he was screwing around on her, she nailed him on it, and God help him if he was cheating on her. When he pulled away from her, she didn't come after him, begging him to tell her what was wrong. She stepped back and waited for him to come back to her. And he did, every time. She didn't beg, wheedle, plead, or whine. If she didn't like something he did, she told him. If she was mad, she'd throw things, cuss, scream, and tear off in her Trans Am. There was no questioning how she felt about something. She also didn't beg him to talk to her. Her attitude was, *You have a mouth that gets you into trouble often enough—if you have something to say, use it.*

Stevie was his match whether his mind wanted to accept that or not. And he'd lost her now. He couldn't fathom her not holding on to Joe; everyone said that she was basically a younger version of Midnight. Midnight had always had a hold on Joe, everyone knew that. And why wouldn't Stevie stay with him? He had money, power; he was a frigging legend in the department, everything Stevie admired. Christian knew he couldn't compare to that. It made him sick to think that he was reduced to comparing himself to his cousin. He'd grown up on tales of what an immortal Joe Sinclair was. His mother had ingrained in him at a very early age that if he wanted to be a good man, he should emulate his cousin, Joseph Michael Sinclair. He'd never reached that, and he never would. How could he?

Disgusted with himself, Christian grabbed another bottle, drinking until he passed out. He woke up the next morning and started over again, growing more and more depressed with every waking hour. He was on a downward spiral, and no one was there to stop him.

Susan showed up two days after the night at the hospital and was aghast as his condition. Christian was beyond the ability to be civil. He answered the door automatically, swaying on his feet.

"Christian!" Susan said, reaching up to touch his cheek. He looked so gaunt she couldn't believe it.

Christian jerked away from her, as if her touch would burn him. He shook his head at her as she stared up at him, searching his face. Finally he walked away, leaving the door open. Susan followed. *X* was playing on the stereo. The song "Gravity" came on, and the words fit the situation better than Susan realized. It talked about the gravity of the situation killing him, and keeping him down.

Christian was falling fast, but his pride wouldn't allow him to ask for help. Not even from Susan, who he considered his best friend in the world. The alcohol in his veins numbed him to the point of not caring about anyone or anything, and that was where he wanted to be. He took any attempt to interfere with that as an attack. As he took Susan's visit.

"Christian…" Susan said, watching him sit with his back against the headboard of his bed, stunned at his appearance. "You can't do this," she said beseechingly. It was obvious he was very drunk, and had been for a while now.

"No?"

"Christian, you'll make yourself sick," Susan said softly.

He shrugged, his face a mask of cynicism. "So?"

"No woman is worth that."

"Who says it's about a woman?" he asked, his words slightly slurred.

Susan canted her head to the side, her look considering. "Why else would you drink yourself into a stupor?"

"Life, liberty, and the pursuit of happiness," he replied, his face contorted in self-directed anger. "Why else?"

Susan sat down on the bed next to him, her deep blue eyes searching his face again. She knew this had everything to do with Stevie. She also knew that he was in the phase where he'd deny pretty much anything. It was a fine line she was walking. Christian could be very angry and violent when he was drunk. She knew she was putting herself in a dangerous place. Dave would probably kill her for doing this. He wouldn't be jealous that she was trying to help Christian; he would be worried for her safety. Christian wasn't known for his adherence to proper behavior.

"Have you eaten?" she asked, knowing the answer.

"Zan," Christian said, shaking his head, "just go home."

"I can't, Christian. You're hurting, and you need me."

"No!" he said, making a violent cutting gesture with his hand, making her jump. "That's where you're wrong. I don't need anyone."

"Who don't you need, Christian?" Susan asked, wanting to help him get to the root of his pain.

"None of you," he said, his lips curling in distaste. "Now get the fuck out."

His voice was so dead, Susan felt the hair stand up on the back of her neck. She'd never seen him this low. It scared her.

"Christian…" she began, already trembling.

"I said get out, Susan. Do it before I make you," he said, his light blue eyes flashing.

"Christian, I can't," she said, pleading with him to hear her.

She saw him tense, and instinctively she stood up. A moment later he jumped off the bed, coming to stand a mere inch from her. His height and large frame in comparison to hers spoke volumes. His hands on her arms were like vices, snatching her up off her feet to lift her to his face, making her cry out. There were tears in her eyes, but he didn't see them, his anger was burning so hot.

"Christian!" she gasped, terrified.

Something in her voice seeped through his alcohol-soaked senses. He set her back on her feet, shoving her away from him forcefully.

"Get out, now," he said, his tone brooking no more argument.

Susan didn't hesitate, moving to the door. She turned to see that he had turned his back to her. She didn't say anything as she left, closing the door then leaning against it as her knees grew weak. She knew that he could have hurt her much more than he had. Christian was very strong, and his anger made him even more so. She heard him give a loud yell, and then heard a thud. It spurred her to move off the door and run down the stairs.

Inside the room, Christian stood staring at the hole he'd just put in the wall. Again his hand was bleeding, and he felt the tingling that told him chances were that he'd just broken a couple of bones. Sitting down heavily on the bed, he reached for the half-empty bottle of tequila on the dresser.

***

Dave Dibbins got home from spending a day on surveillance with Stevie to find his wife lying on their bed with a washcloth on her forehead. He grinned to himself as he walked over, leaning down and kissing her cheek softly. She jumped slightly, and pulled the cloth away as she opened her eyes.

"Oh, David, you're home already?" she said, glancing at the clock, shocked to find that it was actually 5:30 in the afternoon.

Randy had the children that day, having wanted them at Sinclair House for the little carnival her people had put together to entertain the kids. It was why Susan had been free during the day to check on Christian. When Susan had called the office, she had been told by Erin that Christian hadn't been going in at all. Erin had expressed her concern for him, which had prompted Susan's visit to the apartment.

224

The visit from which her nerves were still recovering.

"What's wrong?" Dave asked, sensing her nervousness. He sat down on the bed next to her as she sat up. His arm went to her waist, his eyes searching hers.

Susan took a deep breath, knowing he was not going to like what she had to tell him.

"I went to see Christian today," she said, her voice still a bit shaky.

"And..." he said warily, his eyes narrowing.

"David, he looks horrible. He's been drinking, obviously, for days now."

Dave's head came up slightly as he sensed her evasive tactics. "What happened, Susan?"

Again she took a deep breath, blowing it out in a sigh. "He got angry with me for being there."

"Uh-huh..." Dave said, his eyes not leaving hers.

Susan bit her lip. "David, he grabbed me, but he really—"

"He what?" Dave tensed, his eyes scanning her arms, but the bruises that had already started were under her shirt sleeves. "Where?"

Susan lowered her eyes as she lifted her sleeve. She heard his sharp intake of breath and glanced at the bruise. It was darker than it had been when she'd looked at it earlier.

"David, I bruise easily," she said helplessly.

"He had no right to put his hands on you, Susan," Dave said, his voice barely controlled.

"I know," she said, nodding. "But he was drunk, and I know he's hurting. I just—"

"Don't excuse what he did," Dave said evenly.

"I'm not," she said, knowing she was.

Dave stood up. Susan saw the determined look in his eyes.

"What are you going to do?" she asked, her eyes wide.

"I'm going over there, and he and I are going to talk," Dave said, his tone belying the seemingly innocent words.

"Talk?"

"Susan," Dave said sternly. "He manhandled my wife—that is absolutely unacceptable. I will not sit by and do nothing. He will be made to understand that he has no right to treat you like that, and if it's necessary he'll be taught that the hard way."

"David, please…" Susan said, shaking her head.

It wasn't that she didn't think her husband could handle himself, or for that matter that Christian couldn't hold his own either. But the idea of them fighting, like she'd heard Joe and Christian had, was terrifying. What if one of them was badly injured, or worse? The bruises really didn't hurt that much, and Christian hadn't been in his right mind at the time.

"Susan," Dave said softly, reaching out to touch her cheek gently. "I'll talk first, okay? That's all I can promise."

Susan bit her lip, nodding slowly. She understood Dave's side of this; she just wished it wasn't necessary. It never sat well with her that men were willing to fight other men over her. She abhorred violence in any form, but she also realized that this was a matter of concern for Dave. If he couldn't protect his wife from harm, then he didn't feel like he was doing what was his right to do. It was, after all, very gallant of him. She just didn't feel that she warranted such a gesture.

Dave kissed her softly on the lips.

"I'll be back," he said quietly.

"Please be careful," Susan said, suddenly afraid for him.

Dave grinned. "I'm always careful, honey." He kissed her again and then was gone.

Twenty minutes later Dave knocked on Christian's apartment door. When there was no answer, he knocked again, louder. Finally he heard a muffled shout.

"Who is it?"

Christian sounded fairly inebriated.

"It's Dave."

There was a long pause, then Christian said, "Leave off, Dibbs. I already got my duty call from your household." His tone was anything but grateful.

"That's what I'm here to talk to you about," Dave said calmly. He heard Christian sigh deeply.

On the other side of the door, Christian leaned back against it, looking up at the ceiling. He half expected Dave to kick the door in at any moment.

"What about it?" Christian asked antagonistically.

"It's real simple," Dave said. "If you ever lay your hands on my wife again, I will kill you personally."

Again there was silence.

"Collins?" Dave called. "We clear?"

"Yeah," came the response, the tone defeated. After a long moment, Christian said, "Tell Susan I'm sorry."

Dave distinctly heard tears in Christian's voice, and he knew that he had just made Christian realize the gravity of what he had done that afternoon.

227

"I'll do that," Dave said, nodding.

"I'm sorry to you too," Christian said, his voice less shaky now as he got his emotions temporarily under control. "I had no right."

Dave didn't reply. He knew there was no point in telling Christian how right he was about that. "Look, Collins... if you need to talk..."

"Nah," Christian said, far too quickly, making it obvious that he hadn't allowed himself to even consider the offer. "I'm cool. I just need to get it together," he went on, sounding stronger again. Dave didn't know that he was gritting his teeth and forcing his voice to sound normal.

"Well, if you need us, just give us a yell."

His statement made it clear to Christian that he wouldn't get a visit from Susan unescorted next time; Dave didn't trust him.

"Yeah," Christian said, not sounding like he'd ever take Dave up on the offer. "Thanks."

Dave left a minute later. Christian walked back to his bedroom, picking up a new bottle of tequila and opening it. He thanked his lucky stars he'd found a liquor store that delivered and took credit cards by phone. He finished out his evening the way he finished out most these days: passed out on his bed.

CHAPTER 8

The morning after they got back together, Donovan and Jeanie sat in his living room drinking coffee and talking. Donovan had showered and dressed. He planned to go over and see Randy that morning. It was Saturday, so thankfully he had the weekend to get his shit together before he and Jeanie had to get back to work on Monday. They hadn't addressed what they were going to do on the case yet, still enjoying the feeling of being a couple again. This morning was dedicated to visiting his sister.

Donovan knew he'd been remiss in taking care of Randy during her break-up with Joe. He wanted to see how she was doing and find out if there was anything he could do for her.

"Are you going to tell her about all of this, Donovan?" Jeanie asked, resting her head on the back of the couch and looking over at him.

They were sitting on opposite ends of the couch, their legs stretched out, meeting and intermingling somewhere in the middle.

"Yeah, I need to," he said, sounding resolute. He grimaced. "If nothing else, to explain why I've sucked as a brother lately."

"I'm sure she doesn't think that."

"No, I do," Donovan said, with certainty.

Jeanie nodded, biting her lip. She knew there was no way to assure him at this point. She decided to change the subject.

229

"Tomorrow, will you come with me to trade in my car?"

"You're trading in the Corolla?" She still had the 1995 Toyota she'd been driving since they met.

"Yeah, I think it's time," she said, grinning.

"So what do you want to look at?"

"I don't know," she said, looking thoughtful. "Something sporty. The Trans that Stevie drives is really cool."

"Yeah, and about 30K, babe, and they're not making them anymore, so…"

"Yikes!" Jeanie said, widening her eyes. Then she narrowed them at him suspiciously. "She hasn't been a sergeant that much longer than me, and she can afford one…"

"Uh, honey, Stevie worked for a drug dealer for a year and a half."

"Oh," Jeanie said, looking sufficiently embarrassed.

"Yeah, oh," he said, winking at her.

"Yeah, yeah," she said, giving him a dirty look. "So what are my options?"

"Well," he said, considering it, "you could go for a Grand Am— I think they start at like seventeen thousand—or there's always my personal favorite, the one and only real muscle car."

"Eww…" Jeanie said, making a face. "I can't drive the same car as my boyfriend. That's *so* high school."

"I didn't own a car in high school," he pointed out.

"Neither did I, but still… Eww," she said, grinning.

"Fine, so go buy a Honda or something."

"Haha," she said, wrinkling her nose up, making him laugh. "What about what Blue drives?"

"A Viper?" Donovan asked incredulously, giving her a wry look. "Try 75K, babe."

"Okay then," she said, rolling her eyes. "I'm thinking Grand Am…"

Donovan nodded. "Okay, we'll go have a look tomorrow."

"Cool," she said, smiling.

He got up a little while later, taking her coffee cup and his and putting them in the sink. Jeanie followed. She met him as he was walking back out of the kitchen. He looked down at her for a long moment, then pulled her into his embrace. He kissed her on the top of the head, hugging her close.

"I like the sound of that again," he said after a long moment.

"Of what?" she asked, looking up at him.

"'Boyfriend.'"

Jeanie smiled up at him warmly. "I like being able to say it again."

"I love you," he said softly as he leaned down to kiss her again.

"I love you too, Donovan," she said, kissing him back. She hugged him. "Please don't let me let you go again," she said, with a great deal of emotion behind her words.

"I'll see what I can do," he said, grinning against her hair.

They both knew there had been nothing he could do the last time she'd let him go. She'd applied for the job in San Francisco, and when she got it, she'd thought he'd just transfer to San Francisco Police Department. But since she'd never discussed it with him, he hadn't been willing to uproot his life at that point. They'd been apart for a couple of months when she'd been hurt on the job.

Now she was very glad she had finally gotten him back. She

loved him—she always had. It made her heart soar to hear him say he loved her. It was like hearing it for the first time again.

Later that morning, Donovan walked up the stairs to Sinclair House. He talked to the receptionist, who eyed the brother of the owner/operator with interest. He was dressed in beige Dockers, a hunter green shirt, and brown Doc Martens, with a holstered gun at his hip and his badge clipped to his belt. Donovan Curtis made a striking figure, with his sandy-brown hair and teal eyes set in a handsome face. Women found it hard to resist him, even when he was as reserved as he was at that point.

"Donny?" Randy queried, surprised to see him on a Saturday. Actually, she hadn't seen him much recently. She'd been busy, yes, but she also had the distinct impression that he'd been avoiding her over the last few months as well.

"Hey, sis," he said, moving to hug her.

Randy was small next to his six-foot frame, but with their teal eyes and similarly colored hair, it was obvious they were brother and sister.

"You have time for some coffee?" he asked surreptitiously.

Randy looked up at him, searching his eyes. "Sure," she said, turning to the receptionist. "Jaime, let Derrick know I'll be back in an hour."

"Yes, ma'am."

Donovan walked Randy out to his car. He was quiet on the short drive over to the nearby coffee shop. Randy could sense the tension in her younger brother. She'd called his house a couple of days before to tell Donovan about Rhiannon's miscarriage. Jeanie had answered

232

the phone and had told her that Donovan was really sick with something—"like the flu" was how she'd put it. Randy wasn't sure what was going on, but she was planning to find out.

Once they had their coffee they sat in a corner booth.

"So how are you?" Donovan asked.

"I'm okay," she said automatically. She'd been telling people that for weeks now; it was becoming habit.

"Now that I got the bullshit PR answer," he said, giving her a serious look, "can I have the truth?"

Randy looked back at him for a long moment, then blew her breath out in a sigh, shaking her head. "I'm sorry, Donny. I've gotten so used to pretending that I'm okay, I forget to tell the truth." She hesitated, as if evaluating how she really felt. "I miss him," she said, shrugging. "I guess when you live with someone for over thirteen years, you're so used to their presence…" She trailed off as Donovan nodded.

"Might be that you're still in love with the guy too," he said calmly.

Randy grimaced. "Yeah, that might be it too," she said apologetically. She was still giving him rhetoric.

"So what really happened, Randy? Why did he leave?" Donovan knew he'd never gotten the whole story. She'd told him that Joe hadn't been happy, so he left.

"He left because he thought I didn't want him anymore."

"Was he right?"

"Yes."

"Wow," he said, his expression showing the shock she'd just given him.

233

"I know."

"Why?" Donovan asked, not able to imagine his sister falling out of love with Joe.

Randy shook her head. "I don't know, Donny. I don't know what happened." She spread her hands, indicating her feelings of futility. "Things have been strained since the miscarriage. We just never got back to normal."

"Normal?" he asked, raising an eyebrow.

"Sexually."

"Oh," he said, grimacing.

"And apparently, Joe was already feeling worried about his age. My lack of interest in that area only compounded it for him," she said, sounding truly chagrined at the thought.

"Oh, man," Donovan said, shaking his head. "No wonder things got strained."

"Yes. And he tried to talk to me about it. He even told me he thought I didn't want him anymore." Her eyes showed how she was castigating herself for it. "I couldn't deny it, because he was right." She shrugged. "That was the night he left."

Donovan nodded. "And that's why he's seeing Stevie O'Neil."

"What do you mean?"

"From what Jay told me, Stevie's had a thing for Joe for years. Kind of an idolized crush."

Randy nodded. "So she expressed that and he took her up on it," she said, her tone devoid of anger.

"Probably." Donovan canted his head to the side, giving her a sidelong glance. "Understanding it doesn't make it hurt less."

Randy looked sad. "No, it doesn't. But I didn't stop him from leaving, and I haven't made any effort to fix it, so I don't have any right to complain now."

Donovan nodded, looking unhappy for her. "So what are you going to do?"

Randy took a deep breath. "I'm going to give him a divorce."

Donovan stared back at her in stunned silence. That was the last thing he'd expected. "Rand…" he breathed. "Are you sure he wants a divorce?"

"No, Donny. But he has moved out, and moved on with another woman. So I'd say he's looking for his freedom right now. The situation with him and me hasn't changed or gotten better. So why make him stay?"

"Because maybe he doesn't want to go, sis."

He remembered well when Randy had been having an affair. Joe hadn't been willing to divorce her. He pointed that out.

"Rand, he didn't want to divorce you when you were having an affair on him. And you two have invested another thirteen years into this marriage, not to mention bringing two kids into the world."

Randy looked back at him for a long moment. He could see she was thinking about what he'd said. Finally she shrugged.

"I don't know. I just don't want to hurt him any more than I already have."

"Just promise me one thing then," he said, reaching out to touch her hand.

"What?"

"Before you do anything like file, tell Joe what you're planning to do."

"Why?" she asked. "I don't intend to ask for anything, in terms

235

of property or anything. There won't be anything to contest."

"Except the divorce itself, Randy. I think you need to talk to your husband before you decide his future for him, okay?"

Randy looked shocked for a moment, surprised by his statement. She hadn't thought she was deciding anything for Joe. Hadn't he already made his decision? She realized that her actions and behavior had contributed to it. Randy saw giving him a divorce without making him ask her for it as the decent thing to do. She thought Joe had been more than fair with her, attempting to talk to her about the problem between them. He'd tried a couple of times, in fact. No, the problem lay with her. Just because she didn't understand what was making her feel so detached didn't mean Joe should suffer too. It was obvious he had been before he'd left.

It was clear he'd thought about the situation between them a lot. He'd resolved to talk to her about it, even giving her the opportunity to deny his assumptions. She hadn't done that. The consequence of that was him leaving, which eventually resulted in him having an affair.

Randy had looked at everything from a logical perspective and knew that she was the problem. Much of what she was feeling told her to just to slink away and let Joe be happy again. It hadn't really occurred to her that Joe might still want to be with her. Why would he? He was sleeping with a woman who was about ten years her junior, and who obviously worshiped him like Randy had for years. Why would he give that up?

"I'll see, Donny, okay?" she said.

Donovan nodded, realizing it was probably the best he was going to get at this point. In the end they didn't talk about what had really been going on with him. He didn't have the heart to worry her about the situation. He took her back to Sinclair House and watched her walk inside.

Randy went into the bathroom reserved for her and the staff. There she allowed herself the luxury of crying for a full ten minutes. She'd been avoiding her feelings about Joe, and the situation, and even the actual idea of divorcing him. The conversation with Donovan and brought it into specific relief, however, and she needed to cry to vent her feelings. She'd driven herself crazy so many times, late at night, lying in the bed they'd shared for years, still smelling his pillow every so often and feeling the ache of loss. She'd turned it over and over in her head, and she couldn't find an answer. When no answer would come, she'd push it back out of her head again.

She loved Joe, there was no doubt about that. But she also knew that for a man as virile as he still was, having a young wife who suddenly wasn't interested in him wasn't something his ego could weather. In fact, even at her age, she didn't know how she'd handle it if Joe had suddenly become unattracted to her. She knew it would hurt her, and she knew that she'd be devastated by it. So she understood what Joe was going through. She just didn't know what to do about it.

Ten minutes later, someone knocked on the door. It was one of the psychology students who worked with her. His name was Derrick; he was twenty-one years old, and a junior at UCSD. He was very sweet, always trying to help her. He was very respectful, and although he'd indicated that he thought she was very pretty, he'd never made any overtures to flirt with her. He was well aware that she was married to a very rich, powerful cop, and he joked that he liked his family jewels intact.

Derrick knew that Randy Sinclair was not very happy these

237

days. He suspected that things in her marriage weren't going well. She hadn't told anyone that Joe had left her. She didn't feel that it needed to be public knowledge. Also, she didn't want anyone's pity; it was bad enough that everyone at the department knew what was going on. Randy wanted to keep some semblance of her pride intact somewhere. Derrick did his best to give her the space she needed. He wished he could help, but he didn't want her to feel that he was trying to pry. He made a point, however, of being around just in case she needed him.

***

The day after the incident with Christian, Dave sat on surveillance with Stevie outside the school once again. They'd been there a half hour, making small talk.

"Had an incident with your, ah, ex, yesterday," Dave said casually, stumbling over Christian's status.

"Oh yeah?" Stevie asked, looking over at him.

Dave was relaxed, sitting with his ankles crossed, his usual calm demeanor in place.

"Yeah," he said, nodding. "Seems he was a bit drunk when Susan went over to check on him."

"Check on him?" Stevie repeated, her concern already evident in her voice.

"Yeah. Apparently he hasn't been showing up in the office. Susan was going to go over and have lunch with him. When she called up to make a date, Erin told her about his absence lately." Dave looked over at her, his expression still casual, but Stevie sensed that he was about to drop a bomb. "Apparently, Erin's been really concerned about him lately too. She said he's been drinking a lot."

"Dave," Stevie said sourly, "Erin worships the ground Christian walks on. She'd worry about him if his shirt collar didn't lay right."

Dave grinned. "Blue's clothing issues notwithstanding, Susan went over to check on him."

"Okay…" Stevie said, waiting for the rest.

"She said he was extremely drunk, and looked like he had been for days on end. She said he's lost a lot of weight. She even tried to reason with him," he said, his tone darkening a bit on the last.

"Uh-huh…" Stevie said warily. She knew how Christian could be when he was drunk. He was either very passionate or very dangerous. Sometimes both.

"She has bruises to show for it," Dave said evenly, though his blue eyes flashed.

"Jesus…" Stevie breathed, searching Dave's face. "Dave, tell me you didn't go over there and beat the shit out of him when he was drunk off his ass…" Her tone edged on threatening.

"Steve, he put his hands on my wife."

"Yes, but Susan knows him just as well as I do, and she'd know not to push him when he's that drunk," Stevie said, her eyes flashing.

"So you're saying it was her own fault?" Dave asked, raising an eyebrow at her.

"No," Stevie said, sighing and shaking her head. "You're right—it wasn't. But Jesus, if he was that drunk, there was no way he could fight you. How much did you damage him?"

Dave gave her a measured look, waiting an extra few moments to answer her. Finally he shook his head.

239

"I didn't. He wouldn't even open the door. And in the end he apologized for hurting her."

The relief on Stevie's face told Dave everything he needed to know.

"You still love him, don't you?" he said. It wasn't really a question.

Stevie nodded. "There was just too much shit going on," she said, her sigh loud in the car as her eyes traveled back out to the street, watching the goings-on. "There was this woman in Seattle that was still after him. He wouldn't make any commitment on the house I was buying, wouldn't even bring it up. In fact, the week I was set to close, he conveniently had to go back to Seattle," she added angrily.

Dave nodded. "So you think he was screwing around on you?"

"Yeah, I do."

"Is that why you ended up with Joe?"

Stevie didn't answer for a long moment, leaning her head against the driver's window, looking thoughtful.

"I think that was part of it," she said. "I mean, all the shit was going on with Joe, and Randy not being interested in him anymore. And the fact is, I couldn't believe that. I've thought Joe Sinclair was a god for most of my life—how could his wife not want him anymore?" She sounded almost irate. Dave grinned. Stevie shrugged. "Anyway, we were out at the range, and he was helping me work on shooting with my weak hand, and when he got up behind me to help me line up the shot, I felt like someone had just touched me with a live wire. A lot like when Christian does. I didn't know at the time that he felt it too. Not until we were done and he said he needed a drink." She grinned impishly. "So we went and had a few drinks, and one thing led to another." Again she shrugged. "It wasn't like we set out to sleep

240

together—things just happened."

Dave nodded, seeing how that could happen between two people who had apparently needed each other at that point in time.

"But now it's not so easy, is it?" he asked gently.

"No," Stevie said, shaking her head. "In fact, we haven't even slept together since a few days after the fight he had with Christian. It just doesn't seem right anymore. Now we mostly just hang out and talk. He doesn't feel like he's part of the Gang anymore, and God knows I'm not."

"You still are, Steve. So is Joe," Dave assured her. "But we're like a family, and sometimes family doesn't agree on things. If something major happened, they'd be there for you two, trust me."

Stevie gave him a doubtful look, but didn't say anything.

"So he's bad, huh?" she asked eventually.

Dave knew she was referring to Christian. "Yeah, he is."

"Damn," Stevie said, shaking her head.

She'd been missing him constantly lately. It wasn't just that she and Joe weren't sleeping together. She missed Christian's wry sense of humor, his way of looking at her, his way of kissing her, touching her, and generally his presence. There had been a number of times when she'd had to literally walk away from the phone to keep from calling him. She could only imagine the attitude she'd get from him if she tried. In his eyes, she'd committed the ultimate betrayal, and she wasn't sure he'd ever forgive that. Of course, she felt that in sleeping with the woman in Seattle, he'd cheated on her first, but she knew Christian would say that was far different from her sleeping with his cousin. And deep down, she knew he'd be right.

There was no way out of this, and she knew that chances were

241

very good she'd never get him back. She avoided thinking about it, for fear it would shatter her heart. She hadn't realized how much she really loved him until she'd lost him. "Don't know what you got till it's gone"—the saying held true. And it hurt like hell.

The following afternoon, Dave got a call from Susan. She was worried sick about Christian. He wasn't answering his phone, letting the machine pick up every time. She'd left him numerous messages to call her.

"You didn't go back over there, did you?" Dave asked sternly.

"No, David," she said. "I promised you I wouldn't go back over there without you, and I haven't."

Dave nodded. "Good. Look, I'll see what I can do to check on him, okay?"

"Thank you," Susan said, sounding relieved.

"You're welcome. I'll let you know what I come up with."

A few minutes later he walked into Stevie's cubicle. "Hey, Steve," he said as he leaned against her desk.

"Yeah?" she asked, glancing up from the report she was working on.

"Do you happen to still have a key to the apartment you and Blue shared?" He kept the question casual, but Stevie was alerted instantly.

"Why?" she asked warily.

Dave shrugged. "Susan called me, worried. She said he's not answering the phone now."

Stevie shrugged. "He won't if he knows she's going to hassle him about drinking. That's how he is."

"Yeah, I figured that," Dave said. "But I told Susan I'd check on him..." He trailed off hopefully.

"And you want me to go with you so you can tell her you physically saw him, right?"

"Right," he said, grinning.

"Always willing to do anything for that wife of yours, aren't you?" she said, grinning back.

"Pretty much."

They left a little while later.

When they walked into the apartment, Stevie knew something was wrong instantly. Her hands trembled as she closed the door behind them.

"Christian?" she called, scanning the living room.

Dave went to check the kitchen, and Stevie headed down the hall to the bedroom. She knew, even before she pushed open the door, that she was going to hate what she saw. She was right. Her breath caught in her throat. He was lying sprawled on his stomach, crossways on the bed. His head and arms dangled precariously off the side. His hands were covered in dried blood, and she could see more of it on the sheets.

"Dave!" she yelled as she hurried toward Christian's still form.

There were tequila and beer bottles everywhere—he really had been drinking for days.

"Jesus..." she breathed as she knelt next to his head, touching his cheek. "What have you done, Christian?" she said. "Christian?" she repeated, louder, reaching out to shake his shoulder. "Christian!" she yelled, shaking him harder. Nothing. He didn't move. "Please,

please, please…" she chanted as she reached for his neck to check for his pulse.

It took her a few moments to steady her hand long enough to feel for the heartbeat. She detected a slight pulse, but she thought it seemed thready. Dave came up behind her then.

"Shit," he said as he looked down at Christian.

"Dave, his pulse is thready. We need to get him to a hospital now."

Dave nodded, reaching for his cell phone and making the call.

"What did you do, Christian?" Stevie asked, talking to his still form. "What did you do?" She looked around, noting the partially empty tequila bottle lying on the floor where he must have dropped it. Its contents had spilled on the rug. Her eyes followed the trail of alcohol and stopped at a bottle lying partially under the bed. "Shit," she said, reaching down to pick up the prescription container. She read the label.

"Dave! He took Vicodin," she said, almost frantic. "Damnit. Damnit!" Tears were stinging the back of her eyes.

"They're on the way," Dave said, kneeling on the other side of Christian.

Stevie could see that he was worried too. That scared her more; Dave was always calm, but he didn't look it right now.

The paramedics got there five minutes later, though it seemed like an eternity. Dave and Stevie stepped back out of the way so they could work. They transported Christian to the hospital after a few minutes. Stevie and Dave followed in Dave's car.

Stevie took up a position near the double doors of Emergency. She paced for a while, then leaned against the wall, sliding down to squat, then getting up in agitation and pacing again. Dave called Susan, then paged Midnight and told her what had happened. Within the hour, everyone was at the hospital. No one said anything to Stevie or Joe; there were no looks of accusal, no comments about why this might have happened. Most just walked over to each of them, clapping them on the shoulder or hugging them. Everyone knew what private hell both Joe and Stevie were probably in at that moment.

Joe sat in a chair, his head tilted back to lean against the wall, alternating between closing his eyes and staring up at the ceiling, seeing nothing. It was obvious by the look on his face that he was beating himself up over this. Midnight was the last to arrive, having waited until she could make sure everyone knew what was happening. She walked straight over to Joe and stood looking down at him, searching his face. His eyes were closed, but he sensed her there and opened them. The pain she saw brought tears to her eyes, and she knelt down, hugging him. Joe hugged her back. No one said anything, just watched.

Midnight stood, looking over at Stevie, who had distanced herself from the Gang; she'd stayed near the double doors. She was facing the wall, her forehead resting against it, one arm braced above. It was obvious that she was aching badly too. Midnight walked over and stood at her side. Stevie raised her head, dropping her arm. She stared back at Midnight, her eyes wary, but still deeply affected. Without a word, Midnight hugged her.

"He'll be okay," she whispered.

Stevie nodded. "If he's not, I'm next," she said, her voice ragged but sincere.

Midnight pulled back. "Don't say that," she said sternly. "He made the choice to do this, Stevie—no one could have prevented it.

245

It's in the hands of fate right now."

Stevie nodded, swallowing convulsively. She knew Midnight was trying to excuse her from guilt, but there wasn't anyone who could convince her that this wasn't her fault.

***

Christian woke feeling like he was trying to swim in mud. He groaned in his effort to sit up, and promptly lay back down.

"Try to relax, Mr. Collins," said a female voice.

Christian opened his eyes a mere slit. "Who're you?" he asked, his voice a croak.

"Nurse Capps, Mr. Collins. I'll get your doctor."

She was an older nurse—looked to be in her forties—with staunch brown hair back in a bun and a bland expression.

"Why am I here?" he asked.

"I'll get your doctor, sir. He can—"

"Bullshit, just tell me why I'm here."

The nurse hesitated, then shrugged. "You were found unconscious in your apartment."

"By who?" he asked, his voice taking on an edge.

"Uh…" The nurse picked up his chart and looked through the pages. "A Sergeant Dibbins and a Sergeant O'Neil."

"Fuck," was his only response as he closed his eyes.

So Stevie had got to see his latest failure. Couldn't even manage to kill himself right. *Score one more mistake-slash-failure for Collins,* he thought angrily.

"Look," he said, his voice stopping the nurse from leaving the room. "Do me a favor, will ya?"

"What is that, Mr. Collins?" she asked, almost sighing.

"I'm guessing there's a shitload of people out in the waiting room for me, yes?" he said confidently.

"Yes, sir, there are," she replied, having seen the large group herself.

Christian nodded, looking resigned. "Will you let them know I don't want to see anyone?"

"No one?" she asked, surprised.

"No one."

Nurse Capps hesitated, not sure why her patient was requesting this. Finally she nodded; it was his right to refuse visitors. She made a note on the chart, then walked out, telling him she'd send his doctor down right away.

A half hour later, the doctor walked in. The man was young, looked about thirty-five, with blond hair and glasses. He was a short, bookworm-looking type of a man. Christian watched him pick up his chart and read it, and then the doctor squinted at him.

"Mr. Collins."

"That would be me," Christian replied mildly.

"I know," the doctor assured him. "What happened today?"

Christian looked back at him for a long moment, his stare indicating that he knew what game the doctor was playing. Finally he shrugged.

"I drank."

"You drank quite a lot, Mr. Collins."

"I was thirsty."

247

"Your blood alcohol was off the charts."

"I've always been an over-achiever."

"Mr. Collins, there was a large amount of Vicodin in your bloodstream. We estimate that you took approximately twelve pills. Why?"

"I had a headache," Christian replied, straight-faced.

The doctor gave him a sour look. "You could have died today. Do you realize that?"

"Everyone's gotta go sometime, Doc."

"Were you trying to kill yourself?"

Christian wrinkled his nose up, making a disgusted face. "Too passé for me."

"You do realize that by State law I am required to keep you for seventy-two hours for psychiatric evaluation, don't you?" the doctor said, thinking to shock his patient out of his sarcasm.

"And if I refuse to stay?" Christian asked, his tone not changing a bit.

"Then you can be arrested for attempted suicide," the doctor replied triumphantly, thinking he would shock Mr. Collins this time.

"You mean by the half of the San Diego Police Department in the waiting room?" Christian asked, raising a jet black eyebrow at the little man.

The doctor said nothing for a long moment. He realized Christian Collins was one of those people that wouldn't be cured by way of reality checks—not of the shocking nature, anyway.

"Look, tell you what," Christian said, sounding magnanimous. "You keep everyone in the waiting room out of here, and I won't give you any shit about staying."

The doctor nodded. "That won't be a problem."

"Then I guess we have no problem," Christian said, leaning back and closing his eyes.

He was hiding the mortification he felt. He didn't want to see anyone, to see them looking at him like he was a loser. It disgusted him that he had been stupid enough to botch even the simplest of tasks.

Christian Collins spent the next few days putting on the best act of his life, convincing the doctors that he'd simply been a little bit depressed and hadn't really considered the consequences of his actions. He told them he'd just wanted to sleep, not kill himself. He'd acquired a talent for looking very sincere when he needed to. It worked. Three days later he was released. He took a cab back to his apartment, having to wake the manager from her afternoon nap to get her to let him in.

Walking inside, he was hit with the smell of alcohol. The remnants of his binge were everywhere. His lip curled wryly as he looked around. He wondered just how high his credit card bill was bound to be after this one. He was tired again, but he was already craving a drink.

Spending the better part of an hour looking for a bottle that wasn't empty, he found nothing. Not even a beer left in the fridge. "Fuck, Collins, how pathetic is that?" he asked himself. He walked over to the medicine cabinet and opened it, wincing as pieces of the already shattered glass fell and broke. He stood looking at the contents of the cabinet, pushing bottles aside, picking up others and reading the labels, discarding those that didn't interest him. In the end, he decided suicide by way of amoxicillin just wasn't going to be dignified.

249

In the end he lay down on his bed, suddenly exhausted. Minutes later he was asleep. He didn't hear Stevie come in an hour later. She stood staring down at him for a long time, her face drawn and unhappy. Glancing into the bathroom, she saw the bottles of discarded pills in the sink. She looked back at him, narrowing her eyes. Christian slept on. After a long while, she moved to sit carefully on the bed, wanting to watch him. She felt the need to stay near him, especially since she was sure her instincts had been right.

She was terrified that he would bullshit his way out of the hospital, then come home and accomplish what he'd failed to do the first time. The thought made her sick. It also forced her to risk the confrontation that she'd been avoiding. She'd never forgive herself if he managed to hurt himself again, or, God forbid, kill himself.

Christian stirred, clenching his hands then unclenching them. He rubbed his face, shifting to his side. His outstretched hand touched Stevie's leg, and he woke instantly. He jumped slightly when he noted someone sitting on the bed. Then he realized who it was, and looked up at her warily.

"What are you doing here?" he asked, remembering instantly that she still had her key to the apartment.

"I needed to see you," she said honestly.

"Why?" he asked, not looking directly into her eyes.

"Because I needed to see that you were okay."

"I'm fine," he said evenly, looking away from her.

"Christian…" she said disbelievingly. "You're far from fine."

His light blue eyes flashed then. "What is it you need, Stevie? Huh?"

She searched his face. "I need to know that you're going to be okay, that…" She shook her head.

"I told you, I'm fine," he said tightly.

"And you're full of shit," she said, growing angry herself.

"What the fuck do you want for my life, Stevie?" he asked, moving to sit up, sliding his hand through his hair in agitation.

"That's just it, Christian," she said, her eyes on him. "I want you to have a life."

He turned his head, looking at her over his shoulder. "You want me to have a life?" he said, shaking his head and laughing sarcastically. "Just go, Stevie," he said after a few moments, defeated.

"No," she said adamantly. "Not until I know you'll be okay."

He turned back to her, searching her face for a long moment. He looked away, his eyes on his hands in his lap. "That's not gonna happen."

"Tell me what you're feeling," she pleaded.

"What do you want to hear, Stevie?" he asked, leaning against the headboard.

"I told you."

"You want to hear that I'd give anything for a bottle of tequila right now?" he snapped. "You want to hear that I spent a fucking hour looking for something to drink, something to make me numb again? How I fucking went through every bottle in that medicine cabinet, praying for something stronger than aspirin?" His eyes glittered with malice. "Is that what you need to hear, Stevie?"

Stevie stared back at him for a long moment, her shock showing on her face. It had been what she was afraid of, and hearing it now scared her to death.

"God, Christian, no," she said, shaking her head.

251

"Oh yeah, Steve, trust me."

"No," she said, her voice stronger. "No, and I'm not leaving here until you fucking promise me you won't try anything else."

"I can't do that," he said simply, his eyes once again dropping from hers.

"Why?" she asked searching his face. When he didn't answer, she asked again, louder. "Why, Christian?"

He closed his eyes, shaking his bowed head, wincing almost painfully. His lips tightened, and she knew he was forcing himself to keep silent.

"Goddamnit!" she yelled. "Why?"

He lifted his head at the sheer volume of her voice, his eyes connecting with hers. She sucked in her breath at the depth of pain she saw there. She'd never seen him this vulnerable, never, and it hit her physically.

What he said left her stunned.

"Because I can't live without you," he said, his voice so filled with anguish and self-loathing that she felt it.

She stared back at him for a full minute. His eyes dropped from hers again, and she reached out automatically, taking his face in her hands, turning it back to hers. She stared straight into his eyes, which were glistening with tears.

"I love you," she said. "Please, Christian. Please…"

She couldn't get the words out. She wanted to beg him to forgive her for what she'd done to hurt him so much. But the tears started, choking her. Suddenly he was pulling her into his arms, holding her to him as if drowning himself. She cried, and he held her, rocking her back and forth, gripping her back almost in desperation.

They stayed that way for a long time. When her tears subsided, she leaned against him, her face buried in his shirt, both hands clenched around handfuls of the material. As she turned back into him, she felt his hands stroking her hair, his cheek pressed against the top of her head. If she could have seen his face, she would have seen that he had his eyes squeezed shut, praying that he wasn't imagining this, that he hadn't imagined what she'd said minutes before.

Finally, she risked pulling back to look up at him. He gazed down at her, his light blue eyes shining in the afternoon sun coming through the windows. He was afraid to say anything, afraid the spell would be broken.

"Christian," she said softly, as if loath to shatter the moment as well. She shook her head. "I'm so sorry..."

"I love you," he said, with more conviction in his voice than she'd ever heard before.

She nodded, realizing that they were going to have to talk at some point, but that right now they didn't have to. She laid her head against his chest, winding her arms around his waist, realizing again how much weight he'd lost. His arms closed around her, holding her close. After a while, he lay back against the headboard, pulling her with him. She lay half on him and half on the bed, her head in the hollow of his shoulder. They stayed like that for hours, neither of them speaking. It felt good.

***

Joe went back to work the day after Christian was found unconscious. He worked until 10:00 that night, then went to the gym for two hours. When he got back to the hotel, he worked and read reports until 3:00

253

a.m. He slept for two hours then got up and went back to the gym for another two. He showed up at the office at 8:00 a.m. and started the process all over again.

Kyle pointed out Joe's workaholic practice to Midnight when he got a good look at Joe three days later. Midnight went to see him. Walking into his office without knocking, she sat in front of his desk, putting a booted foot up on it, as he'd done to her enough times in the past.

Joe glanced up then, noting who it was.

"What's up?" he asked.

"I'm taking a survey."

"About what?" he asked, narrowing his eyes suspiciously.

"About how much sleep my staff is getting," she said, smiling brightly.

Joe gave her a quelling look. "Don't start with me, Night."

"Don't make me kick your English ass, Sinclair," she replied sweetly.

He looked back at her for a long moment, then shook his head. "What should I do?"

"In terms of what?"

"Everything," he said, spreading his hands plaintively. "Anything."

She stared back at him, not sure how to respond. "Have you talked to Randy?" she asked gently.

"No," he replied, his face closing off instantly.

"Okay," she said, nodding. "Have you seen the kids?"

"No," he said, sighing. "And I need to. I miss them like crazy."

"Okay, so go see your kids, Joe."

"That easy, huh?"

"That easy. But first take your ass back to the hotel and get some sleep," she said, pinning him with a look.

He stared back at her for a long moment, knowing that if he didn't do what she said, she'd have the entire Gang on his ass next. That headache he did not need.

"Fine," he said, holding up his hands in surrender.

"See?" she said, smiling as she stood up. "That's what I like. Happy, cooperative employees."

"Night?" he said as she turned to leave.

"Yes?" she said, glancing back at him.

"Kiss my English ass," he said, smiling warmly.

"Not even if you beg," she shot back, making him laugh.

"I see how you are," he said, nodding.

"Yes, you do," she said. "Think I forgot that 'And now I remember why' comment?" she added, grinning.

Joe winced. "Have I apologized for that yet?"

"No, and I don't expect you to, Joe," she said, walking around his desk. "I was out of line."

"No, you were worried."

"Yes. But that didn't give me the right to judge," she said, shrugging. "It's just that I was dealing with this shit with Angelica, and I—"

"Angelica?" Joe asked, leaning against his desk, crossing his arms over his chest. "The girl that works with Rick?"

"Yeah." She rolled her eyes. "'Girl' is right," she said sourly.

"Oh-ho," Joe said. "Was she putting the moves on him?"

"And how!"

Joe grinned.

"Shut up, Sinclair. It's not funny," Midnight said, unable to keep from grinning herself.

"So what did you do, *Chief*?"

"What any diplomatic figurehead would do," she said indignantly. "I threatened the little bitch."

Joe laughed. "Why does that not surprise me?"

"Hey, she was messing with my man…"

"She was what?" Rick asked from the doorway.

Midnight glanced over her shoulder. "What are you doing here?"

"Likely the same thing you are," Rick said, nodding toward Joe.

"Oh," Midnight said.

"Oh," Rick echoed, grinning. He knew he'd caught her talking about him. He walked into the office and sat in the chair Midnight had vacated. "She tell you what else she did?" he asked Joe.

"Oh, God, what else?" Joe asked, rolling his eyes and drawing a vile look from Midnight.

"Don't you have work to do, Lieutenant?" Midnight asked, narrowing her eyes at her husband.

"No, as a matter of fact I don't, Chief," he replied, winking at her.

"So, what did she do?" Joe asked.

"I'm leaving," Midnight said, walking toward the door, only to be caught by the hand and pulled into her husband's lap.

"Like hell you are," he said. "So she gets into a pissing match with Angel, right?" Rick said, as if just continuing a story he'd been

256

in the middle of. "And apparently, my loving wife tells Angel to make her best play for me, and if she gets me, she does."

"What?" Joe said, his mouth dropping open. He looked at Midnight as if she were crazy.

Midnight rolled her eyes, shaking her head. "Not before I told the girl that he wouldn't go for it."

"So, what happened?" Joe asked.

"Oh, you know, the usual," Rick said wryly. "Angel pages me and asks me to come to her place to 'talk.' I get over there and she answers the door wearing basically nothin' but a bloody smile—" He grunted as Midnight jammed her elbow into his gut. "Okay, she was wearing a robe for the first minute I was there."

Joe grinned. "But she dropped it?"

"Oh yeah," Rick said, narrowing his eyes at his wife as she tried to look innocent.

"And you resisted, I take it?" Joe said.

Rick gave him a look that indicated he had just asked a really stupid question. "If I hadn't, would I be alive to speak of it now?"

"Probably not," Joe observed.

"For sure not," Rick replied.

"Damn right," Midnight put in.

"That was pretty low, Night," Joe said, shaking his head at her.

"What?" she said indignantly. "The broad wouldn't get it through her thick skull that the man loves me beyond all logical reason." She shrugged, grinning impishly. "I just helped point it out graphically."

"Uh-huh," Joe said, nodding. His eyes met Rick's then, and they both shook their heads as if giving up hope for her.

"Oh, knock it off!" she said, moving to get out of Rick's arms. He tightened his hold, laughing.

"You're stuck with me now," he said.

"Good," she replied, leaning over to kiss him on the lips.

Joe watched them, feeling a tug at his heart. He missed being with the woman who made him feel like that. It made him ache every time he thought about it, which was why he'd avoided thinking about it at all lately.

Stevie had been a temporary healer. She'd made him feel good about himself again. But he was still confounded at Randy's attitude. He didn't know what to say to her, or how to approach it. If she just didn't want him, what could he do?

Joe left the office a little while later. Instead of resting like Midnight had told him to, he went right over to the kids' school. He headed to the office and told the administrator that he needed to take his kids out of school for the day. When he went to their classrooms to pick them up, they ran to him, squealing in delight. He found out that Randy and Susan had been telling them that Daddy was on a trip. They asked him how his trip was. He told them it was just fine.

He called Susan to let her know he had the children and asked her to inform Randy. During the course of the day, he decided he needed some more time with them. While they were back in his hotel room, which he got around explaining when they saw all the neat things they could order from room service, Joe called Sinclair House. He asked for Randy, and a minute later she came on the line.

Joe closed his eyes at the sound of her voice. He hadn't realized how much he missed her until that moment.

"Hello?" Randy said again, thinking the caller had hung up.

"Randy, it's me."

"Oh," she said, sounding shocked.

"Did Susan call you?"

"Yes, she called," Randy said, trying to keep the trembling out of her voice.

"Good. Look, I wanted to know if you'd mind me taking them for a couple of weeks. I feel like I need to get connected to them again," Joe said, feeling the need to explain himself.

Randy was silent for a moment, fighting the urge to ask if he ever wanted to get connected with her again. But she was pretty sure she knew the answer to that.

"Sure, of course," she said softly.

"Thanks," he said sincerely. He glanced at his watch, looking at the date. "I'll bring them back, say, December first, okay?"

"Okay," she said, swallowing convulsively.

"They start their winter break tomorrow, right?"

"Yes."

"Okay," he said, starting to feel distinctly uncomfortable.

Her one-word answers were making him feel like he was bothering her. Or maybe she just didn't want to talk to him anymore either. That thought made him feel sick again.

"Well," he said. "We'll see you December first, then."

"Okay," she said, nodding, tears forming in her eyes.

"Bye."

"Bye."

They hung up, both feeling like hell.

Separation wasn't an easy thing, and they were both just trying to make it through. It seemed like it should be easier, but those weren't the rules to the game.

259

You can find more information about the author and series here:

www.sherrylhancock.com

www.facebook.com/SherrylDHancock

www.vulpine-press.com/midknight-blue-series

Also by Sherryl D. Hancock:

The *WeHo* series follows a group of women from Los Angeles as they navigate the ups and downs of love, life, work, and everything in between.

www.vulpine-press.com/we-ho

The *Wild Irish Silence* series. Escape into the world of BJ Sparks and discover how he went from the small-town boy to the world-famous rock star.

www.vulpine-press.com/wild-irish-silence-series